Previous books by the author:

STARLIGHT (Weidenfeld & Nicolson)
PITBULL (Weidenfeld & Nicolson, Penguin)
OVERGROWN WITH LOVE (University of Arkansas Press)
THE ANGEL OF THE GARDEN (University of Missouri Press)

PULPWOOD

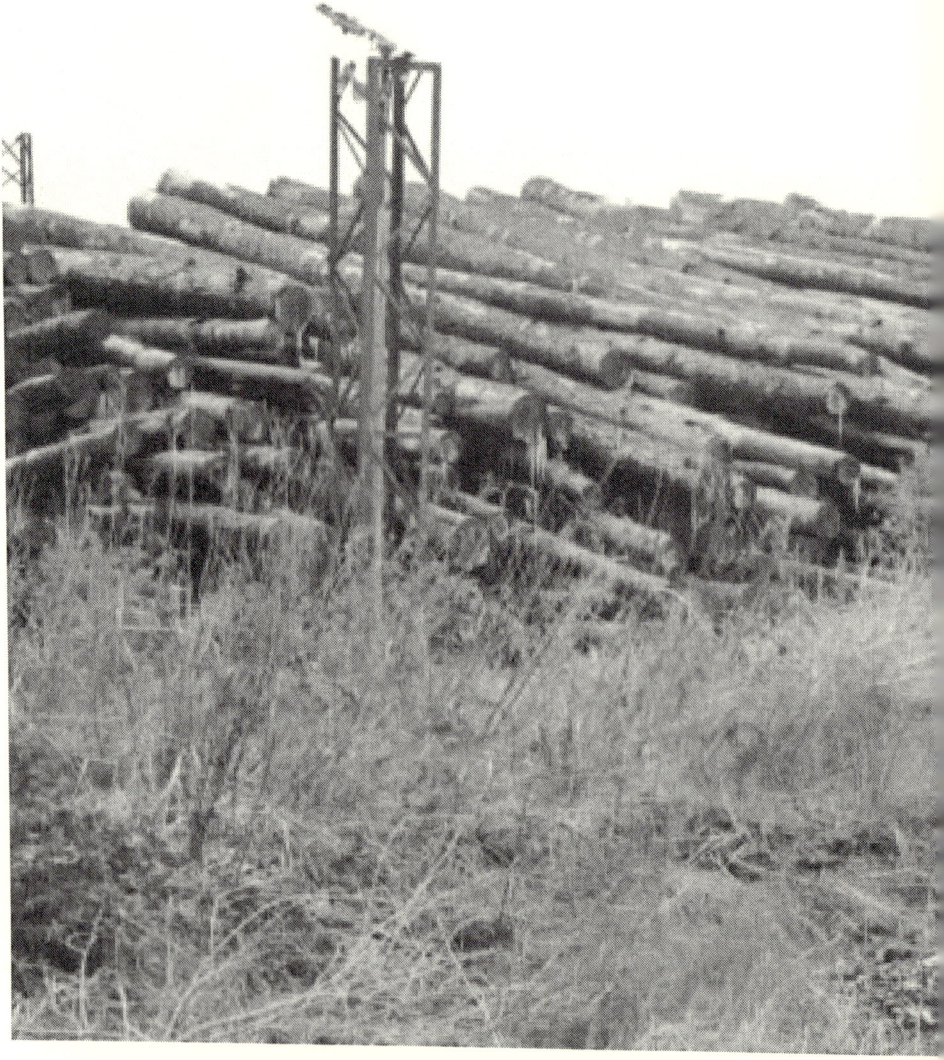

Pulpwood

stories

Scott Ely

Livingston Press
The University of West Alabama

copyright © 2003 Scott Ely

ISBN 1-931982-14-7, library binding
ISBN 1-931982-15-5 trade paper

Library of Congress # 2003108899

This book is printed on paper that meets or exceeds
the Library of Congress's minimal standards for acid-free paper.

All rights reserved, including electronic text

Published at Livingston, Alabama

Hardcover binding by Heckman Bindery

Cover design & layout: Gina Montarsi
Cover photo: Derrick Conner
Typesetting & layout: Gina Montarsi
Proofreaders: Josh Dewberry, Margaret Sullivan,
Elizabeth Drinkard, Jessica Meigs, Daphne Moore

This is a work of fiction. You know the rest: any resemblance
to persons living or dead is coincidental.

Acknowledgements: "Pine Cones" *New Letters* forthcoming;
"Stalingrad" *Antioch Review;* "Rising on Christmas" *Arkansas Review;*
"The Bed" *Shenandoah;* "Walking to Carcassone" *The Southern
Review;* "The Bear Hunters" *The Southern Review;* "Pulpwood" *Five-
Points;* "Queen of the Night" *21st A Journal of Contemporary Photogra-
phy;* "Fishing on Sunday" *The Southern Review;* "The Sweeper"
Antioch Review; "Nicolae and the Devil" *Shenandoah*

first edition
24531

Livingston Press is part of the University of West Alabama,
and as such is a non-profit organization.
All contributions are tax-deductible,
and brothers and sisters, we need 'em.

Table of Contents

The Bed	1
The Bear Hunters	16
Pulpwood	32
A View of the Lilies	48
The Sweeper	63
Rising on Christmas	75
In the Heart of Alabama	92
Stalingrad	109
Land Clearing	124
The Child Soldier	140
Queen of the Night	160
Pinecones	176
Nicolae and the Devil	192
Fishing on Sunday	206
Walking to Carcassonne	223

for Susan

The Bed

Ben Longstreet was standing a few doors down from the oldest house in Charleston, making a sketch of an iron gate, when he heard the woman speak before he saw her, her accent mid-western.

"I've always loved that gate," she said.

She was tall and blonde, almost as tall as he was. She wore heels and a linen dress that a few days before he had seen in the window of one of the shops on King Street. She was definitely not one of the tourists, who in June wandered about the town in shorts and running shoes.

"This town is full of beautiful gates," he said.

They stood talking in the shade of a live oak. He told her he had come to Charleston from Atlanta to start a metalworking business. He had opened a shop on the upper end of King Street. She was Lisa Seymour. A plastic surgeon.

He asked her if she wanted to have a drink, and they went to the bar in one of the big hotels on Meeting Street. He ordered himself a vodka and tonic. She said she would have the same.

"What's your tattoo?" she asked.

She could have seen only a piece of it. He pulled up the sleeve of his t-shirt. The tattoo was a circle. Inside was an open savannah completely empty, just grass and sky, not even a bird circling above it.

"What's it mean?" she asked.

"I was a Marine sniper," he said. "In Nicaragua. Sometimes when there were no targets, I just looked at stuff through the scope."

"We were never in Nicaragua."

"True, we weren't there. But *I* was. My team parachuted in at night."

"To do what?"

"Kill Cubans," he said before thinking.

Immediately he wished he had made up some sort of story about the tattoo. She was a doctor, committed to saving lives, not taking them.

"Why?" she asked.

"They were killing our allies. They did terrible things to the people in those villages. I watched."

"And you killed them."

"Some of them. Mostly officers. The rest were just like me. They killed who they were told to kill. They had no choice."

She took a sip of her drink. He watched her consider what he had told her. At any moment he expected her to stand up and politely tell him goodbye and then walk out of the bar, cool and beautiful in that linen dress, her heels clicking on the marble floor.

"I understand," she said.

He was so surprised that he said nothing at all.

"You don't believe me?" she said.

"Yes, if you say you do," he said. "Most folks don't. Not unless they've done it."

"I do and I haven't done it. But let's not spend the rest of the afternoon talking about killing. Let's walk around and look at gates. My apartment's close to the Battery. I'll give you a glass of iced tea."

So they strolled about the town looking at gates. From time to time he would stop and make a sketch of a piece of interesting ironwork.

Her apartment was on the third floor of an eighteenth century house. The floors were heart of pine, the furnishings spare. Everything was done in white.

"That's how they decorated in the summer before they had air-condi-

The Bed

tioning," she said. "They did the rooms up in white, to make them look cooler."

Now that her practice was going well, she was building a house on the Isle of Palms.

As they sat drinking iced tea on the open porch that ran the length of her apartment, she told him why she understood.

"My father was a sniper too," she said. "In Vietnam."

She was from Montana, where her mother and father had an outfitting business. They took clients into the wilderness to fish and hunt.

For some reason the fact that her father too had seen clearly the people he had killed made Ben feel uneasy. It was as if she might know things about him he would prefer she not know.

"Does he ever talk much about the war?" he asked.

"He doesn't mind at all," she said. "He's proud of what he did."

So what if he had told her everything, he thought. There was no way she could know anything about it at all.

He told her that his father worked in a trailer manufacturing plant and his mother worked in a factory that made batteries. Joining the Marines had been a way to stay out of those plants. When his hitch was up, he had not gone home to the small town in the Georgia mountains but had used the GI Bill to take art and welding classes in Atlanta.

"I'd like you to make me an iron bed," she said. "I haven't seen any ironwork in town that's right for it."

"I'll make you one like nothing you've seen in town," he said.

He thought with satisfaction that he was going to see her again, that this was not simply going to be a single pleasant afternoon. He made a series of sketches of his ideas for the bed, none that she particularly liked, while she talked to him about fishing in Montana and they drank glass after glass of iced tea. Then she had to leave to make rounds at the hospital.

He told her he had a bed in progress at his shop, that she could come by the next day and look at it. He would be there fabricating sections of an iron fence. She said she could come after her office closed. Then they could have dinner.

"It's a shop," he said. He looked in through the French doors at the immaculate apartment. "It's dirty."

"I don't care," she said. "I want to see that bed."

He had run into problems with the fence. It was for an estate out on one of the islands, a huge project that was almost beyond the capacity of his shop. When he saw her car pull into the gravel lot, he and his crew were still struggling to put a curve in a bar by running it through a roller he had designed and built himself. There had been a thunderstorm a few hours earlier, and the water stood in puddles in the lot. She was dressed in a black pants suit. She walked across the lot, picking her way around the puddles.

Ed and Samuel looked at her and murmured something to each other.

"Oh, Boss, but does that doctor lady look fine!" Samuel said.

"Maybe she can fix my nose," Ed said.

Ed had boxed when he was young. His nose had been broken many times.

"She'd charge you three month's pay," Samuel said. "And you'd still be ugly."

The men laughed, their laughter sounding to Ben like barks. Now he wished he had told them nothing about her.

Lisa walked into the shop.

"I don't even have a place for you to sit down," he said. "You could wait in the car. We'll finish bending this bar and call it a day."

"I'll stay and watch," she said.

The bending went smoothly. Then Ed and Samuel went off down the street for a beer. He led her through a labyrinth of machines and stacks of iron bars to the headboard of the bed he had been working on.

"The lady who commissioned this had been to Barcelona," he said. "She wanted something like Gaudi."

The Bed

"It's wonderful," she said. "But I don't want that. I want something no one else has."

He persuaded her to wait in the car while he showered.

They went out to dinner and afterwards drove to the Isle of Palms to her new house. It was three stories, in the process of being framed. The master bedroom on the third floor would have a view of the sea. They stood amid the open studs and smoked Cuban cigars she had obtained from a client.

"The barter system," she said. "This clears his account."

He looked out through the studs, the smell of pine everywhere, at the lights of a ship.

"The bed will go right here," she said. "I'll wake up every morning and look at the sea. I'll be moving in right after the Fourth of July. Can you have it ready by then?"

"I think I can," he said.

He explained that he was working hard just to meet his payroll and pay the rent on the shop. Now he had taken on the fence project. He was afraid if he worked the men too hard they would quit.

"When I finish the fence and get paid for a few other jobs I'll be ok," he said.

They sat between the studs of what was going to be the outside wall and dangled their legs over the edge. He imagined making love to her in the iron bed and waking to the sight of the sea.

Then she began to tell him about her father's encounter with a grizzly while he was bow hunting for elk.

"That bear held him in an embrace," she said. "He stabbed it with a broad head. Got lucky and hit an artery."

"And then?" he asked.

"Sewed himself up with fishing line and walked out," she said. "It took him three days."

"Does he still bow hunt?"

"Every year."

They sat for a time in silence. He could see the white tops of the breakers, illuminated by the lights from the houses, but they were too far away to hear the sound.

"I'll tell my friends about you," she said. "They're all building houses out here. You can make beds and fences and gates. What else?"

"I can do anything with metal," he said.

"Make me something wonderful."

She leaned around the stud between them and kissed him. She tasted of the fine cigars and smelled of them and perfume. He wanted to make love to her right there on the plywood sub flooring.

"I want you too," she said. "But I want to wait. We'll wait on the bed."

"I'll have it by the end of the week," he said.

"When the house is done. You finish the fence. Do some work for my friends."

He felt suddenly exhausted, as if he had just finished a long race. He was not sure if she was serious. If she was he was not convinced he wanted to make such a bargain.

"This sounds crazy," he said.

"To work for my friends?" she asked.

"You know what I mean."

She leaned over and kissed him again.

"I am serious. It's only a few weeks. Indulge me."

He felt there was nothing else he could do but agree. And, he told himself, it was nothing more than a whim on her part. Maybe it was just her way of wanting to know him better before she slept with him.

They sat on the edge of the floor and smoked cigars and discussed his ideas for the bed. Then he took her home.

Over the next few weeks he worked hard on the fence. It was a project that required little imagination, but it would generate enough cash to see him through the summer.

The Bed

At night he made drawings of the bed, which he e-mailed to Lisa. She was never completely satisfied with them. She sent him pictures from museums. Finally he hit on a design she liked. He had found a picture of a thyrsus on the web. The thyrsus, a staff tipped with a pinecone and entwined with vine leaves, was thought to have come from a temple to Dionysus in Alexandria. Now it was in a museum in Germany.

By now the fence was almost ready to install and most of the work, except for the fabricating of the gates, he would be able to turn over to his crew. He had begun to do work for some of her friends. Most of them were doctors or lawyers. Lisa always introduced him as an artist. He was pleased with that because it was what he considered himself to be. But no one else wore snakeskin cowboy boots and black leather pants to these parties.

One couple invited them to a party at their house on the Isle of Palms. He had recently installed a stainless steel countertop in their kitchen. Frank was an anesthesiologist. Nancy was a marine biologist.

"Frank, we've got to have Ben make us a bed," Nancy said.

"You'll have to wait in line, " Lisa said.

"Tell us something about it," Nancy said.

"No, he can't tell you a thing," Lisa said. "I'm not going to look at it myself until it's finished."

Ben wondered if Lisa had told Nancy about their bargain. As Nancy and Lisa went off to look at his work in the kitchen, he wondered if it would be something one woman would tell another.

"Lisa's a talented surgeon," Frank said. "She's got great hands. She's doing well here."

"Only cutting I know about is with a torch," he said.

"Well, you're an artist with it."

The women returned from the kitchen. Then Lisa took him to meet a couple that also wanted an iron pot rack for their kitchen.

After the party he took her home. They sat in his truck and kissed as if they were a couple of teenagers.

"Just remember the house is almost done," she said. "Concentrate on the bed."

"Why are we doing this?" he asked.

"So I'll get the bed on time."

"No, I'm serious."

"I don't know. I want to be sure. It's more than just sex. In a way I'm thinking you come with the bed. I know you're tired of sleeping in that shop."

"I'll sleep somewhere else when I can afford the rent."

"I know that. You'll have plenty of work. All my friends are crazy about what you do."

"I'm not like your friends."

"You shouldn't be. Now go home and get some sleep. You need to finish that fence."

He walked her to the door and kissed her goodnight.

As he drove to the shop, he thought of the two other women he had stopped seeing because of her. He had been sleeping with both of them. He could either go back to the shop and masturbate or call up one of those women, who might not be too eager to see him again since he had made excuses not to go out with each of them on several occasions when they had called. He was so taken with Lisa that he had had no time for them, not even an afternoon in bed after drinking a few beers at a bar. But he had been careful not to break things off completely with Nadine and Sass. He wanted some place to retreat to.

But his plans for calling either one of them were immediately put out of his mind when he listened to his messages. Mr. Demott, the man who had ordered the fence, told him that Ed and Samuel had installed the first one hundred yards of it six feet off the line. Now the posts would have to be dug up and the job redone. It would be difficult to do it without damaging the fence.

In the morning he argued with Ed and Samuel.

"Boss, we followed that line of crepe myrtles," Samuel said. "Just like

The Bed

you told us."

"You were on the wrong side," he said. "Didn't you see the stakes Mr. Demott put out? He paid a surveyor just to make sure something like this wouldn't happen."

"We didn't see no stakes," Ed said. "Kids must've got after 'em."

"You should've checked," he said.

"I don't recall nothin' about no stakes," Samuel said.

Then Ben started to yell and both men quit on the spot.

"You've had your mind on nothin' but that doctor lady!" Samuel shouted at him as he drove out of the lot. "You don't belong with them doctors and lawyers. You're one of us."

He hired a new crew and by the time he had trained them, for there was still fence to fabricate, and they had dug up the old posts (Samuel and Ed had not been lying, the stakes had vanished) it was the end of June.

He had not told Lisa about any of his problems. They went to parties and to classical music concerts, plays, and the ballet. She gave him books to read, but he did not have time for them. The fence was consuming all his energy. But he could not afford to push his crew too hard. There was no time to train a new one. Sometimes he wondered what she would say if he offered to carry her to a stock car race or to a country music concert. Although he still dressed the same way and thought the same thoughts, he felt as if some virus had been planted inside him and one day it would activate itself and he would look into the mirror and see a stranger.

Now he turned all his attention to the fence, ignoring three small projects he had started for Lisa's friends. At night he worked hard on the bed. He had almost finished the headboard. He had used copper left over from a kitchen project for the grapes and silver from an old silver service that Lisa had donated for the grape leaves. He gilded the pinecones at the top of each post with gold. And then on the web he found in a museum in Italy a bronze dolphin, its back curved as it leaped above the waves. He decided he would put it in the center of the headboard and give the dolphin a golden eye.

Then it was July. It looked as if Lisa's house was going to be finished on schedule. After the Fourth he would install the big gate on the drive to Mr. Demott's house. He had already set the posts and had fabricated the gate panels in the shop. Now he was half finished with the footboard. He wanted to spend the Fourth working on the bed, but Lisa insisted that he go with her to a concert at one of the old plantations outside of town. She and her friends were having a dinner catered.

He sat at a long table on the porch of the plantation house. Waiters moved up and down the length of the table filling wine glasses. On the other side of a lake covered with water lilies the orchestra was playing for a huge crowd spread out in a grove of live oaks. The waiters began to serve the first course. As Ben ate his she-crab soup and listened to the orchestra play, he felt comfortable and relaxed. It was almost as if, he told himself, he had been coming here to listen to music since he was a young boy, the oaks, the house and the lake stamped with the remembrance of past July evenings in his mind.

Lisa's house was finished. They were planting big palm trees in the front yard. She was having furniture delivered.

Fitting the gates to the posts proved to be a difficult job. At first he thought he was going to have to dig up and reset one or both of the posts to make the panels fit, but then, after two days of hanging and rehanging the panels, he found a solution. He hung the gates. Mr. Demott made a final inspection and was satisfied.

Ben offered to buy his crew a beer to celebrate. He and David and Earl drove off the island and stopped at a bar on the highway. It was the middle of the afternoon and except for a few people playing the poker machines the place was deserted. They sat at a table and ordered a beer. After a few beers with the men, he would spend the rest of the day working on the bed.

The Bed

He was drinking his third beer when he felt a hand on his shoulder. He looked up. It was Nadine.

"I saw your truck," she said. "Where've you been?"

"Building a fence," he said.

"You were there and then you were gone," she said.

"Let me buy you a beer," Earl said.

"I'd appreciate that," she said. "At least someone's a gentleman."

"I was gonna buy you a beer," Ben said.

"Me too," David said.

They all had another round and then another. Nadine told them about her new business cleaning apartments.

"Wanda got me into it," she said. "She's a smart one for making money."

Ben remembered Wanda, a friend of Sass.

Then David said he had to leave. He had promised his cousin he would help him install a garbage disposal.

"Harry ain't much of a plumber," David said.

"I'll drive Ben back to the shop," Nadine said.

Ben knew something was going to happen. Either she was waiting for the crew to leave so she could get mad at him or they were going to spend the afternoon in bed together. Even if she got mad he decided he would get her to drive him to the shop.

"I've got a condo to do this afternoon," she said. "Why don't you come with me? Then I'll drive you home."

"Why not," he said.

The condo was on the Isle of Palms. The building was right up on the beach so everyone had a view of the ocean. While he sat on the balcony and drank beer, she vacuumed the carpet and cleaned the bathrooms. Then he followed her into the bedroom where they lay together on the unmade bed. He came almost as soon as he entered her.

"My but we're eager," she said. "Hasn't that doctor lady friend of yours been treating you right?"

"How do you know about her?" he asked.

His cock was limp against her thigh. He was worried that she might expect more from him.

"I saw you at the ballet," she said. "During intermission I was standing right behind you. I heard her telling her doctor friends about the new house she's building."

"What were you doing there?" he asked.

"You think I wouldn't go to a ballet?"

"No, I didn't mean it that way."

"Well, what did you mean?"

"You never told me you were interested in ballet."

They had gone dancing and to stock car races. She loved stock car races. She had a poster of Richard Petty in her bedroom.

"I took ballet for six years when I was growing up in Sumpter," she said. "I was good. I just grew too tall."

"You never told me that."

"I don't tell a man everything about myself. We've got to go."

"Don't you want me—"

"No, we don't have time. And besides I don't think you're up to it. I'm behind on my work. You go out on the balcony and drink yourself another beer. I'll change these sheets."

He stayed up all night and finished the bed. Then he disassembled it and loaded the pieces on his truck, which he parked inside the shop. He covered the headboard with a new drop cloth so it would be a surprise to her. When he called Lisa at her office and told her the bed was finished, she invited him for dinner. He turned the ringer on the phone off and muted the answering machine and went to sleep.

He dreamed he was putting an iron fence around the entire Isle of Palms. And when he was finished, he would never have to make another fence again. He would open a studio and gallery on King Street and devote himself to sculpture. He woke covered with sweat. The air conditioner

The Bed

had gone out again.

When he went outside, he saw that it was evening, the temperature outside much cooler than inside the metal building. He opened up the big doors so the place could cool off, and showered and dressed. Then he drove to the Isle of Palms.

He parked the truck in her garage and brought the headboard into the living room. She poured them a couple of glasses of wine.

"Close your eyes," he said.

She put her hands over her face. He pulled off the drop cloth and paused for a moment to admire his work. The dolphin leaped, frozen forever in graceful motion between the vine-covered posts.

"Now open them."

She dropped her hands and opened her eyes.

"Oh, my God!" she said. "It's marvelous! Don't you dare make one like this for Nancy!"

She threw her arms around him and kissed him.

Then she helped him carry the headboard up to the third floor. He brought the other pieces up and they assembled the bed. They put the box springs and mattress on and sheets made with fine Egyptian cotton. She put a spread on it, one she had bought on a trip to Peru.

"Now the room's perfect," she said.

She ran her fingers over the silver grape leaves and copper grapes. She traced the curve of the dolphin's back.

Then they had dinner. She cooked sea bass on a grill along with fresh corn and new potatoes. After dinner they sat on the sofa in the living room. He was feeling guilty about Nadine, but he kept telling himself that the bargain he had made with Lisa was unreasonable. He wondered if she had cheated at some point.

They had coffee and then brandy.

"Let's go to bed," she said.

Now, he thought, everything was going to be all right. They went upstairs, taking their brandy glasses with them. When she lit candles in the room, the light reflected off the dolphin's eye and the silver grape leaves and the clusters of copper grapes.

"Take off my dress," she said. "But don't touch me."

He unzipped her linen dress and slipped it over her head. She stood there in panties, bra, and high heels.

"Now those boots," she said.

He sat on the bed and she pulled off his boots and jeans. She unbuttoned the hand-painted Italian shirt she had given him. She took his cock out of his underwear. For a moment he wondered if the scent of Nadine was still on him. But he had taken that second shower in the evening before he drove to Lisa's house.

"We've waited," she said. "It's going to be worth it."

She held his cock with one hand while she ran her fingers over his tattoo with the other.

"I have a tattoo," she said.

"Where?" he asked.

"On my hip, under my panties," she said.

He knelt and pulled her panties down to her feet. She stepped out of them. In the flicker of the candlelight he made out the tattoo. It was a single number. 29.

"What does it mean?" he asked.

"My father's kills," she said.

She removed her bra and lay back on the bed.

"Now tell me about one of yours," she said.

He stood there for a moment looking down at her and then past her through the French doors that opened out onto the ocean. Far out at sea were the lights of a ship. He could not tell whether it was leaving or approaching Charleston.

"Ben?" she said.

He pulled his underwear over his hardon. As he lay down and put his arms around her, he looked up at the dolphin, its golden eye shining in the candlelight as it leaped above the waves. And then, as they began to move together, he saw himself walking across a savannah beneath a cloudless sky, a line of green forest shimmering in the heat waves in the distance. The savannah was perfectly flat and treeless and covered with short grass, like the rough of a golf course. The only cover was that distant forest. Suddenly he felt cold. There was nothing he could do but walk toward the forest, where he hoped to vanish into that play of light and shadow beneath the big trees.

The Bear Hunters

The boy was studying the rivers of Europe on the computer. He traced the path of the Danube across Europe and watched its seven mouths empty into the Black Sea. Pontus Euxinus it had once been called, the name the Romans used long before Jesus was born.

It was the end of November. Patches of snow were on the ground from a two-inch fall the day before. He was twelve years old and was being educated at home. It had been two years since his mother had moved the boy and his uncle, the mother's younger brother, to the house in the mountains at Sweetheart Gap. His father was dead, killed by a disease in Africa where he had gone to serve as a missionary. He had been an engineer who designed and installed water systems for villages.

"It was something in that water," his mother always said when he questioned her about the circumstances surrounding his father's death.

He had looked up diseases of a like kind on the web and discovered that it could have been any of a number of things: some parasite, an amoeba, a bacterium. He was glad that they drank pure well water up on Sweetheart Gap.

His mother was managing a hotel in a nearby resort town. She had been fired from her job as a schoolteacher, because she insisted on leading her class in prayer. Her picture and an account of her battle with the city of Charlotte were on their church's web site.

From the living room came the sound of the TV. Gabriel, the boy's uncle, a man of twenty-five but with the mind of a child, was constantly before it, sitting there with his Bible in his lap, the Bible he could not read and could only dimly understand if it were read to him.

"Thou shalt not steal," Gabriel said in a firm clear voice.

He always started with that one and then ran through the others. There were times when he got stuck on the commandments and spent the whole day saying them over and over. Some of the boy's earliest memories were of Gabriel intoning passages from the Bible. Once Gabriel had been able to repeat any book or part of a book. He had the entire Bible inside his head. The boy's grandmother, now dead and buried in Atlanta, had discovered how God had touched her son. She was the one who read the Bible out loud to him until he had those books by heart. Gabriel had been on TV many times. But then one day he could remember nothing but the commandments.

Ever since they had come to live at Sweetheart Gap he had been stealing. His victims were the people from Charlotte who owned the summerhouses on the ridge above them. He made no attempt to conceal what he had stolen. He piled the televisions and VCRs and cameras on the desk in his room. On the weekends the boy's mother made Gabriel load the merchandise in her van and she went from house to house making restitution and delivering apologies.

The stealing had stopped when Gabriel grew fat. He had expanded before the boy's eyes, at last growing so large that the walk up the steep road to the ridge where the houses were built was impossible for him. The houses overlooked a famous gorge and on extremely clear days the occupants were presented with a faint view of the gilded top of the tallest building in Charlotte.

Every morning his mother cooked Gabriel stacks of pancakes, country ham, eggs, and grits. The cupboard was always filled with potato chips and cakes. Gabriel spent the day eating and watching TV.

"Gabriel's fat," the boy announced to his mother one day while Gabriel sat before the TV devouring a huge piece of chocolate cake.

"It's better than jail," she said. "It's better than the state hospital."

The state hospital was close at hand in the town at the foot of the mountain. It was a cluster of buildings all constructed of red brick. The grounds were covered with trees and flowers, but there were heavy wire screens over the windows and razor wire at the top of a tall chain link fence surrounding an outdoor basketball court.

Gabriel came into the room. He wore a Charlotte Panthers sweat suit.

"I want to see," Gabriel said. "Please let me see, Lawrence?"

That was a request the boy heard a hundred times a day. Gabriel wanted to look at pornography on the computer.

"Mama's got the password," he said. "I don't know it."

"Do it."

"I can't."

"I'll show you a bear. Show it to Margaret too."

Margaret Cully was a girl of fifteen or sixteen who worked at her father's convenience store. The store was five miles away and mostly uphill. The boy's mother refused all Gabriel's frantic requests to stop when they drove by. When they passed the store, Gabriel scrambled as best he could to the back of the van and watched the store recede in the rear window.

"What bear?" the boy asked.

"Up the mountain," Gabriel said. "There and gone. Before I was fat. Up through the flowers. A hole in the rock where he sleeps."

He had learned to be patient with Gabriel. In the conversation that followed he discovered that Gabriel believed he knew where a bear had his den. He had surprised the bear on the road and it had gone up the side of the mountain.

"Into the flowers," Gabriel had said.

He supposed that meant the bear had vanished into a rhododendron thicket. The rhododendron had not been in flower since the end of June. That was when Gabriel had first begun to get truly large and he had paid some of his last visits to the summerhouses. There were bears in the mountains that were hunted in season by men with dogs, so the bears were wary. But he thought it was possible that what Gabriel had told him was true.

"Let me see," Gabriel said.

"What's there to see," the boy said. "We don't have a credit card."

"Let me see."

"You're sure you know where to find that bear's den?"

"Up in the flowers."

"You'll show me? You promise?"

"Yes."

"Ten minutes. That's all."

He bypassed the parental controls and handed the machine over to Gabriel.

Then he went into the living room and sat in front of the TV and waited for the ten minutes to pass. Gabriel had been watching a show about antiques. An auction was in progress. A wardrobe was being sold. Ten thousand dollars flashed up on the screen.

When the time was up, he returned to the room. Gabriel was watching two naked women kissing each other. The boy could not understand why anyone would want to watch that. He took the mouse out of Gabriel's hand.

"More," Gabriel said.

"No, now you show me where that bear lives," he said.

He expected that Gabriel would somehow give him directions, for it was impossible for Gabriel to lead him to the bear's den.

"I'll show you," Gabriel said. "Come along."

Gabriel went out of the room. The boy followed his slow progress through the house and out the kitchen door and into the garage where he had a difficult time going down three low steps. It was cold in the garage. Gabriel's breath came out in white puffs.

"How're you gonna walk up a hill?" he asked.

Gabriel grinned and walked across the empty garage and opened the door to the storeroom. He pulled from a shelf a stack of boxes they had used when they moved and then reached up and brought down something made of metal with plastic-coated steel cables attached to it.

"Come along," Gabriel said.

Then he understood what the object was. He had once seen it demonstrated on TV.

"We're gonna winch you up those hills?" he said.

"Come along," Gabriel said.

Then he laughed, his breath coming out in large white puffs.

"You want to see the bear's hole?" Gabriel asked.

The boy thought about the bear, wondering if it all was some sort of fabrication on Gabriel's part.

"How did that bear run up the hill?" he asked.

"Up through the flowers," Gabriel said.

"No, how? Show me. How did its legs move?"

Gabriel got down on all fours on the concrete floor and gave a slow but correct imitation of a bear's gait. His front and back legs moved in unison, just like a bear's. But then he slipped and fell heavily on the floor and lay there for a time like a seal basking on an ice floe until with some help from the boy he got to his feet again.

"I'm a bear," Gabriel said. "Up the mountain fast."

"No, you're not a bear," he said firmly.

Sometimes Gabriel got stuck on something, and he became like a loop of videotape, playing the same scene over and over. He did not want to listen to Gabriel saying he was a bear for the next week.

They walked slowly along the road, now completely clear of snow. He carried the come-along and a camera that he planned to use to take a picture of the bear's den. Gabriel had put a box of doughnuts and several cans of Coke in a backpack he carried slung over one shoulder because even without his winter clothes on he was much too large for it to fit.

Above them was the long thin ridge that held the summerhouses. The oaks and hickories were bare, but in places the mountainside was covered with thick stands of rhododendron. Water trickled out of the mountain and made puddles on the road that at night would freeze. Patches of frozen seep water still lay on the shady side of the road.

"No bear up there," Gabriel said.

"I wasn't expecting there to be," he said.

He was irritated with himself at allowing Gabriel access to the pictures of women. And if that piece of stupidity was not enough he was out here in the cold proceeding along the road at a pace not much faster than a small child could crawl. Gabriel was already breathing hard and the road ran perfectly level at this point. He was going to fall behind with his schoolwork. He reviewed in his mind the principal rivers of Europe.

"There's gonna be a bear," Gabriel said. "Up in the flowers."

"We're not going to see a bear's den," he said.

"No! No! Up in the flowers!"

Gabriel stopped and turned to face him. He looked as if he was on the verge of tears, and the boy was sorry for what he had said.

"Yes, maybe we'll see that ol' bear," he said.

"Up in the flowers," Gabriel said. "Down in the rock."

A truck came along the road and slowly passed them. The boy waved at the men inside and they waved back. He had seen the men, those gaunt hunters, before. There was a metal dog box in the truck bed. Through the air holes he saw pieces of dogs: an eye, a tongue, teeth, a tail.

"Bear hunters," he said.

"No, not my bear," Gabriel said.

"Yes."

"No! No!"

Gabriel was now in tears. The boy went up and stood before him, the immense bulk of his uncle towering over him.

"You made me let you see," the boy said.

"The bear," Gabriel said.

"Yes, but you could have just shown me the bear."

"Kill the bear."

He was crying harder now.

"No, bear season is over," the boy said. "They're after coons."

The boy had no idea what the men were hunting. Perhaps at this time of year all the bears were asleep in their dens.

"Coons," Gabriel said.

"Yes, coons," the boy said.

Gabriel wiped his eyes and his nose on first one coat sleeve and then another. The boy patted him on the leg as he might have done to a horse. Gabriel smiled down at him.

It was noon and they were still on the asphalt road, which now was running slightly downhill. They had been on the road an hour and besides the hunters only two other trucks had passed. He sat down in a patch of sunlight on a rock and Gabriel sat in the shade. He had two doughnuts out of the box and Gabriel ate the rest. They drank one of the Cokes apiece.

"How far?" he asked.

Gabriel, his back turned to him, was urinating into the ditch. That was something the boy's mother had to struggle with constantly. He looked up and down the road, thankful no one had appeared.

"Close," Gabriel said.

He checked to make sure Gabriel had zipped up his pants.

The road dropped more sharply. The slope above was a rhododendron thicket. He heard water running but could not see it. They came upon a gravel road that ran off to the right, going up at a moderate grade.

"Here," Gabriel said.

"Up in the flowers?" the boy said.

Gabriel nodded his head.

At first it seemed to the boy that Gabriel might be able to go up the road unassisted. He moved ahead at his maddeningly slow pace, impelled, the boy imagined, by the thought of those ten minutes at the computer. The boy resolved that he would never be persuaded again.

But then Gabriel stopped. He tottered there on the road, the gravel crunching under his feet as he attempted to put the next foot forward. He sank to his knees.

"Pull me," Gabriel said.

The boy walked up the road and attached the come-along to a tree. Then he ran the cables back and attached the hook on the end of them to a piece of rope he tied around Gabriel's waist. Gabriel struggled to his feet. The boy worked the lever and Gabriel ascended the road with a smile on his face.

It was easy, but the boy considered how long it was going to take them at twenty yards a pitch to get wherever they were going. But he soon discovered there were level stretches where Gabriel could walk as the road ascended the mountain in a series of switchbacks. They crossed a bridge over a stream, where they rested for a time. While Gabriel drank another Coke, the boy looked for trout holding in the eddies behind the bridge footers.

They went up, the road sometimes running between dense rhododendron thickets or leafless stands of hardwoods. When he asked Gabriel how far the bear's den was, he received the same reply over and over.

"Up high," Gabriel said. "Up high."

The boy's satisfaction with the efficiency of the come-along soon disappeared as he was confronted with the tediousness of the operation. He checked and double-checked the attachment of the hook to Gabriel's harness. He imagined Gabriel slipping out of it and tumbling down the road, perhaps even off the road where in a rhododendron thicket even his great body would be brought to rest by the net of branches. He wished the hunters would appear and give them a ride in the back of their truck.

The higher they went the more snow there was. Finally patches of snow began to appear on the road. He had almost ceased to think about the bear's den. What occupied him now was getting to that place where he would make one last pitch with the come-along. His arms and shoulders were tired from working the lever.

They reached another place where the road ran level, but this place was obviously not a switchback. On the uphill side there was a huge rhododendron thicket and on the other open timber. Far below he saw a piece of the gravel road and farther off there was the highway and beside it a farmhouse looking like a toy set at the edge of a field of bright green winter wheat.

Gabriel started off along the road.

"Up high?" the boy said. "Up high? What's higher than this?"

"Come along," Gabriel said and walked away laughing.

The road curved and then instead of another rhododendron thicket there was a house. They were on the top of the ridge containing the summerhouses. Gabriel had tricked him by bringing him up the back way.

Filled with outrage the boy stepped in front of Gabriel and brought him to a halt like a handler stopping an obedient elephant.

"There's no bear," he said. "You came to steal."

"Thou shalt not steal," Gabriel said.

"But you're going to steal. I won't help you back down the hill if you do."

"I'll tell Elizabeth. You let me watch the girls."

The same pleased look was on Gabriel's face as when he had pulled the come-along down from the shelf.

Whatever Gabriel had come up to steal could not be heavy, the boy reflected. Something light and portable, that he himself could easily return as his mother had so many times. If he were lucky he would be able to do it without his mother's knowledge. There was no way he could stop Gabriel from doing whatever he had come all the way up the steep road to do. At least he was sure that Gabriel could be appeased somehow to keep silent about the computer.

They walked along the road. The houses were all on one side for the view. He looked for the gilded tower of the tallest building but there was a bit of haze in the air off towards Charlotte, so he could see nothing of the city.

He imagined that Gabriel would pick a house at random and start looking for something to steal. The first year they had moved to Sweetheart

Gap it had been chain saws. He recalled driving along this road with his mother with three chain saws in the back of the van. She stopped and asked at each house until she had returned two of the saws and they had come to the end of the row of houses. The owner of the third came for it the next weekend.

Gabriel paused and looked at a house. He shambled up the stone walk to the door and looked through the window set in it. Then he went all the way around the house, looking in the windows. The door to a utility room in the back was unlocked. Gabriel pushed it open. Tools hung on hooks set in wallboard. A chain saw was on the floor.

"There it is," the boy said, pointing at the saw. "Get it and let's go home. But I'm not carrying it."

Instead Gabriel took up a sledgehammer.

"That's not worth much," the boy said.

Gabriel ignored him and walked out of the room, leaving the door ajar. The boy closed it and followed Gabriel around to the front of the house. Instead of going on down the road, Gabriel walked up to the front door. Before the astonished boy could say a word in protest, Gabriel drew back the hammer and smashed the lock. The door sprang back and hit the wall. Gabriel dropped the hammer, which made a clang when it hit the brick porch. Then he walked into the house, leaving the boy standing in the mid afternoon sunlight. He looked out to the deserted road. He looked toward the houses on either side, cut off from his view by a thick growth of hemlocks. The sound of the hammer on the door was long gone, but the boy could still imagine it and thought that at any moment some human voice would rise in protest over what Gabriel had just done. But nothing happened. Two crows sailed lazily overhead, cawing softly to each other.

Then Gabriel emerged from the house with a chair. It looked puny and insignificant in his hands, almost like a child's chair. The wood was elaborately carved, and the boy knew at once that this was an object much more valuable than a chain saw.

Gabriel, oblivious to the fact that the shattered door was behind him and there was a remote chance that someone might come along on the road, sat down on the porch steps. He was still breathing hard from the exertion required to smash the door. He took off his gloves and ran his hands lightly over the carving.

"Leave it," the boy said. "Take the chain saw."

Gabriel shook his head. Then under the boy's questioning he explained why he had stolen the chair. He had seen the owners obtaining an estimate of the value of the chair on a TV show. He had recognized them for they had come to the house to retrieve the chain saw that was now sitting in their utility room.

"Five thousand dollars," Gabriel said.

"What would you do with five thousand dollars?" the boy asked.

"Margaret Cully," Gabriel said.

He spoke the girl's name with reverence as if he were saying a prayer.

"ATV," Gabriel said. "I'm gonna ride up to see Margaret."

A person could drive an ATV without a license. He imagined Gabriel riding it along the highway to the store on the shoulder of the road. All the gravel roads would be open to him. He could steal a few chain saws every day.

"Look at that door," the boy said. "They'll catch you. They'll take you to that house in Leesville."

Gabriel knew what that was. Usually the threat of sending him there made him afraid, but his only reaction was to smile.

"Can't walk up the hill," he said.

"They'll find out," the boy said.

He tried to take the chair out of Gabriel's hands but his uncle was much too strong.

"Margaret Cully," Gabriel said.

He imagined Margaret recoiling in horror from Gabriel's attentions. He wanted to kiss her like the women on the computer were kissing each other. Gabriel was trapped. And this time he might end up behind the razor wire.

The Bear Hunters

"Put it back," he said.

"No," Gabriel said.

"Then let's go home."

At least if they were home before his mother returned from work there might be some way for him to return the chair. He left Gabriel and carrying the come-along walked to the edge of the cliff. He tossed it out over the treetops where it fell into a rhododendron thicket. No one would ever find it.

"Let's go home," he said.

Gabriel smiled.

"Margaret Cully," he said.

"Yeah, you're gonna ride your ATV to see Margaret Cully," the boy said.

They went down by the familiar gravel road that the boy hoped was shorter than the way they had come. It was now late in the afternoon and the sun was behind them, their shadows enormous on the gravel. Gabriel went down with difficulty, his breath coming out in white puffs and his knees popping.

Then they were at the paved road. Gabriel sat down. His sweatpants were wet across the bottom and there was a dark patch between his shoulder blades where the sweat had soaked through his heavy jacket. It grew darker as the sun fell behind the mountain. The boy put the chair down and sat on it, his head level with Gabriel's for the first time that day.

"Mama's going to be coming home," he said.

It was dark now when his mother came home. He was not wearing a watch and it was hard to gauge the exact time with the mountain between them and the sun.

"She'll be late," Gabriel said.

"You better hope she is," he said. "Get up."

Gabriel moved his head from side to side, reminding the boy of the way a cow might regard him through a barbed wire fence. His face was covered with sweat; his breath still came out in fast white puffs. The boy realized that Gabriel was not going to be able to move for a time. He sat on the chair and waited for Gabriel to recover. A breeze came down the side of the mountain, rattling the leafless branches of the hickories.

"Cold," Gabriel said.

"Walking'll warm you up quick," the boy said.

Gabriel got up and they went along the road, the slight uphill grade causing him to begin to breathe deeply again after only a few yards. But despite Gabriel's complaining the boy managed to persuade him not to stop and rest. Once they stopped when the boy heard a car approaching. He hid the chair in the rhododendrons and they stood together, Gabriel breathing hard, and waited for it to pass.

It was the hunters. The truck slowed down as it passed and the man on the passenger side smiled and waved to them, but the driver just stared. The truck slipped slowly past them in the fading light and again the boy saw those pieces of dogs through the holes in the grate of the shiny aluminum dog box. Then the truck was gone, the taillights disappearing around a bend in the road.

"Bears," Gabriel said.

"Coons!" the boy said savagely. "Or foxes. Maybe even just rabbits. You've never seen a bear. You never will."

"Up through the flowers."

"You just keep on eating those big stacks of pancakes Mamma fixes you. You'll be bigger than any ol' bear."

The boy regarded the chair Gabriel held in his hands, an alien thing, a mark set upon both of them. He wished he were standing at the edge of the cliff where he had thrown the come-along. He imagined the chair turning in the air as it fell into the rhododendrons accompanied by wails from Gabriel.

"Down in the rock," Gabriel said.

"Yeah," the boy said. "That's where you're gonna wish you were."

It grew dark. They saw no more traffic on the road, and Gabriel shambled along at a slow but steady pace. And then to the boy's amazement they were home and there was no sheriff's car, its blue light flashing, sitting in the driveway. The house was dark. He hoped that this was one of the nights when his mother was late.

Once the boy had hidden the chair in the storeroom in the garage, he went into the house and started a fire in the wood stove. Gabriel had disappeared into his room. The boy walked down the hallway to Gabriel's room. The door was open. Gabriel lay asleep on his bed, still dressed in his clothes. The room was filled with the stink of Gabriel that the boy had smelled all his life, that was always on his uncle. It was always a constant struggle for his mother to persuade Gabriel to bathe.

He went back out to the garage and took the chair out of the storeroom. He set it on the concrete floor and stood there and looked at it.

They'll come here first, he thought. *But no one will believe he walked up that hill. Is that enough?*

He went over their journey in his mind. The hunters, the come-along lying in the rhododendron, the shattered door. At any moment the lights from his mother's van would fill the garage. He thought of the brick buildings of the state hospital standing in the valley among the leafless trees, the moonlight caught up in the razor wire.

My uncle, he thought.

It would be a long time before his stink would leave the bedroom. If Gabriel could just sleep the rest of the winter like the bear he claimed he saw, sleeping through the snow and rain, warm in a den hidden deep in a rhododendron thicket, and emerge thin and bright of mind from his winter's sleep. And then he could walk or take a car to visit Margaret Cully, driven there by that force which the boy did not understand, the same force that had made Gabriel climb the mountain.

He went into the storeroom and returned with a handsaw. Then he quickly sawed up the chair into lengths the same as the wood stacked in the garage. He liked the smell the wood made as he cut into it. Once he finished, he swept up the sawdust and put it in the trashcan. Then he went into the house and fed the wood into the stove. It was clear to him now that his mother had to work late and that there had been no need to rush. The flames quickly died down in the stove and soon there was only the red glow of the hickory logs through the window.

His mother called and asked him to fix supper for himself and Gabriel. He went into the kitchen to make macaroni and cheese but found that he was not hungry. He went to the living room to watch TV, but when he sat down and scrolled through the channels he found nothing to interest him. He turned the set off. From Gabriel's room came the sound of snoring. He realized that burning the chair had been a futile gesture. It was true that no one would believe that Gabriel, even with his help, had climbed the hill and now the chair was gone. But Margaret Cully was still there.

We can live here, he thought. *We'll be fine here.*

But he knew that was not going to happen. No matter where they lived there would be neighbors with things to steal and girls. He imagined them living in some desert landscape, the only neighbors miles away, the only roads to their houses running over high mountain passes. They would never live in such a place. Gabriel was headed for the state hospital or jail.

Gabriel was muttering something in his sleep. Then he was silent. He got up and walked to the open door of Gabriel's room. Gabriel lay on his back, sleeping soundly and not snoring. His face was covered with sweat, for now the house had warmed up.

He went into the room and pulled off Gabriel's gloves and knitted cap. He unzipped his jacket. Gabriel murmured in his sleep but did not wake. He lay down beside his uncle and pulled a blanket over them. It smelled of Gabriel and something else he could not identify, perhaps just the scent of old wool. He closed his eyes and waited for sleep. And then he was asleep until he was awakened by the sound of Gabriel's voice.

"Down in the hole," Gabriel murmured.

Gabriel was still asleep. His face was dry and his breathing slow and relaxed.

"Down in the rock."

The Bear Hunters

The boy reached out and put his hand on Gabriel's big shoulder.

"A hole in the rock."

Now sweat broke out on Gabriel's face and his legs moved as if he were struggling to climb a hill.

"Up in the flowers," the boy whispered. "Up in the flowers."

Gabriel slipped back into a deep sleep.

The boy left the room and returned with the Bible his mother had given him on Easter. Then he woke Gabriel, which was hard, because Gabriel resisted, turning his face into the pillow. But finally the boy got him out of the bed and into the living room.

"We'll start with Genesis," the boy said. "You could say that one perfect. You'll be back on TV."

"Can't," Gabriel said.

"You got up that mountain. You can learn this book. It'll be easy. You already know it. It's inside your head."

Gabriel placed both hands on the top of his head.

"I can feel it," Gabriel said.

"That's right," the boy said. "It's there. Now listen close. You raise your hand when you need to let your brain rest."

"In the beginning God created the heaven and the earth." the boy began. "And the earth was without form, and void; and darkness *was* upon the face of the deep."

He read on while Gabriel listened, the boy reading with expectation toward the death of Joseph, filling Gabriel's head with the words that might save him.

Pulpwood

Breland was cleaning seatrout when Sally walked over from her house. She commented on the number and the size before she got down to business. While she was talking, he watched a boat run up the bay and pass under the highway bridge that spanned the mouth of Bay St. Louis and out into the open expanse of the Gulf.

"Nice boat," he said.

He wished he were on it, going out after lemon fish off the Chandeleur Islands.

"You just up and quit?" she asked.

"That's right," he said.

"What will you do?"

"Fish some."

"And after that?"

"I don't know. I'm just going to let it happen."

She started to say something but thought better of it. He watched her think. She was choosing her words carefully.

"That doesn't make any sense," she said. "You had a good job."

For fifteen years Breland had been in charge of the dormitories at a military school in Gulfport. He also taught tennis and boxing to the cadets."

"I'm thinking about going down to South America," he said. "Do some hunting and fishing there before I get too old. You can still hunt jaguar in

Pulpwood

some places. I've wanted to do that since I was a boy."

"You're going to lose this house," she said.

"I suppose," he said.

A few years ago he had bought the small cottage in Bay St. Louis. Sally Suzaneau lived in a house she had inherited from her parents two doors down. She owned a nursery and landscaping business, also inherited from her parents. Sally and Breland had been lovers for a year. They had talked about getting married, but lately she had been reminding him of his mother. It was the way she always sat ramrod straight on the edge of her chair. He had noticed that when they first started going out together. And just the other day, the way she sniffed at her coffee to savor the aroma. That too was the perfect picture of his mother. He had been unable to eat his breakfast.

"Working at that school can't be that hard," she said.

They had talked about whether he would go into the nursery business with her after they were married. It was not something he had looked forward to. He was not interested in growing things.

"Whether it's hard or easy, I'm not doing it anymore," he said.

He was not going to miss running the dorms. And he was not going to miss teaching tennis. It was the loss of those young boxers that he knew he would regret from time to time. He believed that boxing taught the students something useful about themselves, respect for their own skills and their opponents'. It was something they did not learn from tennis.

"Is it because you don't want to get married?" she asked. "Is that what this is all about?"

"No, that's not what it's about at all," he said.

"Then what?"

"I'm not sure."

"Go to South America this summer. Hunt and fish all you want."

He had showed her pictures of the enormous trout to be had in Argentina.

"It wouldn't be the same." he said.

"When you stop talking crazy, come see me," she said.

She turned and walked across the yard, disappearing behind a clump of oleanders.

He tried not to think about her as he finished filleting the fish, instead concentrating on smoothly sliding the knife blade along the ribs toward the tail. He packed them in plastic bags and then cleaned his tools and washed his hands.

He moved out of the house and into a room at the YMCA in Gulfport. He sold the furniture, his boat, and his guns and fishing rods. It was easy to find a buyer for the house, but he did not make much off the sale. After he paid his debts, he found he had ten thousand dollars. Even as he liquidated his possessions, he was aware of being driven by the fear of something he could not even name. It was as if he had gone out beyond the islands into the really deep part of the Gulf and on a moonless night had dived deep to the very bottom where it was cold and perfectly dark. He believed that if he could reduce his life to the simplest possible terms, he could avoid sinking down and coming face to face with that unnamable thing. The only possessions he kept were his truck, an unabridged dictionary and the collection of Greek and Roman classics he had inherited from his father.

Every morning he woke early and masturbated. He yearned to wake to the warmth of a woman beside him, to her soft voice and her caresses, but if he tried to live that sort of life, he thought, his little money would soon be gone.

At the gym he jumped rope and did some work on the heavy bag. He concluded his workout with a five mile run on the beach. Afterwards he went to the library where he spent the day reading one of his father's books. The margins were filled with notes made with a fountain pen, the handwriting so hurried and careless he could only read a few of them. Every day he half expected to come upon a note that might explain his father's suicide, but the only clear ones were his father's observations upon

Pulpwood

the conduct of men in battle. His father was a harsh critic.

It was because of his father that Breland had read Thucydides when he was a freshman in high school. And the British poets of World War I. He could not exactly remember when he had started reading his father's library, but it had been at an early age, before he went to high school. His father had been a pharmacist.

One evening in June, the summer before Breland started the first grade, his father had locked himself in his study and shot himself with his service revolver. He left no note. No one ever had any idea why he did it.

He and his mother slept together that night. Breland was used to crawling into the big bed when he had a nightmare. This time he woke to the sound of her sobbing, and he walked across the hall and into her room where she lay crying in the dark. He went to sleep with her arms wrapped around him, waking in the morning to watch her sleeping in her peignoir. She had not removed her make-up, and he found it strange to see her painted face in bed.

He waked her, and they had breakfast. That afternoon her sister arrived from Alabama. That night the women slept together. Later he realized that his mother was a woman who had no female friends. That was why she had found herself alone with him in the house. She preferred the company of men. And from time to time, long after his father was buried and the sister went back to Alabama, she would ask him to sleep with her because she was scared of the dark. He still had memories of his mother in her peignoir and the smell of her body: usually a lilac soap smell mixed with the lingering scent of her favorite perfume. He was relieved when Wilson, who was to become his stepfather, moved into the house. She and Wilson had had no children. He had died soon after Breland went off to college.

Although he tried to be careful, the money disappeared faster than he thought possible. At Christmas he visited his mother in Jackson. He did not tell her that he had quit his job. During dinner he watched his mother sit in the chair in the same way she always had, and when she served the coffee and performed her ritual with the cup, he was sure he had done the right thing in breaking off the affair with Sally.

By Easter his money was almost gone. Yet he kept up his morning regimen, rising early every day, trying to keep inside him the rhythms of his fists against the bag until just before he walked into the library. As he read there was that good feeling of emptying himself, of the weight of the gloves on his hands and the smell of the bag and his own sweat. Somewhere in one of those books he thought he would find something that would tell him how to live.

The week after the Fourth of July he was down to his last hundred dollars. His truck still ran all right, but it had so many miles on it that he did not think it was worth selling.

He met a woman on the beach and asked her out to dinner, planning to spend all the money on that, and hoping she might invite him to spend the night with her. For the first time since Sally had disappeared behind the oleanders, he felt that he could not spend another night alone.

Margo wanted to go dancing at a place on the beach where they played blues music. She was, he guessed, four or five years younger than he, a social worker at the VA hospital. He had told her he had just got back from Saudi Arabia where he had been doing engineering work for the Saudis, repairing Gulf War damage. And for some reason, though he had always prided himself on speaking the truth, Breland took great delight in this fabrication.

They were on the floor dancing to someone doing an imitation of Otis Redding when he saw Sally sitting at the bar. He supposed Sally would think Margo was the reason for his strange behavior. He steered Margo to the other side of the dance floor.

He planned to suggest they go to a restaurant famous for stuffed flounder. But when he found Sally sitting at their table, he composed himself

Pulpwood

and made introductions. Sally had a date who was going to join them.

"It's Cecil Barnett," Sally said.

"That lawyer who likes to sail?" Breland asked.

"That's the one," Sally said.

"I love sailing," Margo said.

"Then you'll have to come with us sometime," Sally said. "All four of us could go."

"I'm not that interested in sailing," Breland said.

"I'm not surprised," Sally said. "I hear that you live at the Y and spend the afternoons in the library. You can't have much money left."

"Oh, no," Margo said. "The Saudis paid him plenty."

At that moment Sally's date appeared, and the band started to play again. Sally started to ask Margo a question about the Saudis, but Cecil swept her off onto the dance floor.

Breland took Margo to dinner. They ate flounder and drank two bottles of good wine.

In Margo's bedroom, after love, she wanted him to tell her about what he was doing at the library.

"It was a joke," he said. "Sally likes to joke."

"Are you going to be here in the morning when I wake up?" she asked.

"Only if you promise to ask me no more questions about the library," he said.

She did and for the first time in almost a year he went to sleep with his arms around a woman.

In the morning he left while she was still asleep. She might not ask him any more questions, but he would never be able to explain why he was broke.

He returned to his room at the Y and retrieved his things. He pawned his watch and a ring. All this gained him only enough money to live a few weeks. As he treated himself to a big breakfast of shrimp and grits, he pondered what his next move might be. He might go back to work. He could get another job, probably at a school somewhere. He could count on good recommendations from the military school. But he had found nothing in the books or in his father's gloss that would teach him how to live, how to swim down to the deepest part of the Gulf and to smile at that dark thing. And he often reflected that the books had done his father no good at all.

After sitting on the beach wall for a long time, watching people fly kites and wind surf, he decided to ask his mother for money. Fifteen years ago, she had had the family farm near Hattiesburg planted with pine trees for pulpwood. The land had been covered with longleaf pine when his ancestors helped log it around the turn of the century. On the cleared land they had done some cotton farming until the poor soil was exhausted. Now all that was left of the farm was the trees. The farmhouse had burned, leaving nothing but the chimney and the brick piers that formed the foundation.

When he visited her in Jackson at Christmas, she had been talking about selling the trees.

He called her collect from a pay phone at the Y.

"Mama," he began. "I want to talk to you about those pine trees."

To his surprise she did not interrupt him or even sound shocked. She let him talk until he had nothing left to say.

"You can have the money," she said. "They're already cutting. Down on the back side toward Mr. Goodline's place. But I want something in return. I want a week at Pecan Hill."

That was what she called the farm. He had been there a few times to hunt deer. There were no pecan trees, the house site marked by a couple of big black walnuts. But there was a hill. Although the farm was mostly bottom land, the house itself was built on a low hill just above the hundred year high water mark.

"Mama, it's the middle of July," he said. "It's going to be too hot for you."

"I don't need air conditioning," she said. "I don't even need a fan. Your father took me to dinner there once. That was in August. After supper a nice breeze came up from the creek. They told me that happened every night."

He wondered at the ability of her aging mind to create delusions.

"There's not going to be a breeze, Mama," he said. "It's going to be hot."

"You're broke," she said. "I'll buy all the supplies. We'll need a tent and food and a lantern."

He argued with her some more, but she was adamant. If he wanted the money, he was going to have to spend a week with her at Pecan Hill. So he acceded to her demands. She was going to wire him some money. Next Monday he would drive to Hattiesburg and meet her at a country store.

The temperature was close to a hundred when he left Gulfport and drove inland toward Hattiesburg, a hundred miles to the north. The truck needed a new ring job, and he left behind him a cloud of bluish smoke. The air conditioner had long ago failed. Soon his shirt was stuck to the back of his seat, and the blast of hot wind in his face gave him no relief. He didn't expect that his mother would last more than one day at the farm. It was likely to be too hot to sleep at night, especially inside a tent. One night, he thought, that would be enough. Then she would retreat to her air-conditioned house in Jackson.

She was waiting for him at the store, dressed in khaki safari clothes and a man's Panama hat. He threw his arms around her, feeling her frail, old woman's body through her clothes. She appeared to have no weight at all, as if she were made out of paper instead of flesh and bone.

"What a beautiful day," she said.

He looked up at the sky. There was not a cloud in it, no hope of an afternoon thunderstorm to cool things off.

"It's pretty hot," he said.

"Why this is nothing," she said. "And this evening it'll be cool at the house. You'll see. Now tell me about Sally Suzaneau."

So he told her while they stood together in the sun, she looking up at him with her pale blue eyes from under the brim of her hat. She looked as cool as if she were standing on a block of ice.

"Well, you found out what Sally Suzaneau was made of," she said. "You take the money from the trees and go away someplace. Out of the country. That's what you should do. I think you should go to Italy."

He stood there hatless, feeling as if the sun were drilling a hole in his head, and tried to understand her reaction. He had expected her to be furious with him for abandoning his job and then coming to her asking for money. Now she was giving it to him as if it meant nothing at all to her, as if what he had done was the most normal thing in the world. And suggesting that he go to Italy. He had never heard her mention Italy before. As far as he knew she had never been out of the South.

He followed her to the farm. She drove her old station wagon packed with camping equipment. She turned off the highway onto a gravel road. A logging truck passed them loaded with freshly cut pine logs. When the road turned to dirt, he followed the twin plumes of dust raised by her car. The dust had been pounded talcum fine by the passage of the logging trucks, and the leaves of the trees and honeysuckle lining the road were coated with it. The dust had a slightly sweet taste as if it had absorbed some of the nectar of the honeysuckle flowers.

They met another logging truck, and he smelled the sharp scent of the resin. Ahead in the dust cloud her brake lights came on and the right turn indicator began to flash. He made the turn, and they drove out of the dust cloud and into the bright sunlight again. They were driving through a pasture. Up ahead were the twin black walnuts, along with a big magnolia in bloom. The chimney stood between the walnuts. All around them were the pines.

They unloaded the station wagon. Off in the distance he heard the sound of trucks and the rattle of chain saws, along with the cough of a bulldozer they were using to cut a road to carry out the timber. She had bought everything necessary to set up a camp. The tents, which she showed him how to pitch, were mostly mosquito netting.

"We can go to sleep looking up at the stars," she said.

Inside a mosquito-netted enclosure, they ate the ham sandwiches she had made for their supper. It was evening now. Bats swooped in and out of the circle of light thrown from the gasoline lantern he'd hung from the ridge pole.

"I wonder why I feel such a connection with this place," she said. "I don't imagine I set foot out here more than five times. The house burned before I could really get acquainted with it."

She pointed toward the creek where there was still a faint bar of light over the oaks and hickories.

"Your father said he and his brothers used to swim there," she said. "He was going to show me where. But he never got around to doing it."

A cool breeze came up from the creek, shaking the leaves of the walnuts.

"See, just like I told you," she said. "I wonder where that cool breeze comes from?"

"It's always cooler in the bottoms," he said. "It's nothing more than that."

"I've never even seen that creek."

"Maybe we'll go down there tomorrow."

"Yes, we could. I don't imagine it's changed any since your father swam in it."

Later he lay on his back on an air mattress and looked up at the stars. Now there was no scent of lilac soap and perfume. The dominant smell was insect repellent and sunscreen. She had undressed beside him while he lay with his back turned to her, remembering those nights in her bed and the warm feel of her body against him, sometimes welcoming but sometimes carrying with it a cloying heaviness.

A meteor shower began at the foot of Orion. He wanted to call out to her, but she was asleep. Her snoring competed with the whine of the cicadas and the trilling of the tree frogs.

He closed his eyes and slept too.

In the morning he awoke to the smell of coffee. The cutters had not begun work yet, the only sounds those of the birds singing their morning songs. The pasture between them and the creek was covered with patches of fog. It was not hot yet, but he knew that soon it was going to be.

"I want to see how much they've cut," she said. "We'll go while it's still cool."

They walked away from the creek, through the orderly rows of pines, all of them about a foot in diameter. It was still dark and cool beneath the trees. They had not gone a hundred yards before they startled a doe. She darted away through the trees, her white tail flashing.

Off in the distance he heard the sound of a diesel motor starting. A few yards away he saw the end of the trees, an open space filled with light. They walked out of the trees together, she in the lead.

Before them was a wasteland filled with stumps and branches. The scent of resin was everywhere. Far away he saw a yellow bulldozer moving across the wasteland, puffs of black smoke shooting out of its smokestack as it pushed a collection of stumps into a pile. A breeze brought them the stink of diesel fuel.

"I hate pine trees," she said.

"Why?" he asked.

"Oh, it's not the longleaf I hate," she said. "Once the whole of south Mississippi was covered with a longleaf forest. It's these trees we plant for pulpwood that I don't like. Commercial trees. It'd be different if what I planted was going to become houses, but they turn it into newsprint or toilet paper. I'm going to let live oaks grow here. This land has had enough of pines."

They returned to their camp and had breakfast.

She took a plastic sack and some tubing out of the car.

"You go down to the creek and fill this up," she said.

She explained to him that it was a portable shower, designed to be hung from a tree limb. The sun would heat the water inside the plastic bladder.

"I don't mind being hot," she said. "But I can't stand being dirty."

He walked down to the creek, which was mostly dry. He climbed down into the bed and walked up it until he came to a deep pool of black water. Frogs jumped at his approach and turtles dived off a log. He wondered if this was the pool, where water striders skated over the surface, that his father had swum in as a boy.

When he returned, he hung the bladder from the limb of one of the black walnuts in a position to catch the morning sun. Just before noon she took a shower. He hoped that none of the cutters would wander up through the woods and startle her.

They spent the rest of day sitting in the screened shelter reading, she a novel and he Livy's account of the Second Punic War. His father had written his name in the book in a large bold hand. They waited until dark and had supper inside the shelter.

Then they went to sleep, he watching the stars in hopes of another meteor shower that never came.

The rest of the week went this way. They read, ate, and talked until early in the morning when it had cooled off enough to sleep. And she still sat in a camp chair with the same posture she used at home and still sniffed at her coffee in the same way, exclaiming in delight over the aroma.

The sounds of the cutting came closer and closer until finally the bulldozer, trucks, and men with chain saws were working a few yards away. They moved on, leaving only the black walnut trees and the magnolia standing.

On the morning of the seventh day, they woke to a scene as desolate as any battlefield. The birds were gone. Only a solitary mockingbird sang from the top of one of the black walnuts. The air was full of the smell of diesel fuel and resin.

"I have to leave soon," she said. "I play bridge this afternoon."

She turned away from him for a moment to regard the clear cut land.

"I meant what I said about you going to Italy," she said.

He started to protest, but she silenced him with a wave of her hand.

"Go," she said. "Go while you have a chance."

He had no idea what he would do, probably continue to live at the Y.

She looked across the cleared land beyond the walnut trees.

"Your father killed himself because he stayed in Mississippi," she said.

She had never said anything like this before.

"Where did he want to go?" he asked.

"He wanted to go back to Florence," she said. "He was there during the war. He wanted to write poetry. When he came home from the war, he was serious about it. But he said that he was a man with a family, responsibilities, that he couldn't spend his time on frivolous things. So he studied to be a pharmacist. And I agreed with him. Because I was afraid."

"Afraid of what."

He watched a dust devil traverse the wasteland, picking up pieces of branches. She turned to watch it too. It grew dark and thick with the earth. Then it moved upward into the sky and disappeared.

"Afraid of the same things he was afraid of," she said. "Lack of money. I was pregnant with you at the time. But I was really afraid of something else. It was his excitement for it, the passion he had. I suppose you could say I was jealous, but that's not exactly the right word."

"So he shot himself because he decided not to write?" he said. "Was there a note you never told anyone about?"

He found himself angry.

"No, I'm just guessing," she said. "That's all. But he burned his manuscripts before he died. He did it in the middle of the night, the night before he shot himself. I woke and he wasn't in bed. I saw the glow from the fire. Out at the back of the yard. We hadn't used that wire trash burner for years. It was against the law to burn trash in the city. I imagine that breaking that law made him nervous. I watched him until he finished and then he came back to bed. He cried when he told me what he had done. I'd never seen your father cry before. It was a thing he was ashamed of and I comforted him the best I could. Then we went to sleep. He woke us all in the morning."

She had told it in a calm controlled voice, as if she were a historian recalling some distant event.

"I'm not going to kill myself," he said.

"I believe you. But I think you need to get out of Mississippi for a time. He'd spent the war in Africa and Italy but there was nothing he could take from that but death. He needed something else, but he never found it."

"I'll take your money. I'll go."

He was lying.

"Good."

She looked toward the creek and its border of hardwoods.

"No, I'll not plant pines here again," she said. "We'll have live oaks."

He tried to imagine a live oak forest that neither she nor he would ever live to see.

Then he thought of actually going to Italy, how he could travel on what surely would be a modest amount of money. He might go to Florence first and look at the art and then later when it turned cold he would go on to Rome. He imagined himself riding in second class on a night train to Rome, the speech of the passengers as unintelligible to him as the songs of the birds. There would be snow in the Po Valley. If he were lucky, he might see pheasants, brilliant against the whiteness, as the train passed through the farm land. When he arrived, he would take a room in a cheap hotel near the station. He would have breakfast in a café and drink coffee in the sunshine. When he returned to his room, he would feel lightheaded from lack of sleep and the coffee, but not sleepy at all. He would go out and wander about the city.

She went to take a shower but discovered that the bladder had ruptured. She returned holding it away from her body with obvious distaste, as if it were a dead animal.

"I'll return this thing," she said. "I feel so dirty. I think I'll swim in the creek before I go home. You show me the way."

He led her to the creek. They stood together on the edge of the dark pool. Water striders skated across the surface. It was cool in the creekbed, the banks rising well above their heads and the trees interlacing over them and closing out the sky. The pool was perfectly still, looking like a piece of polished black metal.

He stood with his back to it while she took off her clothes.

"Your father once swam here," she said. "Just think of that."

He heard her entering the water. And then she was swimming. He turned and watched her swim to the center of the pool. She stopped and treaded water.

"Oh, it's so cool," she said. "There must be a spring that feeds it."

He had not noticed that the water was particularly cool, but he had filled the bladder in the sun-warmed shallows.

"You swim too," she called.

He shook his head.

She did a surface dive and disappeared. It seemed to him that she had been under a long time when she emerged, laughing and gasping for air.

"It's deep!" she cried. "I never touched bottom."

She swam towards him for a few strokes, which brought her to the shallows. She stopped and stood, the water level with her shoulders. Then she walked toward him, gradually emerging to stand before him, the water at her knees. He stood transfixed, like a deer in a spotlight, gazing at her wrinkled breasts and at the blonde hair of her pubis, which had turned mostly white.

"Your father always thought I was ravishing," she said.

Pulpwood

He did not reply, but turned and ran, going up the bank and into the undergrowth as quickly as any deer. He broke out of the trees and into the wasteland, his arms pumping and his legs churning, while far away he heard the sound of her voice: high and insistent and pleading.

A View of the Lilies

Big Red strained on the lead as he pulled Ben away from the river, out of the hickories and gums and up on the bluff where there were pines. Joe was behind him, he and Sugar caught in a tangle of grapevines. Joe was a large man, better able to control the dog, but Ben was more adept at slipping through obstacles such as briars or grapevines or sweet gum thickets.

They went on, Joe still in the lead because he was faster. He had run cross country at Clemson. The bloodhounds were following the scent left by their fellow deputy. The dogs were silent, for they had been bred not to bay. Up they went, following one of the lanes formed by the pines that twenty years ago had been planted in orderly rows, the needles thick beneath their feet.

"He's headed for the rock," Joe called.

Ben did not reply. Instead he concentrated on keeping up with the dog.

Now the land ran level and off to the east he could see the open space above the river. If Russell were a criminal, he would be trapped on the rock with no place to go. The only alternative would be to risk a leap into the treetops below. He came out of the pines onto the rock. There was Russell standing on the bare granite, his head thrown back and laughing. Then the dogs were all over him. The men pulled them off and praised them.

Ben and Joe sat down on the rock, both of them still breathing hard, for it was a hot afternoon in the middle of June in South Carolina. They drank from their canteens while Russell petted the dogs.

"I thought I'd lost you in Maury's Creek," Russell said. "Lord, but I ran right over a big water snake. Did you see it?"

"No," Joe said.

"The dogs went straight down the middle of the creek," Ben said. "Folks who don't believe bloodhounds can track over water should've seen 'em."

"There's the Ball Man," Russell said.

He had taken out a pair of field glasses and trained them on the river below. Ben and Joe stood up and looked where Russell was pointing.

Down in the river among the lilies were two canoes, one yellow and one red. A species of spider lilies, which grew only in a few places in the world, were abundant in the shoals below. This time of year they were in full bloom, the shoals turned into fields of white.

Stephen Foster's canoe was piled high with balls. He was a photographer, his pictures of birds of prey and other animals well known in New York and Europe, but he was more famous in the county for collecting balls that had been washed or thrown into the river and donating them to needy children.

"Who's that with him?" Joe asked.

"Don't know," Russell said.

Russell handed him the glasses.

"Too far away to tell," Joe said.

"Let me see," Ben said.

Joe started to hand him the glasses, but as he did they slipped out of his hand. He caught them with his other hand just before they hit the rock.

"Watch out for my glasses," Russell said.

Ben put the glasses to his eyes and scanned the river. Everywhere there were lilies but the canoes had vanished.

"They've gone behind that island," Russell said.

From where they were standing they could see the head of the island but not the foot.

"Let's give the dogs some water and run 'em again," Ben said. "They need the work."

"Let 'em chase Joe this time," Russell said.

"I'll go through the gravel pits," Joe said. "Let 'em pick me out while their noses are full of the scent of all that diesel fuel and dynamite."

Joe took a long drink from his canteen and then walked off into the pines.

Ben found his wife Judith shooting baskets in the dusk at her outdoor goal. The strip of concrete in front of the garage was well lighted, but sometimes she preferred to play in the dark. This year, after she had quit her job at the nuclear plant, she often could not sleep and went out to play in the middle of the night. He would be awakened by the sound of the ball on the concrete and the squeak of her shoes.

Once he had gotten up and walked to the kitchen, intending to go out the door to speak to her, to ask her what was wrong. But he was arrested at the sight of her in the dark, her body in ceaseless motion as if she were playing against an entire team by herself. She drove down one side of the driveway toward the basket, spun away, and then hanging in the air shot the ball, which went in beautifully, catching nothing but net. It was a move he had watched her make many times ten years ago at Clemson.

Then she circled back to do it again, dribbling through a crowd of imaginary defenders. He saw her face, partially illuminated by the security light at the edge of the yard. It had such a look of anguish he could not bear to look at her again and so turned away and returned to bed.

She had quit her job to become a consulting engineer, but almost a year had passed and she had done no consulting. She had complained of boredom out at the plant. Not once during the year had she complained of being bored with staying at home. She had spent a good deal of her time cooking the game he had stored in the freezer. He had tired of duck, dove, deer, and turkey. Now she had started to talk about farming, the business that had bankrupted her father, but she had no land to farm.

Stephen Foster did, land he rented out. Stephen had been at college with them. And today his friend Joe had pretended to drop the glasses so he could not see that it was Judith in the yellow canoe. Joe had not known that Judith had been going out on the river with Stephen for weeks. Had not known that Ben knew and had even encouraged her to go.

She stopped playing and switched on the lights. He got out of the truck. The smooth skin of her muscular legs and upper arms glistened with sweat.

"Look at this!" she said.

She held out the ball for him to see.

"It's a game ball," she said. "From when we beat Alabama. We all signed it. See, I'm right there."

As she read off the names of the other girls, he imagined her hanging in the air, her body in the same position that night he had watched her from the kitchen window.

"You and Stephen found that today?" he asked.

"Yes, there it was, sitting right in a clump of lilies," she said.

She bounced the ball and then spun it in her hands.

"Now how do you suppose it got in the river?" she said.

"You could put a notice in the paper," he said.

"Nope, now this ball belongs to me."

"We were on the rock right after lunch."

"You must have seen us right before we found it. On the back side of that island."

And what did you do today besides pull basketballs out of the river, he thought. *Should I just ask her? Has he promised her the farm?*

Big Red and Sugar whined from the dog cage in the back of the truck.

"Did they do good today?" she asked.

"Yes, they tracked Russell over water," he said. "All that scent coming off his head just hangs there. It was easy for them and the creek kept 'em cool."

"Dumb as rocks. Smelling machines are what they are."

"They're good at what they do."

"I wasn't saying anything against them. You've said the same."

She was right. It was his expression.

"I know," he said. "I guess I'm tired."

"I'll go make us a couple of gin and tonics," she said.

He took the dogs out of the truck and put them in the kennel where he fed and watered them. As they ate, he sat with his back to the wire and a dog on either side of him. He imagined sleeping with the dogs on the pine needles on the bluff above the river, drifting off to sleep listening to the regular heavy sound of their breathing.

He wanted their life to return to what it had been before she quit her job. She had come to hate the sight of the huge blue cooling towers. He did agree with that. They were like grotesque metallic mushrooms that had sprung up overnight out of the gently rolling land. He thought of how they had built the house on ten acres of land. She was using her degree; he was working the dogs. Everything had been perfect.

He heard her calling him.

"Good night, darlins," he said.

He petted them one last time. Then he went out the gate and across the dew-wet grass to the house.

In the morning they woke to light rain and low clouds.

"I guess you won't be collecting with Stephen today," he said.

"No, and besides he's got film to develop," she said. "I'm spending the day on the web. It's about time I should be getting some work."

He said nothing in reply, for he had heard her talk like this before. At least she was not talking about farming. Then the phone rang. A child had disappeared.

"I'll have dinner ready," she said. "Deer tacos. You're not getting tired of them are you?"

"No, that'll be fine," he said. "And maybe we'll find the child right away. Take her home to her family."

He kissed her and went to put the dogs in the truck.

The country where the child was lost was below the fall line, where the land was flat and the soil sandy. Fields of cotton and soybeans stretched away on either side of the road toward distant tree lines. The rain fell gently on the fields. Only a little water had accumulated in the fields and ditches.

He met Joe at a farmhouse. A helicopter hovered overhead and then flew off over a stand of trees. A group of people on the porch, relatives and friends of the family, watched them intently as they stood together in the rain.

The five-year-old girl had wandered out of the yard with her dog. The dog had returned but not the girl. The woods behind the house, leased to a hunting club, stretched all the way to the river five miles away.

"Low-shoulders in them woods," Joe said.

"Yes," he said.

Here, below the fall line, there were cottonmouths in addition to copperheads and rattlers. They always worried about the dogs, but so far they had never lost a dog to a snake.

They drove along a muddy track past the house and to the edge of the woods. There he let the dogs sniff one of the girl's socks. Then he and Joe followed the dogs into the woods.

It was all oaks and hickories. The leaves kept out the rain, but water dripped from the trees and the bushes and the leaves were wet. They jumped a doe out of a honeysuckle thicket and she bounded away, her white tail flashing. The dogs ignored her.

"They're on her," Joe said.

Ben wondered if he should ask Joe directly about Judith and Stephen. *If it's true*, he thought. *What then?*

Then he pushed the thought of Judith and Stephen off into a remote corner of his mind. He concentrated on Sugar who did appear to be on a scent; he watched the ground for snakes.

They came out of the trees into a small soybean field. At one end of the field was an earthen dam marking a pond. Trucks were parked by the dam. A diver stood on it in a wet suit.

"Rushing things, ain't they," Joe said.

"Yes," he said. "I hope the dogs don't take us there."

The dogs took them away from the pond on a dirt track used by farm machinery to the far end of the field. But instead of going back into the woods, the dogs followed the track along the edge of the field toward the pond. The trucks of the rescue squad had recently used the road. Although he looked hard, he could not find a single track made by the little girl.

They followed the dogs up onto the dam. A group of men were watching the diver.

"We followed her tracks up here," a man said.

"Somebody might've told us," Ben said.

"We came through the woods," Joe said. "One of these dogs could've got bit by a cottonmouth."

"We're sorry," a second man said. "We found these tracks and called in Angela. I hope she don't find her."

"Look!" a third man said.

The diver was ascending, her passage marked by a trail of bubbles through the clear, coffee-colored water. As she came to the surface, they all saw that she carried with her the body of the child. The child's long blonde hair streamed out behind her, her body limp, her face in peaceful repose. And as always with the dead, particularly children, Ben felt as if he were looking into the heart of things without understanding what he was seeing.

"Aw, it's a shame," the first man said.

He imagined the dogs finding her, the child laughing as they licked her face. That was the image he had tried to keep in his mind since they had arrived at the farmhouse.

They lifted the child out of the diver's arms. The dogs sniffed at her as the rescue squad zipped her into a body bag. The dogs were glum, their heads down and their tails lowered. They were always like that when they found a dead person instead of a live one.

The insects were loud in the grass; swallows swooped low over the pond, dipping their beaks to drink. The clouds had thinned overhead; it had stopped raining. The men had grown less solemn. One of them laughed at something quietly and the others joined in. That indifference. He could never get used to it.

He and Joe took the dogs into the woods. While Joe held the dogs he walked off into the trees and hid in a cane thicket. The dogs would work better on the next search if they ended the day finding a live person. He sat on the soft leaves for a time, listening to the water drip from the trees. He heard Joe's voice far off in the woods and then the sound of the dogs' paws on the wet leaves. Then Sugar, followed by Big Red, came bursting into the thicket. As they licked his face, he discovered that he was crying.

"Good darlins," he said. "Good darlins."

As he drove toward home, the clouds grew thick again. It began to rain hard. The dogs, after they had licked themselves dry, had gone to sleep in their cage. The truck smelled of wet dogs, a smell he liked.

Stephen Foster, he thought.

He could confront Judith this evening. But he wondered what he would do if she admitted that Stephen was her lover. He could leave her or suggest that they go for counseling in Charlotte. Counseling did not right now seem attractive to him. The image of the dead child, her hair streaming out behind her, suddenly appeared before him. Two people fell in love and had a child who they loved and now she was dead. He wondered if the couple had other children.

But today Judith was not collecting balls with Stephen. Stephen was at home developing film. She could be with him. His house was over in the next county. He would go there and if it were true he hoped that Judith was there with Stephen.

Stephen's house was old and grand and in ill repair. It needed painting and the hurricane a year before had damaged the roof, which was still covered in one place by a blue plastic tarp. He wondered if that was the result of Stephen's indifference or a lack of money.

The house sat on a square plot of land filled with live oaks, magnolias, and pecans. Ancient camellias grew in profusion beneath the trees. And around that husbanded square of lush foliage stretched fields of cotton and soybeans.

His father's ancestors had built the house and cleared the land around it. His parents and grandparents were dead, he the last of his line. With his death, Ben imagined that the farm would be sold to some stranger. And then like the shock of plunging into a creek in December to follow the dogs, an image appeared before him of Judith standing in one of those fields, watching a picker move through *her* cotton.

He drove along the circular driveway lined with camellias. Stephen's truck was not in the front of the house. Neither was it under the roof of the big shop shed where a cotton wagon was parked half filled with balls of every description. A yellow and a red canoe were on the ground beside it.

He returned to the house and rang the bell. Then he tried the door and it swung open. Stephen was probably the only person in the county without an alarm system. He walked across the heart-of-pine floor and out of the entryway into the big living room. The furniture was covered with dust and the room looked like it had not been lived in for a long time. It was the same with the room on the other side of the big hall and also the dining room; the chandelier covered with dust and spider webs.

Then he went into the kitchen, which was neat and clean, and into the bedroom, which was the same, an open wardrobe filled with Stephen's clothes. There were paintings on the walls but no photographs of birds.

He went upstairs to explore the rest of the house. He did not care if

A View of the Lilies

Stephen came home and found him there. They would sit down and talk about Judith over coffee. And then he would go home, what to do about Judith settled in his mind.

Stephen had turned several of the upstairs rooms into a studio and darkroom. One room was filled with photographs of hawks, falcons, ospreys, and eagles. The one Ben liked the best was of an eagle, taking flight out of the lilies as patches of fog hung low over the water.

Then on a table in Stephen's workroom he found picture after picture of Judith. Most of them had been taken in the woods on the opposite side of the river from the big rock. Here the land was lower. Once there had been a gristmill there. The only access, besides walking in five or six miles through the woods from a county road, was by water. There was a series of photographs of her standing or sitting on the foundations of the ruined mill. Others were of Stephen sitting on a blanket amid the remains of a picnic at some place in the woods Ben did not recognize, a clearing amid a stand of pines, and out beyond Ben, over his shoulder, was a view of the river and the lilies, a field of white shining in the light. And there were basketball pictures, taken at their house. She hung suspended in the air as she put up her famous jump shot.

He went to the window and looked out on the fields.

Has he promised her this? he thought.

The pictures meant nothing. They would be expected to have a picnic if they spent the day on the river gathering balls. Anyone would expect him to take pictures. But then there was Joe's conduct with the field glasses. It would be no use trying to talk with him or Russell. Neither of them would want to get involved. They would tell him to talk with Judith.

He left the house and drove home, intending to ask Judith directly if she and Stephen were lovers.

He found Judith at home. She was excited about an interview with a Charlotte engineering firm that specialized in environmental work. She had made reservations at a restaurant in Charlotte so they could celebrate.

"They're very interested," she said.

He wanted to tell her that the time for celebrating should be when she got the job, but he did not want to discourage her efforts.

"We wouldn't have to move," he said.

"That's right," she said. "It'll be perfect. Did you find that child?"

"Yes, she drowned in a pond."

"I'm sorry."

"The dogs were depressed. We let them find me and that helped some."

And it seemed to him that he should tell her how he felt when he watched the diver bringing the child's body up out of that coffee-colored water, but then he realized that he did not have the words to do it.

"It was raining," he said. "And a diver brought that little girl up out of the pond. Stephen should have been there to take a picture of it. I can't describe it. It was horrible and beautiful at the same time."

"I'm sorry," she said.

"It's always hard with children," he said.

"I know."

She put her arms around him. As she did it he imagined that he would burst into tears, but instead he found himself suddenly strangely detached as he imagined himself watching Stephen taking a photograph of the drowned child.

The evening that followed was a good one. She talked about some of the projects she might work on and he found himself enjoying her enthusiasm. They returned from dinner and made love. She was bright and happy, her old self. He could not bring himself to ask her about Stephen. And if there had been something, the new job might be the end of it. He would not have to decide whether he wanted to forgive her because he would not know.

Later that night he woke to find her gone. He went down to the kitchen and looked out at her shooting baskets in the dark. This time as she dribbled down the side of the driveway and went up for her jump shot her face, illuminated by the security light, did not have that look of despair. Her

A View of the Lilies

face was shining.

On the day before her interview, she announced at breakfast that she and Stephen were going to spend the day on the river. She would not be home until after dark. Stephen was going to try for a new record on the number of balls he could collect in one day. A shoe manufacturer had promised to donate one pair of shoes for every basketball he found. He had been on the river since sunrise. She was going to meet him and they would collect basketballs until dark.

He went about his duties for the sheriff's office that day and tried not to think of them together on the river. He returned home and fed the dogs. Then he had dinner, sitting at the kitchen table and looking out on the basketball goal. Afterwards he sat in front of the TV and idly scrolled through the channels.

But there was nothing that caught his interest, so he decided to go to the river. He would take the dogs and if he found Stephen and Judith having an innocent picnic he could say that he had taken the dogs out for exercise. That was something he often did in the evening after it cooled off.

He put the dogs in the truck and drove to the river. There he left them in the truck and climbed the bluff, taking with him a pair of field glasses. Once he reached the rock, he discovered there was no need for the glasses. A red canoe and a yellow canoe were drawn up on a gravel bar on the far side of the river.

Back at the truck he put one of Judith's T-shirts he had taken out of the clothes hamper and sealed in a plastic bag, a canteen, and the dogs' leads in a backpack. Then he let the dogs out of the cage and made them heel, and they walked down to the river. They loved the water so it was no trouble to persuade them to follow him across the shoals. It was an easy walk among the lilies, for seldom was the water more than waist deep. Only he had to move carefully at times for the rocks were slick with algae and the soles of his trail-running shoes did not grip them.

Once he reached the bank and the canoes, he brought the dogs to heel again and headed for the old mill. They could be sitting on a blanket eating fried chicken or she could be sitting atop him, the way she liked to do, his fingers on her nipples.

If I see that I will turn way, he thought. *I will go home and have a drink and go to bed.*

But they were not at the foundations. He put the dogs on their leads, held the T-shirt for them to sniff, and gave them the command to find. The dogs pulled him off into the trees. When he found them, he would tell them that he was hunting Russell.

Fifteen minutes later the dogs were still on the trail, pulling him south along the river. He began to wonder if they were following a false trail. There was no good reason for Judith and Stephen to walk so far. Then the land started to rise and soon they were out of the hickories and gums and into rows of planted pines. He could see they were headed for the top of a hill, a prong that jutted out above the hardwood forest below, and that was where he now expected to find Judith and Stephen, at the place with a view of the lilies.

He brought the dogs to heel. They protested but obeyed. Then he circled off to the northeast, intending to approach the prong from the even higher ground above. It was easy walking beneath the pines, which had grown beyond pulpwood size. Soon they were above the prong and as they moved forward along one of the avenues of pines the western side of the lily-covered river gradually came into view. Off to the northwest he could see the face of the big rock, but the place where he had stood earlier in the day was hidden by a screen of trees.

Slowly he and the dogs walked down the avenue of pines and more and more of the river came into view. Some sort of large raptor sailed with fixed wings over the river toward him, the light from the setting sun caught up in its feathers, and then disappeared from view. Then he saw them a hundred yards away, lying in a hammock strung between two pines. The cords forming the hammock were white and the hardware and the var-

A View of the Lilies

nished wooden stays glistened in the light. Yesterday it had been on the shelf in a store.

He heeled the dogs, put them on their leads, and made them sit. They had caught the scent of Judith and Stephen. They held their heads high and sniffed the air. Big Red looked like he was going to bolt, and in whispers Ben scolded him.

He trained the glasses on the hammock. The attitude of their bodies was that of after love. She, her upper body bare, rested her head on his chest and he had thrown one arm across her back. They were so still that he wondered if they were asleep. They could be simply murmuring endearments to each other or silently regarding the beauty of the field of lilies, that vista of rock and flower and water that stretched out before them at their feet.

For some reason he could not understand, he felt calm. He continued to look at them through the glasses and waited for the anger to rise within him, but it did not. Instead he felt strangely detached. Perhaps it was the distance or their immobility. They were like a pair of statues in a museum.

Then when he least expected it, anger against both of them filled him, a violent shock, like a cottonmouth sinking its fangs into his leg. He unsnapped the dogs' leads.

"Find, darlins!" he said. "Find!"

The dogs raced off along the avenue. He retreated back up the slope and threw himself into a clump of briars. He brought up the glasses on the hammock just as the dogs reached it. They went straight for Judith, Big Red leaping into the hammock followed by Sugar. The hammock overturned as he heard Stephen yell. Judith was shouting at the dogs.

As Judith pulled on her T-shirt, Stephen stood and looked up the slope. Ben lowered the glasses to prevent him seeing the flash of the sunlight against the lenses.

"Ben!" Judith shouted. "Ben!"

He crouched low in the briars as she continued to call his name. Then, fearing that she might run up the slope after him, he crawled away until he was certain that he was concealed behind the curve of the hill.

Then he blew the silent dog whistle and ran through the pines. Before he had covered a quarter of a mile the dogs were at his side. He ran hard, as if he were competing in a cross country race. He retreated into that regimen, clearing his mind of everything but the act of running, listening to his body, so it was impossible for any thoughts of Judith to intrude. When he reached the beached canoes, he felt loose and relaxed, ready to run for miles if it were necessary.

He entered the river, still thinking that this was a race and that he would not permit himself to let the image of Judith and Stephen in the hammock enter his mind again. But at mid river it was necessary to pause to adjust the backpack. He sat on a rock and took a drink of water. The lilies grew in profusion around him, their heads heavy with flowers bobbing in the current. As he considered what lay ahead, it seemed to him that it was like a long and difficult cross country race he did not possess the speed or endurance to win. He realized that by setting the dogs on Judith and Stephen he had made it harder, not easier. He looked up toward the prong, but it was hidden from view by a screen of big poplars.

Sugar licked his face and whined; Big Red was lying down in a shallow pool. Then the dog came out of the water and ambled over to be petted. He shook, spraying them both.

"Yawl found her," he said. "Good darlins, good darlins."

And he sat there on the rock, talking quietly to the dogs.

The Sweeper

The summer before I went off to college my father got me a job as the assistant operator of a street sweeper. He had been deep into Savannah politics for years, along with running a Ford dealership, and I got the job because someone owed him a favor. I wanted no part of selling cars and he knew it. He was not even particularly angered by my failing, just bewildered by the fact that his son, his only son, could not sell.

"That boy couldn't sell lifejackets on the Titanic," he said to my mother over breakfast, as if I were not there.

Many of his sayings and jokes were nautical, stemming not from a tour in the Navy but from his own yearning to go to sea, some elemental stirring in his blood. Maybe it was because he grew up poor in South Georgia, in those piney woods, where his father worked in a lumber mill. I could imagine him sitting outside the unpainted pine bungalow where they lived, on one of the stifling, windless summer days, and dreaming of ocean breezes.

Caught up in the science craze of the sixties, I had decided in my junior year in high school that I wanted to be a meteorologist. To my father this called up images of TV weathermen. For me it was a fascination with hurricanes. I longed to be on one of those planes which flew into the eye of the storm, buffeted by winds, shaken as if by a giant's hand, to emerge into that perfect calm of the eye with clouds piled high all around. I never studied meteorology, never flew in one of those planes, but the eyes of hurricanes were much on my mind as I rode the street sweeper with Enoch

Guice from nine o'clock at night to six in the morning.

Enoch Guice, a man who loved his work as my father did his, came from those same piney woods of South Georgia. He was a gifted mechanic who performed his own maintenance on the sweeper. I think he preferred to be alone and sometimes resented that he had been forced to carry an unneeded helper about the city.

My father said it was like I was working in Russia where the government made work for people.

"Who'd ever have thought that Democrats and Rooshians would be the same," he liked to say.

Then he would laugh so hard at his own joke that I wondered if he was going to be able to finish his ham and eggs.

Enoch loved the sweeper, which was essentially a big water tank on wheels. In the city shop he made modifications that tripled the amount of water he could direct from its nozzles. He installed those larger pipes to better play the game that made his job enjoyable. The game was flushing bums and drunken sailors off sidewalks and out of doorways where they had curled up to sleep. It amused him, and me too at the time, to watch that sudden flood of water lift a sleeping man off the sidewalk and deposit him wet and cursing several yards away in the gutter.

We started working beyond Chatham Square, the most distant square from the river, and made our way east toward Bay Street, where on those little side streets and alleys the hunting was usually good. So all through the closing hours of the night, I would sit beside Enoch as he steered the sweeper through the squares and watch the town go to sleep. We might talk some then, but after midnight we hardly talked at all. I gave myself over to dreams of flying into hurricanes while Enoch drove and dipped snuff.

Then later, when we drew closer to the river, we would always come upon some sleeper, and if Enoch managed the nozzles just right he could send the man into the gutter and down the street like a surfer riding a wave. A sailor might wake, his drunken dreams brutally interrupted, and

The Sweeper

could not be blamed for imagining that he was at sea and had gone to sleep on his watch and suddenly had been swept off the ship by a giant wave.

All of them complained of their ill treatment, sometimes in English but more often in other languages. Most crawled into a doorway and went back to sleep, but others wanted some sort of satisfaction from Enoch. Some were content to curse him while others tried to climb into the cab. Enoch kept a hickory club to deal with the latter. He was a big man, not fat, just big and loosely put together as if someone had taken a human skin and filled it with billiard balls. Yet he swung that club with the expertise and precision of a Ted Williams or a Mickey Mantle. One tap and it was over.

One August morning, a little after midnight, we came upon a man asleep on the sidewalk. It was a hot night, every street lamp surrounded by a vortex of insects that seemed to be swirling about the light faster than usual.

Enoch slowed the sweeper and raised the brushes. Sometimes one of his victims would awaken when we approached and ruin the game. But I could see this man was not going to be awakened by anything so soft as the sound of the sweeper. He was dressed in a new pair of jeans and a sleeveless T-shirt and work boots. He looked about Enoch's age, old enough to be married and have young children. I guessed that he was a sailor.

Now Enoch slowed the sweeper to a crawl and maneuvered it closer to the curb. I had seen him drive it up onto the sidewalk so he could catch a man at just the right angle. He brought the sweeper to a halt and directed his attention to the nozzles. The man slept on. I remember thinking at the time that we could run the brushes over him and he would not move.

Enoch looked at me and grinned as he put his hand on the lever that controlled the nozzles. He pushed it forward, the water coming out in a rush and the machine trembling beneath us slightly as it always did. The sleeping man rose on the crest of a wave in a perfect effortless way that I had seen happen only one or two times, and was borne on it across the sidewalk, barely missing a light post, and into the gutter where the flood carried him a good thirty yards before he was gently deposited, one leg on the curb and his head in the street.

"Goddamn," Enoch said softly. "Goddamn."

This was undoubtedly the apogee of the entire summer, Enoch's greatest moment. We sat on the sweeper, the machine in neutral, and waited to see what would happen next.

"If we'd have been on Bay, I'd have sent him all the way to the river," Enoch said.

But I only half heard his boast, because all my attention was directed at the man, who was slowly getting to his feet. He stood and looked at us, pushing his long hair out of his eyes and shaking his head in the way an exhausted bull might regard the bullfighter approaching with the sword.

We waited for him to do something, but he just stood there and stared at us. Enoch put his hand on the end of the club. I had never seen that before. He prided himself on waiting for the last possible moment to make a decision.

The man walked toward us, not fast, not slow, but steady. I imagined that I could hear the water squishing in his boots, but I knew this was just dreaming on my part. The noise from the engine was too loud. He came on steadily and stopped on Enoch's side of the cab.

I saw he was going to speak, hoped that he would curse us in some foreign language so it would be just so much noise in Enoch's ears, no more than the sound of jays incensed against a cat, giving Enoch no reason to use that hickory club.

"Why did you do that?" he asked.

He was a small man, not half the size of Enoch.

"You ain't allowed to sleep on the sidewalks," Enoch said. "There's a city ordinance against it."

Enoch held onto the steering wheel with his left hand and the club with his right, holding it so tightly his knuckles turned white.

"There was no need to do what you did," he said.

"You were sleeping," Enoch said, clinging to a blind parroting of the

The Sweeper

ordinance.

"I wouldn't be proud of doing what you did," the man said. "I wouldn't be proud at all. Ain't you ashamed of teaching this boy such ways."

"I ain't ashamed of nothing I do," Enoch said.

Already there had been more words exchanged than with any drunken sailor Enoch had ever sent floating down the street.

"You're the child, not him," the man said.

He pointed at Enoch. I noticed that Enoch had released the club. The water dripped from the man's clothes and made a puddle at his feet. Somewhere close by someone had a flower garden in a courtyard. The sweet scent mixed with the smell of the diesel fumes from the sweeper. It was getting on toward the time of the morning when I liked to sit and dream of hurricanes.

"Why don't you just go on back to sleep," Enoch said.

Off on the river a ship blew its whistle, a deep sound that barely reached us, filtering along the sides of old houses and slipping through ironwork and the branches of the live oaks.

"I wish I could," the man said.

Then Enoch did something I never expected. As he did it he glanced at me and I saw a look on his face that frightened me. He reached into his pocket and pulled out his wallet. He held out a twenty-dollar bill.

"You get yourself some coffee," Enoch said. "Get yourself some food and a place to sleep."

The man looked at the money in a way that made me certain he was not going to take it. And I knew he was not going to take it before Enoch knew, who still held the bill in his fingers. The man was looking at it as if Enoch held a fist full of snakes instead.

"I ain't hungry," the man said.

"What do you want with me?" Enoch asked.

I wondered why Enoch did not draw him closer and then tap him on the head with the club.

"Just talk to you and this boy," the man said.

"Well, say what you got to say," Enoch said.

"You take me down to the river," the man said.

He put one foot up on the step. I expected Enoch to reach for the club, but he made no move.

"This ain't a taxi," Enoch said. "We won't even be there until around sunrise. We got work to do."

"I ain't in a hurry," the man said.

Enoch looked like he was about to cry. The sweeper throbbed beneath us. Water still glistened on the man's face in the purple glow from the streetlights. His wet T-shirt clung to his lean muscled body, the body of a lightweight fighter. There was a whitish scar on his left arm, causing me to imagine a knife fight at midnight in some South American port.

"You come on up," Enoch said. "Take the boy's place."

The man came into the cab. He smelled of tobacco and whiskey, the way my father and grandfather smelled in the evening after supper. Both Enoch and I smelled of sweat, but underneath the tobacco and whiskey smell the man had a clean watery scent to him.

Enoch put the sweeper in gear, and we began to make our way through the squares. As he drove, the brushes working furiously beneath us and the water sluicing through the gutters, Bass Faircloth began to talk.

First he told us about growing up in the Mississippi Delta where his father grew cotton and soybeans. His father had failed at farming and had drowned himself in the Quiver River, a small stream that fed into the Yazoo.

"Like something a woman would do," Enoch observed.

And instead of getting mad, Bass agreed it was. He pointed out that a man should use a pistol or drive a car into a tree or off a cliff. Such violent and furious means were acceptable.

I could not quite understand why Enoch had allowed him aboard the sweeper in the first place. But as he talked, and I can call up even today the sound of his musical flute-like voice wrapping itself around us like that hot summer night, I began to understand why Enoch had let Bass on

The Sweeper

the sweeper. His voice was so compelling that I could imagine him telling stories at night after supper aboard a ship and no one caring to do anything but listen to him while the ship made its steady and inexorable progress through the hot night across some perfectly calm southern sea.

Enoch stopped the sweeper just as we reached the east side of Orleans Square. He turned and looked at Bass.

"What were you doing, a man like you, sleeping on the sidewalk?" Enoch asked.

"There was this girl . . ." Bass said.

Enoch nodded his head like he understood perfectly. But I did not understand. That was before I had fallen in love.

Miranda, he told us, was the daughter of a crop duster, who often dusted his father's fields. Her mother had disappeared on Miranda's first birthday, gone, her note said, to California, and no one ever heard from her again. When Bass met Miranda she was attending a private school in Memphis.

One June day Bass watched the crop duster's plane touch down on the grass strip behind the house. He thought nothing of this since he had seen the plane land there many times, but he was surprised when he saw Miranda get out of the pilot's seat and her father from the passenger's.

Miranda stepped out of the plane and Bass took one look and fell in love.

"She didn't pay any mind to me," Bass said. "But she cast a shadow just as white as the cotton in my daddy's fields."

I had never heard anyone talk like that about a girl. It was like something out of a book.

She paid no attention to him at all, walking up to the house past him with hardly a glance in his direction. And that made Bass desperate and wild, the first time a girl had made him feel like that, thinking to himself that he was going to be completely lost if he were not allowed to have her near him every day. So when his father suggested that he show Miranda the deer, he was overjoyed.

They drove up on the federal levee in his truck and then down off it and through fields protected by a private levee. It was dusk by the time he eased the truck around the side of a stand of cottonwoods. There, caught in the lights in a field of new wheat, were the deer, which stood for a moment, their eyes glowing red in the lights, before they ran and disappeared into the trees, leaving the field empty. It was as if they had never been there at all.

And she had cried out in delight and clapped her hands together.

"It was the deer that did it," Bass said. "It was like we had looked right inside each other."

That did not make much sense to me. But Enoch believed it. He did not say *amen* like in church but something close to it, an inarticulate sound made deep in his throat.

As Enoch carefully drove the sweeper through the deserted streets, Bass talked and we listened.

During the next few weeks Miranda came with her father and each time Bass took her to look at the deer. Then unexpectedly she came alone, for she was an expert pilot, and took him flying over the river and down to Greenville where she flew the plane under the bridge. Their passage was to Bass a blur of girders, a giant spider web of steel that looked like it was going to catch them for sure, with the brown water below and the blue sky above, and then everything getting mixed up, so even when she put the plane into a steep climb over the willows on the Arkansas side, he was not certain they were going up or down. Bass swore that he would never fly with her again. But he did and she continued to display a sort of recklessness that defied explanation. It was as if she believed that she and the plane were exempt from the laws of physics.

"Your daddy'll skin you if he finds out what you're doing with his plane," Bass said.

That was after she had flown the plane sideways through a narrow gap at the end of a soybean field.

"It's just doing what it was designed to do," she said.

The Sweeper

And he came to believe that in her hands the plane could do almost anything. She refused to allow him to drive up to Memphis to see her. So he resigned himself to waiting until she landed the plane behind the house.

They became lovers toward the end of the summer. She landed the plane on a grass strip belonging to a hunting club and they walked down to the river where late in the evening they made love on a sandbar.

Bass was thinking of marriage, of the children they would have, when she stopped coming. He sat for a week on the porch, waiting to hear the sound of the plane approaching low and fast over the cotton. When he called, the phone rang and rang or he got her father, who always promised to have her call him.

Finally she did call, early one morning, telling him that she wanted him to drive up to Memphis and visit her at her house. Her father had gone to Yazoo City. She would be waiting for him, she said, in her bedroom on the second floor.

"I burned up that highway," Bass said. "She lived with her father in a house near Rhodes College."

Bass drove up through the late July heat, those endless fields stretching across the perfectly flat land, interrupted only here and there by clumps of cypresses or farm buildings. And then he was in Memphis and found the number of the house. He opened the door and went through the silent foyer and mounted the stairs. It was when he reached the second floor that he heard the sound. He almost turned away and went back down the stairs, but something, he was not exactly sure what, compelled him to walk down the hall and push open the door.

There in her girl's room, pink curtains on the windows and a travel poster of Rome on one wall, she lay on the bed, her legs wrapped around a man's waist, his identity a mystery to Bass for only a moment, the man turning but still moving on her, and Bass looked straight into the face of her father.

He bolted for the doorway and the stairs, hearing the man's curses behind him and her laughter, rising loud and shrill. He reached his truck and as he put it in gear and started to drive away, he saw her father, a pistol in his hand, and dressed only in a pair of khaki pants, come running across the lawn. But Bass pushed the accelerator to the floor and the truck shot down the street, the houses and trees going by in a blur, and in the rear view mirror he saw the father standing in the street, holding the pistol at his side, a figure of arrested outrage.

"I went to sea," Bass said. "I ran away to New Orleans and lied about my age and got my seaman's papers."

"What about the girl?" Enoch asked.

"I don't know what happened to her," Bass said.

"Have you ever been back?" I asked. "I mean did your parents know what you were doing and where you were?"

"I wrote them letters," Bass said.

"You ever think about that girl?" Enoch asked.

"I love her," Bass said.

I thought that was the craziest thing I had ever heard anyone say. This girl was sleeping with her own father and then laughing about it. Bass claiming he still loved her was crazy.

"You never went back to see her?" I asked. "Not even once."

"Once I did," Bass said.

He went back to Memphis that one time, after he learned that her father had been killed in an accident. He had flown his plane into high-tension lines. Miranda, he discovered, was married to an aviation mechanic who worked at the Memphis airport. She was teaching sixth grade. One afternoon he sat in a rented car and watched her bring her class out for recess. She walked with the same determined springy step. He wanted it to mean that what happened between her and her father had not touched her at all, that contagion leaving no mark on her. He knew he should not get out of the car and go talk to her and he did not.

"You think she did it with her father every day?" Enoch asked.

Bass turned and looked at him and Enoch sort of shrank down in his seat. It was the only time he ever looked small to me.

The Sweeper

"You let me off at the corner," Bass said.

We had just left Johnson Square and were only a block from Bay. Enoch stopped the sweeper at the corner and I got out. Bass climbed down from the sweeper and stood on the sidewalk beside me. His clothes were still wet and there was now a musty smell to him. I looked at him and tried to imagine him as that boy climbing the stairs to the girl's room, but I could not.

"I hope you were paying attention," Bass said. He motioned with his head to Enoch, not even bothering to look at him and keeping his eyes on me instead. I think his eyes were brown, but it was hard to tell in the purplish glow from the streetlights. "He's never going to understand."

I turned and glanced at Enoch, who just sat there and looked at us, both of his hands on the wheel.

Then Bass turned and walked away. We both watched him until he turned the corner on Bay, headed back to his ship I supposed.

I got back on the sweeper with Enoch. We flushed no more drunken sailors that night, even though we had two good opportunities. We also did not talk. I had no idea what Enoch was thinking about, but I suspect it was Bass walking in on that girl and her father.

I sat there trying to understand what Bass was saying about love. But it was hopeless. Not until much later did I come to understand how love could make a man go off on a ship and turn his back on his family and how it could make him lie down on a sidewalk in a strange town to sleep.

The only thing I clearly did understand was that I should not ride on the sweeper any more and take part in the game. So I quit my job. As punishment my father had me start washing cars at the dealership. Then two of his salesmen quit and out of desperation he had me put on a coat and tie and I actually sold a couple of cars for a good price. And then I sold three more and discovered that I could sell.

Now my father is dead. So is Enoch Guice, who had a heart attack early one morning and was found, slumped over the wheel of the sweeper. I have a wife and children and plans to open another dealership in Charleston. But sometimes during hurricane season, I wonder how it was that I never studied meteorology, never rode on one of those hurricane planes. It is then that I wonder what became of Bass Faircloth, whether he is on a ship somewhere, moving through mountainous waves into the very eye of a storm.

Rising on Christmas

Benson Green was running the river in the snow. It was Christmas Eve and northern Arkansas had received six inches of snow two days before. The temperature had risen into the forties and the roads and the sky were clear, but the snow still lay thickly in the woods along the river and on the tops of the huge boulders scattered here and there on the riverbank. He had come to see the big icicles, some longer than a man, which formed on the face of Skirum Bluff in the winter. It was a trip he made at least once a year.

He was an expert canoeist and the river was low, so there was no real danger of losing control of the boat. He enjoyed manipulating the predictable force of the water to place the canoe exactly where he wanted it. But just in case he made a mistake he wore a wet suit and carried a change of clothes in a waterproof bag. His wife was going to meet him at Nectar Covered Bridge at sundown.

Benson was a microbiologist in charge of the lab at the county hospital. Lillian ran the farm, inherited from her father, where they lived. They had two chicken houses and grew some tomatoes and peppers. Occasionally she would plant a crop of sorghum and make molasses at the mill her father had built.

He had gone a good way down the river and was in a narrow gorge, the walls rising sheer on either side, when he came around a bend and saw smoke at Steele Creek Falls. He wondered if it was some canoeist he knew, out on the river to view the icicles. As he approached the falls, which had to be portaged at low water, he saw a figure standing on the little rocky island where the river split into two sections. The man, dressed in camouflage, was joined by a dog. Both of them stood motionless and watched him approach. The bluish smoke from a fire rose behind them. As Benson paddled closer, he saw that the man, who now was squatting oriental fashion on the rock, was not one of his canoeing friends.

He looked like an Ozark man, who might never have ventured far outside the mountains. He might have gone to Little Rock once or twice in his life. The hill people were suspicious of outsiders. Several months before this suspicion had blossomed into violence. The canoe shop a man from Missouri had built at the Little Rock Highway Bridge had mysteriously burned.

The burning was caused by the theft of a steer. Someone butchered it in a pasture a little downstream from Skirum Bluff. Whoever did it had taken the meat away by water, because the only way from the pasture to the highway was a single dirt track, ending at a locked gate. On a sandbar the farmer found the tracks of a single man and the marks left by a beached canoe. So the theft was blamed on a canoeist, some outsider, even though plenty of locals owned canoes and were accustomed to using them on the river.

Benson, who had been raised in Arkansas, was familiar with such attitudes, but never had completely understood them. He had gone off to school in the North and had returned with his degree and faith in the scientific method. He had abandoned even the unemotional brand of religion practiced in the Episcopal church. The hill people favored extremes. Snake handling was practiced in some of the local churches. They hated, loved, and worshipped with a fervor that sometimes made Benson uncomfortable. If he had not met Lillian on a canoe trip on this very river, he would probably have lived in a city like Little Rock or even Memphis. But she wanted to live in her father's house. He did like having the river so close at hand.

Benson put the canoe into the slack water at the head of the island. A few strokes brought him close to the man, who was dressed in an insulated deer hunter's jump suit and wearing an olive drab watch cap pulled down low over his forehead. Now the stranger stood up, a little man with black stubble on his face. His eyes were like two bits of polished coal. The pit bull's eyes were yellow. Benson halted the canoe with a paddle stroke and took a good look at the dog. The man looked down at the dog and then back at Benson.

"He ain't a bad dog," the man said. "You come on and have some breakfast."

Benson, with a couple of quick strokes, drove the bow of the canoe up onto a slab of rock at the head of the island. As he stepped out onto the rocks, he saw that the man had camped there, sleeping in the open on a blue tarp spread out on the sand at the bottom of the falls. A battered aluminum canoe was beached beside the tarp, a sleeping bag thrown across the gunwales to dry. A freshly cut cedar tree lay in the bow, the bole roughly cut as if by a beaver, taken down with a hatchet or a machete.

The little man, whose name was Konrad Skirum, had spent the night on the island. Without Benson's having to ask, Konrad began to tell him how he made a living. He trapped otters and mink. He set lines and nets for catfish and carp and gar.

Benson wondered what connection he had with the Skirums, who were in the strip mine business. They were well off. He wondered if this man was some cousin they would rather not claim.

"I wouldn't eat a gar," Konrad said. "Carp's not bad though. I wouldn't eat pond-raised cats. Meat on river cats is white as snow and firm. Soybean fed cats taste just like soybeans."

He sold the fish to markets that catered to the poor, who were not particular about the sort of fish they ate.

Konrad had spent the night paddling the canoe upstream from eddy to eddy and checking his traps. He had risen before sunrise to hunt from a tree stand for deer. He hunted year round with no regard for game laws.

"I hunt for meat, not for fun," he said. "That makes it right."

The tree was for his trailer where he lived with his wife and five children below Nectar Covered Bridge. He pointed out that the trailer and the land it sat on were paid for.

Benson sat by the fire and watched Konrad cook country ham and eggs in an iron skillet. The dog sat gravely by Konrad's side.

"Go ahead, you can pet him," Konrad said.

"What's his name," Benson asked.

He was not sure he wanted to pet the dog.

"Ain't got a name," Konrad said. "I'm waiting to see what it's gonna be. He come up to the trailer a month ago. Was all skin and bones. Had been fought and hurt bad."

"Go on, he won't bite," Konrad said. "He sleeps with my littlest boy."

Benson petted the dog cautiously on the head, feeling the puncture marks in the dog's skull with his fingers.

"There'll be a reckoning one day for them that do that to dogs," Konrad said.

Benson agreed that there should be.

As they ate the ham and eggs Konrad explained that he was camped on the island because of stolen steer. The landowners up and down the river had vowed to prosecute anyone who set foot on their property. He was a suspect. The sheriff had visited his trailer.

"I showed him my freezer," Konrad said. "Nothing but deer and catfish in it. I told him he should be looking for them that burned down that man's business."

The dog left them and made his way up the slope where he stood looking upriver, his nose in the air.

"Maybe smells a deer or a wild hog," Konrad said. "A man could use a dog like that to hunt wild hogs. Ain't afraid of them tusks. Bore right in and grab 'em by the ear or the nose. Won't let go. God put that in that dog's blood. He didn't put fighting other dogs for men's pleasure in it. They'll pay for that, them that does it."

Benson agreed again he thought they would surely pay.

As they ate the ham and eggs, Konrad pointed out that he knew Benson was married to Lillian Snead. The Sneads were bankers and Konrad made it clear he did not think much of them.

"You come to see it?" Konrad asked. "They been all over the river this month."

"See what?" Benson asked.

"That deer in the wave."

Konrad explained that a deer was trapped in the hydraulic, a powerful wave created by the water flowing over a smooth granite slab, just above Skirum Bluff. It had been there since Thanksgiving.

"It's a miracle," Konrad said. "Brother Whitefield says it's gonna rise on Christmas day."

Benson had heard of Brother Whitefield. The year before a woman had been bitten on the ear by a rattlesnake as she was handling it in his church. Luckily the snake caught her with only one fang, so she received only half a dose of venom. She survived, but she lost the ear.

Benson explained to Konrad how the hydraulic would hold anything that washed into it: a log, a man, a canoe.

"What's the miracle?" Benson asked.

Konrad looked at the dog and then up at the sky. He pulled off his watch cap and ran his hands over his straight black hair.

"It ain't rotted," Konrad said softly. "It's perfect. God is gonna snatch it up to heaven."

Benson wondered at the ignorance of Brother Whitefield's followers. The cold water had preserved the deer, and the fluid dynamics of the wave held it in place. But he knew better than to try to explain that to Konrad.

"I didn't know there were animals in heaven," Benson said.

Konrad petted the dog on the head and grinned at Benson.

"If He wants 'em there then it'll be," Konrad said. "We'll go down the river together. I want to see *you* when you see it. You see it, then you'll understand."

Konrad began to pack up his camp while Benson portaged the falls.

They went down the river. The dog sat motionless just behind the cedar tree while Konrad knelt, supporting himself on a thwart. Four mink lay stiff at his feet. Benson was surprised at how well the little man handled the canoe. There were plenty of places where someone who did not know what he was doing could lose control of a boat.

When they were in sight of the hydraulic, Benson saw that the big house-sized rock on the left hand side of the river was filled with people. Konrad went on down past the hydraulic and into the pool at Skirum Bluff. Benson caught an eddy just above the hydraulic and pulled the boat up on a rock. The people on the rock were talking and pointing at him, but he could hear nothing because of the rush of the rapids.

There were fifteen or twenty of them. Some had brought lawn chairs. He saw old people and children and one woman with a baby. They had built a fire on the rock, and people stood around it warming their hands. One man dressed in an army overcoat, which still had staff sergeant's stripes on the sleeve, held a book in his hands. He was bareheaded. He had red hair and bushy eyebrows. He began to talk, pointing down at the deer from time to time. Everyone stopped and listened. Benson supposed this was Brother Whitefield.

Benson looked down at the deer held by the wave slowly turn over and over. He could see no mark on it. It looked perfect, as if it had drowned only a few minutes before. The tines on its antlers glistened in the sunlight. Brother Whitefield pointed at the deer and then at Benson, and everyone on the rock looked at him. Benson wondered if Brother Whitefield was using him as an example of an unbeliever.

He wondered what they would do if he paddled up into the hydraulic and pushed the deer out with a paddle blade. It would be a dangerous maneuver, although he had put the canoe in the wave many times before. A person had to know how to slide the canoe across the face of the wave and escape from the grip of the hydraulic out one of the ends. And no one would be inclined to save him if the boat overturned and he was caught by the wave. Yet the look on Brother Whitefield's face might be worth the risk.

But he decided to leave the deer alone. They could stand on the rock until New Year's and the deer would not go anywhere. He supposed Brother Whitefield would explain the deer's failure to ascend to heaven as a result of a lack of faith on the part of his flock. He was sure the preacher had explained the woman's suffering from the rattlesnake bite in the same way.

He wondered how they would react if he had them all in a classroom and with diagrams charted the physical forces that held the deer and explained how the temperature of the air and water had kept it from decaying.

When he returned to the canoe, he decided he would drop into the hydraulic and ride the wave with the deer. Konrad was standing with them now. They all waved him off, pointing to the path Konrad had taken into Skirum Bluff pool. The only one who was calm was Brother Whitefield, who stood watching him with his arms folded, his red hair electric in the early afternoon sun.

He dropped into the wave and leaned hard downstream, spinning the boat so the bow was pointed upstream. Then he righted himself, and using the paddle as a rudder, held the boat steady in the wave. It shuddered beneath him and the bow took on a little water, but then it rode smoothly on the face of the wave. He turned to see what kind of expression Brother Whitefield had on his face.

Suddenly the boat bucked under him. In an instant it overturned and he was in the river, the cold water filling the space between his wet suit and his body and taking his breath away. Then he was tumbling over and over. He looked up and saw the blue sky. Again the wave pulled him under, down into the cold darkness. He felt himself slide over the deer. For a moment he found himself looking into the deer's eye, his eye fixed to it as if it were a peephole. The eye was calm and placid, like the eye of a cow, no longer a wild thing. He saw yellow and purple amorphous shapes.

Just as they were about to form into something definite, the wave jerked him away.

He and the deer rolled over once and then twice in a grotesque underwater ballet. He shucked his life jacket as he was presented for a third time with a view of the blue sky and the people on the rock. Benson sucked in a breath of air. As the wave pulled him under, he dove for the bottom where he knew the water was flowing downstream.

His tactic worked. The water no longer tugged at him. His lungs burning, he kicked himself to the surface in the middle of Skirum Bluff pool. He was facing the bluff where the enormous icicles hung, now melting fast in the sun, the water dripping down the face of the bluff. He turned and saw Konrad paddling across the pool toward him. Brother Whitefield, with a smile on his face, was pointing at him. The people around him were nodding their heads.

Konrad paddled Benson about the pool as he searched for his canoe. The canoe had vanished. Finally he found a piece of one of the ash gunwales and the waterproof bag. The canoe had probably gotten pinned under a ledge at the bottom of the hydraulic, its plastic hull ripped and twisted by those enormous forces. There was probably nothing worth recovering.

Two men held a blanket as a screen while he changed into dry clothes. There were no more major rapids, so it made no sense to stay in the clammy suit. When they lowered the blanket, he found himself face to face with the preacher. Brother Whitefield pointed at him and then turned to the crowd gathered in a semicircle with their backs to the woods.

"Jesus has touched this man," Brother Whitefield said.

The crowd murmured.

"Jesus is in that deer. Yawl all saw this man embrace that deer. Here is a man who has embraced Jesus."

A woman in the crowd gave a little cry. Benson listened to the rush of the river. Out of the corner of his eye he saw the deer turning slowly in the

Rising on Christmas

grip of the hydraulic.

Brother Whitefield faced Benson

"What did Jesus say to you down there?"

For a moment Benson considered telling the people about the deer's eye.

"*I* got myself out of that place," Benson said savagely.

Brother Whitefield smiled at him.

"Jesus has put his hand on this man."

Benson was uncertain what to do or say. He wished he were in the windowless lab at the hospital, listening to the hum of a centrifuge. Then he found himself standing before the crowd and explaining to them the physics of the wave and why the deer had not decomposed. They listened politely until he finished. There was a long silence. Konrad, who had a grin on his face, squatted on the rock with his arms over his knees, the dog sitting at his feet.

Brother Whitefield pointed his finger at Benson and addressed the crowd.

"This man will rise with that deer!" the preacher shouted.

"Sweet Jesus, sweet Jesus," a woman's voice crooned.

Benson retreated to the water's edge where Konrad's canoe was pulled up on the rock. Konrad was by his side. Brother Whitefield and the crowd seemed to have lost interest in him. They were all gathered now on the edge of the rock above the wave. The preacher was pointing down at it and explaining something to them.

"I'll take you down to the Nectar Bridge," Konrad said. "I'm coming back tonight. Brother Whitefield is gonna have a vigil on the rock."

"What will you do if that deer ascends to heaven after midnight?" Benson asked.

"Be glad I'm saved."

"If it doesn't?"

"Try to have more faith. None of us has got enough."

"What if you see me flying up to heaven?"

"Can't ascend until you're dead. You ain't dead yet. He's got that all wrong. Even a preacher ain't perfect."

"Well, I'm not dead and I'm not going to be for a long time. Let's get on down to the bridge. You don't want to take the chance of missing anything here."

"That's right."

They turned their backs to the group on the rock and paddled across Skirum Bluff pool. Benson and the dog were in the bow and Konrad in the stern. The cedar tree was stored amidships.

They came out of the gorge, and the river soon flattened out some, the banks gently sloping instead of precipitous walls of rock. Beyond a thin screen of trees there was pasture on both sides. Benson saw cattle, the low afternoon sun illuminating their drool as they stood at metal feed troughs.

There were well-worn trails on both sides where the cattle had come down to the river to drink. When Benson had floated the river in the summer, he often came upon them standing in the water to escape the heat. They came upon a pasture lined with new orange no trespassing signs. Someone had nailed one to every tree along the river.

"That's where somebody stole that steer," Konrad said.

The dog, which had been dozing in the bow, suddenly sat bolt upright. Then it sprang into the water, nearly upsetting the canoe. Benson kept them from going over by thrusting his paddle out parallel to the water like an outrigger.

Konrad yelled at the dog as it swam strongly for shore, but it paid no attention to him. It reached the bank. Without bothering to shake itself dry, it scaled the bank in a few bounds and disappeared into a honeysuckle thicket.

"I don't know what's got into that dog," Konrad said.

Benson looked at his watch. It would be dark in an hour. The covered bridge was less than half an hour away. Lillian would not be too worried if rounding up the dog delayed them. She would sit in the truck and read and wait for him to arrive. He had been late at pickups before.

"Might have smelled a wild hog," Konrad said.

They sat in the canoe for a few minutes, listening for some sign of the dog. But there was nothing. The snow seemed to have silenced everything. A squirrel ran round and round the base of a big gum, its claws making rattling sounds on the bark, then darted up the tree, disappearing from view in the topmost branches.

"We best go find him," Konrad said.

They made their way up the bank. They walked in the dog's tracks through a grove of poplars where pieces of rusted farm machinery were scattered here and there, half-covered by the snow, and past the remains of a wooden outbuilding. They came out into the pasture and saw the dog, upriver from them, loping across the pasture. The cattle had gathered in a tight knot by a feeding station, all their heads turned toward the dog.

Konrad yelled at the dog, but the animal continued his steady progress across the pasture. The dog reached the tree line and disappeared. The cattle lowered their heads again. The pasture was a smooth expanse of thick grey grass, here and there dotted with patches of snow that lingered in the dips and hollows. The sun had now dropped into the branches of the single leafless tree by the feeding station, making the tree appear to be on fire. He imagined that off in the trees, where the dirt track wound up a hill, there were men with rifles.

"I don't like being on posted land," Benson said. "Every farmer up and down this river is itching to get a shot at a rustler."

"I got to find my dog," Konrad said. "He won't go far. Besides he'll be easy to track in the snow."

Konrad started across the pasture at a trot and Benson followed him. The dog's tracks through the patches of snow were as straight as if they had been laid out by a survey team.

Benson was relieved when they reached the cover of the woods. The dog's tracks crossed those of deer and rabbits, but the dog never swerved to investigate their scents. It was growing dark fast. Konrad whooped like a man calling hogs. Then he yelled, "Hey dog! Hey dog!"

"We can't find him in the dark," Benson said.

Konrad reminded him the moon would be up soon.

"It'll be like high noon with all this snow," Konrad said. "Until then I've got a light."

The dog continued to travel upriver. They were in the trees the whole time, and Benson was thankful not to be wandering about in someone's pasture. By now Lillian was probably thinking of calling the sheriff.

They entered the gorge again. A trail ending at Skirum Bluff ran along the river. The moon rose above the hills, the light falling down through the leafless trees and producing the effect Konrad had predicted. Konrad turned off his flashlight, and they walked on the trail in the moonlight, following the dog's tracks.

Then the dog began to travel at a trot, clearing the fallen logs on the trail at one bound. Soon they would be at Skirum Bluff. Perhaps one of Brother Whitefield's followers would have a phone he could use to call Lillian. He urged Konrad to walk faster.

"That dog can't go nowhere but back to us or to Skirum Bluff," Konrad said. "He'll be there waiting for us. Faster'll get somebody a broken leg."

Benson realized that Konrad was right. The sides of the gorge were too steep for the dog to scramble up, and he would have no reason to swim the river. The trail was slippery with patches of snow. It would be a bad place to get hurt.

He told Konrad of his hope that someone at Skirum Bluff had a phone.

"Brother Whitefield has got one," Konrad said. "Carries it with him everywhere he goes. Wants to keep track of them that is born and them that dies."

Benson imagined Brother Whitefield was more interested in deaths than in births. He wondered if the preacher had convinced himself that he could see a soul. Was it something like the blotches he saw when he stared into the deer's eye, or was it more like the pasture in moonlight, austere and simple, a play of light and shadow?

The trail twisted and turned through the boulders. Then up ahead, they heard the heavy rush of the hydraulic. They came out of the trees and onto the shore of the big pool. Now that they were still, Benson felt cold for the first time, despite his jacket and cap.

The people were gathered tightly about the fire. Benson knew that those within the circle of firelight would have no view at all of anything out in the darkness. He looked up at the big icicles bathed in a mixture of fire and moonlight. Some had broken in half and the pieces crunched under their feet as they made their way along the foot of the bluff. The dog was nowhere to be seen.

"Where is that son of a bitch?" Konrad said with a heat that surprised Benson. The whole time they had been trailing the dog Konrad had not said a word against him.

They climbed the rocks past the hydraulic. People were playing lights on it. Benson saw the flash of the tines as the deer rolled slowly in the wave. Then they saw the dog standing at the edge of the river. Here, just above the hydraulic, the river necked down and flowed fast. On either side was nothing but bare rock.

Konrad ran forward toward the dog. The dog looked at him over his shoulder and then leaped into the river. It swam fast, the current bearing it downstream. It paused in an eddy behind a midstream rock, the same rock where Benson had stood and watched the deer, before the dog swam strongly into the current again. It gained the slack water on the other side and bounded out of the river. After shaking itself, it trotted over to join the people on the rock.

Benson yelled to the people there. They played their lights over him and Konrad.

"Call Lillian Green!" Benson shouted through his cupped hands. "Tell her I'm all right! Lillian Green! Lillian Green!"

Someone yelled back at him, but Benson could understand nothing over the rush of the water.

"They can't hear you," Konrad said.

Benson told him about how worried Lillian would be.

"We can swim across," Konrad said. "Dry our clothes at their fire. That dog's gonna run off on me again if I don't get over there."

Benson told Konrad he was not going to make the swim. Then he explained to Konrad why the dog had been so successful, how somehow he knew not to fight the current but to swim straight for the other side. How Konrad should let the current carry him into the eddy.

"You do like him and you'll be all right," Benson said.

He told Konrad the number of Lillian's phone and had him repeat it back several times.

"I'll get myself to that fire," Konrad said. "Get dry quick. You know, Plumb Creek Road's not but a quarter of a mile up the hill. You swim on over with me and she could meet you there. It's a long walk back to my boat."

Benson pointed out that at least he would be dry. He told Konrad to tell Lillian to give him a couple of hours to reach the Nectar Bridge. He looked forward to making the rest of the run in the moonlight, something he did often on midsummer nights.

Konrad took off his boots and tying the laces together slung them over his neck. He jumped into the icy water and swam strongly for the other side. As had been the case with the dog, the current carried him into the eddy, where he paused. But instead of striking out for the other side, he lingered there. He looked back at Benson. Konrad's face was a pale oval in the moonlight.

The people on the rock played their lights over him. Benson heard shouts but could understand none of the words. He hoped Konrad would climb up on the rock. A few minutes in the water could kill a person. Soon he would be too weak to make the swim. Konrad put his hands on the rock as if to pull himself out of the water. Then he just hung there.

Benson stripped down to his long underwear and leaped into the water, the shock of it a blow to his body. He put all his energy and determination into the swim, the current seizing him and bearing him downstream. Then, thankfully, he was in the eddy. He put his hand on Konrad

Rising on Christmas

and spun him about.

"Go!" he shouted. "Swim! Now!"

Konrad looked at him and raised his arm. On the rocks, not twenty yards away, there were men standing, making motions for both of them to swim. Benson put his arm over Konrad's chest. Benson kicked them though the eddy line and into the current. Konrad was flailing his arms, interfering with their progress. Benson saw the lights on the rocks and heard the men's shouts. Konrad had stopped struggling, as if he had somehow realized how close they were to being saved.

Benson gave Konrad a push out of the current and into the slack water along the rocks. Konrad glided forward into the outstretched hands of the men. But the push sent Benson backwards, and the current grabbed him. Within seconds he was in the hydraulic. He felt himself slide over the body of the deer. He planned to dive deep again.

He relaxed his body and waited for the right moment to make his dive. But something seized him, and he was pressed against the side of the deer. When the deer rolled, he was carried with it. He held his breath and caught another one as he and the deer came to the surface. His eyes were filled with lights; he heard shouts. Then he went down again, embracing that heaviness, that enormous weight. He felt cold and heavy as if his stomach were filled with lead shot. He thought he heard the preacher's voice, but he knew that could not be so. Then he no longer felt cold, and he imagined on the next roll or the one after that he would free himself from the embrace of the deer.

The people stood on the rock and watched the deer and Benson turn slowly, the tines entangled in Benson's long underwear. As Konrad repeated Lillian's phone number to Brother Whitefield, the dog began to howl. Konrad spoke to him sharply, and the dog lay down at his feet.

The preacher dialed the number on his phone, standing off away from the others. But even though Konrad was still shivering he edged away from the fire to hear what the preacher was going to say. He told her that her husband was at Skirum Bluff where they were keeping a vigil. Mrs. Green had probably heard about the vigil, he said, about the deer that Jesus had caused to be incorruptible. Then he noticed that Konrad was eavesdropping and he glared at him and strode away to the other end of the rock, to a thicket of river birches, where, Konrad reflected, if it had been summer he would have been enclosed in a shady green cave. And there the preacher said other things to her.

Whitefield walked up to Konrad, who still stood a little off from the group.

"What'd you tell her?" Konrad asked.

"That her husband is gonna rise," Whitefield said.

"Why'd you do that?"

"Because it's true."

"That man was right. It's like that deer has been in cold storage. I've been in that water. I know how cold it is. Besides to her it ain't the rising that's important. He's drowned."

The people had lost interest in Benson and the deer and were now beginning to realize that Konrad and Whitefield were having an argument.

"Tomorrow is His day," Whitefield said. "When they rise it will be a sign from Him. That man believed in nothing at all. But He will make him rise."

"Only rising he's gonna do is when the rescue squad shows up," Konrad said. "Besides, there's no rising until Easter."

Whitefield gave Konrad a look of contempt.

"Since you know what's gonna happen, maybe Jesus is speaking through you," Whitefield said

"No, he don't speak through me," Konrad said.

Konrad turned and started up the trail from the rock with the dog. He was wearing Whitefield's army coat. The preacher had put it on his back with his own hands. Someone had given him a pair of running shoes, which were much too big, to replace the boots he had lost in the river, and he knew it was going to be hard to walk up the hill in them.

He expected he would meet Mrs. Green on the trail. He would tell her what awaited her at the river. Then he would walk back down with her or they could wait together for the rescue squad.

"Konrad, you send that woman down here so she can see," Whitefield called after him.

Konrad did not reply. He put his head down and continued to walk, knowing that if he kept moving soon he would be warm.

In the Heart of Alabama

Josie Gibson was bringing her two sons home from school. She drove along a road that ran perfectly straight through a forest of pines planted in orderly rows.

"Stop today, Mom," Jason said. "You promised."

"You promised," Andrew said.

Jason was twelve and Andrew was fourteen.

"Mr. Tiomkin might not even be at home," she said.

"We could still look at the skulls," Andrew said.

The boys were wild to take a closer look at a line of antlered deer skulls nailed to the side of the barn at the old farmhouse where Alexander Tiomkin lived. He was a sculptor. She had met him at a faculty party a few weeks ago. He was not tall, standing only a little taller than she. He had a thick chest and big shoulders and his hair was that shade of black that was almost blue. Alexander had said he would drop by her house but so far he had not. She liked him. The boys' desire to see the skulls would be a good excuse for a visit.

This was her first year teaching political science at a small Alabama state university near the Florida line. She had expected to find a better job, but she had had only one offer. She had just completed her Ph.D. Her dissertation, which was on Cuba, might with a little more work be in shape for publication. That would change everything. At least she had stopped asking herself what a person with a degree from Cornell was doing teaching in Alabama.

She had known ever since the party that the barn with skulls on it belonged to Alexander. He had not mentioned the skulls, but the moment he described his house she knew where it was. She drove by it every day on her way to take the boys to school. She was renting a house not far away that belonged to an anthropologist and his wife. The Youngs and their two daughters had gone to Africa for a year. Dwight Young specialized in primitive hunting techniques. He had sent her an e-mail from Africa telling her that the people in the area where he was living still preferred wild game to domesticated meat. Soon, despite everyone's efforts, there would be no game left.

She had offered to pay the Youngs rent, but they had refused. A house sitter was what they wanted they said. And since Josie was broke she felt it was an offer she could ill afford to turn down. She had refused to accept alimony from her husband when they divorced while she was completing her dissertation.

They were out of the pines now. Fields of soybeans and cotton were planted on either side of the road, an alien landscape to someone who grew up in Boston. Then there was a forest of hardwoods, and they crossed the river with its stands of feathery-topped cypresses on either side. The land on the left was planted in corn and on the right the passage of the river in the distance was marked by a line of cypresses. Then she saw the old farmhouse with its rusted tin roof and the barn and pieces of Alexander's work (he worked exclusively in cypress) scattered about the yard beneath the live oaks.

He had told her about himself at the party. His father had been a gamekeeper on a hunting preserve not far from Moscow, reserved exclusively for the use of important members of the Party. His grandfather had held the same position, and his great-grandfather, all the way back to a Tiomkin who was the property of a family of gentry. Their estate had been combined with several others to form the preserve.

Alexander had shown early talent in art and had been sent off to Moscow to study. He was beginning a successful career when the Soviet

Union broke up. He had made friends with a French sculptor, who also worked exclusively in wood. With his help Alexander went to France where he spent a few years and from there to this teaching job in Alabama. He preferred cities to the country and talked about living in San Francisco or New York.

She saw him walking out to the driveway to meet them.

"The boys wanted to see the skulls," she said.

She introduced them and they shook his hand.

"Did you shoot those deer?" Andrew asked.

"No, the man who owned this house did," he said. "I shot a doe last year for meat. I am not interested in horns."

They talked as the boys examined the skulls.

"It was a lucky day for me when the system collapsed," he said. "I would never have been permitted to produce decadent art."

He indicated the pieces beneath the live oaks with a wave of his hand.

"But you are an admirer of Castro," he said. "They make state art there too. Bad art."

"I study Cuban politics," she said. "Not art."

"The politics are simple," he said. "We had Stalin. Cuba has Castro. It is the exercise of absolute power."

She wondered why he was attacking her.

"My father is a history professor," she said. "When I was a child he told me a story of taking a course under a Cuban professor when he was at Georgetown. "This professor went to school with Fidel. The professor had recently returned from Cuba. He had gone over with some Cuban nationalists based in Miami. They were going to slip into the country and blow up things and recruit from among those who were dissatisfied with Fidel. They imagined there were many of them. The CIA had trained this man and his friends.

"As they were approaching Cuba a man who had served with Fidel pointed out to the professor that they were all going to die. 'No one knows those mountains like Fidel,' he said. And it was then that the professor was sorry he ever left Miami. He didn't want to die a useless death.

"They missed their contact that night and returned to Miami. The professor gave up on the movement and decided to get a job.

"I was always fascinated with that story. And I was fascinated how Fidel has managed to survive so long, how he's maintained the loyalty of the Cuban people."

"Those who are not loyal are dead," he said.

"It's not that simple," she said. "You can read my book when I'm finished."

"At least you are not one of these American university Marxists who drives a BMW," he said.

"No, I drive a Ford and I'm not a Marxist," she said. "My car doesn't want to start in the morning. Do you know anything about cars?"

"No," he said. Then he paused, a smile on his face. "Do you know that everyone here is a Baptist," he said. "Missionaries came here to convert me when I moved in. Have they come to Dwight's house?"

"No," she said. "I'm a lapsed Catholic. Maybe they know that."

She liked his smile and the abstract shapes he had formed from the cypress logs.

The boys had abandoned the skulls and were playing on his pieces.

"A comment on my work," he said. "Good playground equipment."

"Do you know Dwight Young?" she asked.

"Yes, we hunt together," he said.

At the Youngs' house guns and bows were locked up in a case with glass sides. He had left a note saying that the combination to the lock was not written down anywhere in the house and that the glass was designed to foil the attempts of the most determined thief. The boys loved to stand in front of the case and stare at the weapons. There were pictures in the house of the Youngs' daughters, who were in their teens, dressed in camouflage and posing with ducks, deer, doves, and quail they had killed. The boys knew nothing about hunting but they were desperate to learn. Most of the boys in their class at school had killed deer. But neither of them had ever shot a gun. Until she came to Alabama she had not known anyone who owned a gun. Perhaps Alexander or someone like him might offer to teach them.

For weeks the boys had been dressed and out of the house before she had risen, gone off to play in the pine forest that started at the edge of their backyard. They were drawn by the mystery of the woods. She worried about snakes, but her neighbors' children played in the woods and no one seemed concerned. She did not understand the attraction something like the deer skulls held for them. They returned from the woods with tales of deer they had seen. Sometimes they brought back a turtle and once the skull of an animal a neighbor identified as a possum.

"This year I'm going to bow hunt," Alexander said.

"Dwight has bows," she said. "With pulleys on them."

She would steer clear of Cuba for a while.

"No one hunts with reflex bows anymore," he said. "Not even in Russia." He looked at the boys playing on his sculptures. "Let's have lunch tomorrow."

"Yes, I can do that," she said.

She left wondering if seeing him was such a good idea. She had promised herself not to get involved with anyone until a year had passed. Her husband Philip was a successful broker. He had blamed the breakup of their marriage on her pursuit of a Ph.D. Neither of them had taken a lover. It had been more insidious than that. They had just drifted apart. But that last year of graduate school, after the divorce, had been the loneliest period of her entire life. Fortunately at the time she was taken up with completing her dissertation.

When they met for lunch, he arrived with an envelope full of pictures. The owner of an important gallery in New York had become interested in his work so Alexander was preparing to e-mail him the photographs. She looked at the pictures while they waited for their food and he smoked cigarettes.

"I don't add anything to a log once I start to work on it," he said.

In the Heart of Alabama

"So your art has rules," she said.

"No, I wouldn't call them rules. Just a task I set myself."

"Not like the rules of Soviet realism."

He smiled.

"No, I permit myself anything."

She was beginning to think how nice it would be going to sleep with him after love. They would talk about their work: his plans for a cypress log or a chapter from her book. He would understand her work in a way that Philip had never been able to. Yet at the same time she resisted such fantasies about a man she hardly knew. She had been wrong before. There had been the interpreter in Havana last summer. It turned out that he was married and had three children. And she would not have been surprised if the hotel room had been bugged.

"I will take you and your sons turtle hunting on Saturday," he said. "Can you go?"

"Where?" she asked.

"On the river, the one you drive over every day."

"What will we do with them?"

"Eat them."

He went on to describe the soft-shelled turtle they would be after. The turtles had a leathery carapace instead of a hard shell. They liked to lie on the bottom of the river half buried in the sand. They would hunt them by wearing snorkeling gear and drifting with the current until they spotted one of the turtles. A hunter caught one by grabbing the carapace from either side and keeping away from the head. The big ones, and there were turtles in the river three feet in diameter, could give a nasty bite.

"Dwight showed me how," he said. "We will borrow his canoes."

The canoes were stored on racks in the garage. She had not been in a canoe since her days at summer camp.

"Aren't there snakes?" she asked.

"Yes, but most are harmless," he said. "The alligators stay in the small creeks and sloughs. They're shy of humans. Dwight's children swim in the river. Come this Saturday. We will have turtle stew for dinner at my house."

They decided he would come to her house on Saturday morning and use his truck to transport the canoes to the river, where they would launch them below the bridge.

They had a long lunch and split a bottle of wine. After lunch they walked back to campus together. The thermometer on the bank read one hundred degrees, and the humid air felt thick in her lungs. She imagined how nice it would be drifting along in the shade of the big trees that lined the banks of the river.

They parted at a fountain in the center of campus.

"Tomorrow," he said.

"Yes, the boys will be thrilled," she said.

She returned to her office and tried to read, but the wine had made her sleepy. No one had classes on Friday afternoon, and she did not expect to see any students. She lay down on the sofa next to the window to take a nap. She had to pick up the boys in two hours.

There she fell asleep and dreamed of swimming in a Russian river with Alexander. They were naked, standing in the water up to their waists, a dense birch forest on both banks, and he was telling her how on hot midsummer days like this his father would catch big fish with his hands by carefully feeling for them in shady places up under the bank.

"Come," he said. "I will show you."

He took her hand and led her out of the sunlight into the shade, the bank rising over their heads.

"Here," he said. "Here."

She stretched out her hand into an underwater crevice among the tangled roots of a big tree. The water was cold.

Then she woke. She looked at her watch and realized she would have to hurry to be on time to pick up the boys.

They launched the canoes below the bridge. The river at this point was narrow and full of snags. They had dropped off her car at a low water

In the Heart of Alabama

bridge five miles downstream

"Boats with motors can't use the river here," Alexander said. "After it goes into Florida it becomes wider and much deeper."

She looked out at the river, which was flowing with a slow but steady current. She told the boys to put on their life jackets.

"Are they good swimmers?" Alexander asked.

"Yes," she said.

"Americans are so safe they can not enjoy life," he said. "The river is very shallow in most places. They can stand up if they fall out. Besides, we will soon be hunting turtles."

"He's right, Mom," Andrew said. "Please."

"I can swim all the way across this old river," Jason said.

She gave in. Jason got in the boat with Alexander and Andrew with her.

They went down the river. She discovered that she remembered how to handle a canoe, at least in this gentle current. They picked a path among the maze of snags and left the bridge behind them. Soon they could no longer hear the traffic crossing the bridge. There was just the gurgle of the water against the snags and the songs of the birds, the sounds almost as alien to Alexander, she imagined, as they were to her.

"When do we start?" Andrew asked.

"Later, when the river broadens some," Alexander said. "This is not a good place for turtles."

The river widened but was still filled with snags and continued to meander in lazy loops across the flat land. She liked watching the muscles in Alexander's back work as he maneuvered the canoe. They all drank cokes and swam when they got hot. She was surprised that the water was so cool, almost cold. It felt delicious.

"Are there springs that feed it?" she asked.

"I do not know," Alexander said. "Dwight would know."

They stopped for lunch at a place where there was a sandbar on one side of the river and a low bluff on the other. There was a rope swing tied to the limb of a magnolia. Alexander told her that the Youngs' girls had made it. She remembered a rope swing at camp and that moment of weightless suspension as she paused at the top of the arc before falling towards the water.

They sat in the shade and ate lunch while the boys played on the swing. Andrew climbed high into the tree and picked magnolia blossoms, which he dropped into the river. Some floated downstream. Others were caught in an eddy, creating a raft of blossoms against the dark water. Finally she made the boys stop and eat.

She lay back on a blanket and closed her eyes. She thought of making love to him on the sandbar, looking up at that tree full of blossoms, as they lay entwined on a blanket. Then his voice brought her out of her dream.

"It is time to hunt turtles."

They packed up their gear and began the hunt. At first it was she and Alexander who drifted with the current out in front of the canoes. She liked floating along, watching the sandy bottom of the river only a few feet away. The water was as clear as out of the tap. She drifted over a long, colorful snake lying stretched out on the white sand. It did not move as she passed over it. She swam over to Alexander and put her hand on his shoulder. They stood together in the river.

"I saw it," he said. "It is a banded water snake. Harmless. I know that one from Dwight."

They continued their hunt but had no luck. They let the boys take a turn.

Alexander was telling her about how his grandfather had fought and died at Stalingrad when Andrew, who was in front of Alexander's canoe, dove. Alexander stopped his canoe by slipping over the gunwales into the water, and she did the same.

She was concerned that Andrew did not immediately appear. Then he rose to the surface twenty yards downstream. He held a turtle the size of a laundry basket by the shell. The turtle's legs were flailing as it tried to escape. Alexander threw the painter of the canoe to Jason and went to help.

After a brief struggle they put the turtle upside down in the bottom of the canoe. It was a strange looking creature with its leathery shell and long, snake-like neck.

"We're going to eat that?" she asked.

"Sure, Mom," Andrew said. "It's going to be great."

They ate turtle stew over rice. He had made it with tomatoes, corn, and turnips from his garden. She had not been able to watch Alexander and the boys butcher the turtle, but she ate two helpings.

After dinner she and Alexander went out on the screened porch while the boys watched a movie. He lay in a hammock and she sat in a rocking chair. It was a still, hot night. The whippoorwills were calling from down by the river.

"We do not have that wonderful bird," Alexander said. "You do not have nightingales. Should we do something again soon? Next week?"

"Tomorrow," she said. "Andrew is old enough to look after Jason."

"Nothing to do in this place tomorrow except go to church."

Their laughter mingled with the calls of the night birds.

"I'll cook dinner for us," she said. "Here."

"An American dinner?" he asked.

"You want borscht?"

She tried to recall the meals people ate in the nineteenth century Russian novels she had read.

"No, I am making a joke," he said.

"Do you eat ducks in Russia?" she asked.

"Yes, but they do not eat them here."

"Well, I suppose it will have to be a surprise."

"I like surprises."

They sat together and talked about her book. Then the boys appeared on the porch. She took them home.

"He's a nice man," Jason said.

Andrew had gone to sleep, stretched out on the back seat. This was something new, his needing so much sleep.

"Yes he is," she said.

"Next time I'm going to catch a turtle," he said.

"We'll go again."

"With Alexander?"

"Yes."

"Good."

They drove toward home as Jason talked about turtles.

Alexander proved right about the scarcity of ducks. The one grocery store open on Sunday afternoon had no ducks. She called the Wal-Mart Super Store thirty miles away. They would not have any until Monday. So she decided on chicken. But when she returned from the store, she remembered that the Youngs had a freezer full of game. They had told her to help herself to it.

One of the bags was labeled JANET'S MALLARDS. She put the two ducks in the sink and started running cold water over them. She also found what looked like a good bottle of wine in the Youngs' wine rack. It was not possible to buy wine on Sunday.

She left the boys after giving Andrew a lecture about his responsibility toward his younger brother.

"You're having a date with Alexander?" Andrew asked.

"Yes," she said.

"You hardly know him," Andrew said.

"We teach together," she said.

"We spent the whole day on the river with him," Jason said. "We ate turtle stew at his house."

"So there you are," she said.

When she left the boys were watching a movie. They gave her perfunctory goodbyes.

She had never cooked wild duck before. Although she had come armed with a recipe from one of the Youngs' cookbooks, she allowed Alexander to help when it turned out that he had cooked wild duck many times. He made a broth with the liver and lights, organs she would have thrown away.

They ate out on the porch on a table he had made out of cypress planks. There were fireflies this evening in the live oaks and the whippoorwills were calling again out in the soft darkness. They finished one bottle of wine and started on another. They had peach ice cream for dessert. Then they drank coffee. He lay in the hammock and smoked cigarettes.

"My father is dying of cigarettes," he said. "I will go see him during Christmas break or in the summer."

"And you still smoke," she said.

"A habit I cannot break."

He put out the cigarette.

"Come sit with me," he said.

She lay in the hammock with him. For a long time neither one of them said anything. They lay there listening to the calls of the birds.

Then they began to wriggle out of their clothes as the hammock swayed back and forth. Her arm was caught in the sleeve of her blouse. She thought about getting up to slip out of it but did not want to take the time, did not want to do anything to interrupt the moment. And then she almost tipped them over.

"Careful," he said.

Some animal screamed from the woods. The sound rushed over them, raising the hairs on her arms.

"What is that?" he asked.

"You don't know?" she said.

"I am Russian. You are the American."

Then it made the sound again. This time she thought it was beautiful instead of frightening.

"It's a bird," she said.

"You are guessing," he said. "A wildcat. That is what I think it is."

They put their arms around each other. The word *love* came into her mind, but she thought she would be like a man, concentrate just on his body and hers. That was what he was doing. She was sure of it.

The animal screamed again but she took no notice of it. Then it was silent. They made love while choirs of whippoorwills sang in the dark woods.

The boys in Andrew and Jason's classes at school were preparing to hunt doves. The season opened on the Labor Day weekend. They complained that they were going to be excluded.

So when Alexander offered to take them with him on opening day, not to shoot but to watch, she agreed. He also offered to teach them to shoot.

"It is the custom here," he said. "I will teach them as my father taught me."

They were sitting in the room where the gun safe stood in a corner next to the fireplace. He walked over and worked the combination and swung it open. He took out a shotgun. Then he called the boys into the room.

He worked the action of the shotgun and shucked out two shells. Then he gave the boys a lecture on gun safety. After he finished he put the shotgun back in the rack and took out two BB guns. He explained to the boys how they worked. He gave a gun to each of them and they walked out of the house with the barrels pointed at the ceiling.

As she worked at her desk, she watched the boys shooting at a beer can Alexander had set on a fence post. They moved carefully and stiffly in accordance with his directions. She was pleased that now they would not be isolated from the other children.

The boys became hunters with shotgun and rifle and bow. When she brought them home from school in the afternoon, they practiced shooting their bows at a Styrofoam deer. Alexander was strict with them. She never saw them treat a broad head arrow or a gun or a knife in a careless manner. Now the boys knew the combination of the gun safe, which was only locked when everyone was away from the house. By the middle of October, Andrew had killed a deer with a bow and Jason had killed one with a rifle. Alexander marinated the venison in milk and juniper berries. It seemed to her that they ate game for at least one meal a day. The boys loved deer tacos. She seldom bought meat at the grocery store. Andrew and Jason were happy with their new identities. She was happy too.

And then, just before Christmas break, Alexander's work won a prize. Soon after it was taken by the important gallery in New York, the one that had been interested in his work back in August. He was unable to go to the opening, because he was sick with the flu. She moved him into her house until he felt better. All his pieces quickly sold and there was an article about him in the arts section of the *Times*.

Suddenly he was flush with money. He bought the boys shotguns for Christmas. After Christmas there was another exhibition of his work. He went up to New York for the opening. And she discovered that she was jealous. She imagined him with other women in New York.

While Alexander was in New York, he received news that his father had died. He flew to Moscow. She exchanged a few e-mails with him. They talked on the phone.

"How's Moscow?" she asked.

"Cold," he said.

"New York?"

"All my pieces have sold and they want more of them. I am thinking about taking leave for the spring semester."

"So you can work."

"Yes. It will be good to be back in Alabama."

She was relieved that he was planning to return but did not say so.

"It is hard to be away so long," he said.

"We'll have the whole spring semester together," she said.

"Yes, but then you are going to spend the summer in Cuba."

"I'm going to finish my book."

They both paused. She looked out the kitchen window at some kind of bird circling over the pines. She did not know what it was. If the boys had been home, they could have told her.

"You know that I have a high regard for you," he said. "I think we have a high regard for each other."

"Yes, that's what I feel too," she said.

She thought about flying to Moscow. She could send the boys to Philip. He had wanted them over Christmas anyway. That was an important time to him. They had fought over that.

"Let us wait until I get home," he said. "Then we can talk seriously about us. Matters of the heart should not be discussed over the phone."

"Yes, you're right," she said.

She was thankful for the opportunity to delay whatever conversation they were going to have about love. She found herself telling him some university gossip that had nothing to do with either one of them, and he told her of a visit he had paid to one of his teachers.

Then they talked about the boys. He was concerned about them. He wanted to be sure someone was going to take them duck hunting. She assured him that had all been arranged. As they were talking, she imagined him taking some old girl friend out to dinner.

"Goodbye," he said. "I will come home to flowers blooming."

"Yes," she said. "Flowers in the winter."

"Goodbye, Josie. I will be thinking of you."

"And me of you."

She put the phone down and she wondered if she was in love with him. But perhaps, she thought, he was right about not talking of such things on the phone, not before they had been said in person.

In between those infrequent e-mails and phone calls, she found herself focusing on her book. As she worked she thought from time to time of Alexander's understandable but overly simplistic views about Cuba. She also thought of what her summer would be like in Cuba. Would she run into the interpreter again? What would they say to each other?

One day, after she had had a particularly good afternoon, she thought about how she had distracted herself like this in graduate school. She and Philip were getting a divorce and the boys were being troublesome and in the midst of all that she did some of her best work.

Then she received an e-mail from Alexander telling her that he was not returning for the spring semester. There was too much money to be made in New York. He wrote that he hoped he had helped her and the boys learn to live in Alabama, that he had the highest regard for her. He was thinking about starting to work in metal. He thought that his "cypress" period might be over. But he was going to keep his house in case he decided to work in wood again. There was a good supply of cypress logs stored in the barn. He had arranged for a friend to teach the boys to hunt turkeys when the season opened in the spring. It was the only game with which they were unfamiliar.

The day she received the e-mail she stayed up all night with her book and fixed, she thought, a chapter that had always been weak. She felt good, she told herself. After all she had not been in love with Alexander. Besides, she was not sure she wanted to be in love with anyone right now. Her life was going to be much less complicated without Alexander in it. She had Cuba to look forward to in the summer. Alexander had never really understood anything about Cuba. It was not, as he supposed, simply an extension of the Soviet Union. She watched the sunrise over the pines but kept working until mid-morning, filling herself with the book so there would be no room for Alexander. Then she left the boys a note on the door not to disturb her. She lay down on the daybed and slept until late afternoon, waking to the gathering darkness.

One Sunday afternoon in February the boys had gone out with .22 rifles to roam the woods. As she sat at her desk, she saw them returning, the sunlight flashing off the blued rifle barrels. It was warm out, and the camellias planted along the edge of the yard were in bloom. Flowers in the winter. She loved that about the South just as Alexander had.

Jason was carrying something in his hand, but it was partially hidden by a patch of waist-high scrub oak the boys were walking through. When they came out of the scrub, she saw they had shot a crow. They had broken one of Alexander's rules, shooting something they did not intend to eat. They came on into the yard, walking past the camellias loaded with scarlet blossoms, the bird limp in the attitude of the newly killed, its feathers blue-black, the color she suddenly realized of Alexander's hair. She started to speak his name, but instead, to her surprise, as unexpected as that colorful snake appearing before her eyes in the clear, cool water, she heard other words.

"My children!" she cried. "My children!"

Stalingrad

When I was a boy in Mississippi, I had a friend named Wolfram Varderman. His father had disappeared off the face of the earth during the battle of Stalingrad. He had not returned when the handful of Germans who had survived capture by the Soviets had been repatriated to Germany. He may have died in some labor camp in Siberia, or I suppose his bones may still lie there outside the city where the German 6th Army was encircled and destroyed.

Wolfram's mother, who was a Berliner, sometimes spoke of her former husband Albert as if he were still alive. Wolfram told me this. He told me too that his mother often dreamed of Albert. In her dream he was a lone figure walking across a snow-covered landscape with a sack thrown over his shoulder. She even knew what was in the sack. She always awoke to the scent of apples. Even then I thought it was strange a mother would tell her son her dreams of a father who was surely dead. Wolfram thought the same thing and said he wished his mother would keep her dreams of his father to herself.

When Wolfram was a baby, his mother had fled before the advance of the Soviet army, carrying him in her arms. I wonder if Wolfram, if he is still alive, ever has dreams about that. It seemed to me that every chance she got his mother would tell the story of her running through the rubble as Soviet artillery shells fell like a heavy rain.

Later when I was at Ole Miss, I remember thinking of Wolfram when

I listened to President Kennedy's speech. "*Ich bin ein Berliner,*" he said. I thought at the time that I knew two Berliners. But I had not seen Wolfram since he left with his family for California at the end of the 10th grade.

Wolfram's stepfather was an American army colonel who had met his mother during the occupation. Wolfram loved his stepfather. They hunted and fished together. He taught Wolfram how to throw a curve ball. My father had been killed during the invasion of Normandy. He was buried in France. At the time I had never visited his grave, but I knew what it looked like, one of hundreds of white crosses arranged in perfect rows across grass that was greener and thicker than the St Augustine grass on our front lawn. My mother had not remarried. She did not seem to be interested in men at all, only in her job at the state office building in downtown Jackson where she worked for the Commissioner of Agriculture. If she dreamed about my father, she never told me.

Fortunately for me Colonel Varderman taught me to throw a curve ball too. Whenever he took Wolfram hunting or fishing I got to go along.

Wolfram and I both lived out in one of the new subdivisions built in Jackson not long after the war. Ours was five or six miles outside the city limits, on a pine-covered ridge only a couple of miles from the Pearl River.

During the school year we spent our weekends in the woods that ran unbroken from the edge of the subdivision to the river. The pines quickly ended and were replaced with gum and oak and cypress. The land was a maze of creeks and oxbow lakes.

It was late May. It had been raining for several days, but had cleared in time for the weekend. Like always Wolfram tapped on my window just before sunrise. I looked up and saw his dark shape, taller by four inches than me, through the screen. I dressed and unhooked the screen and climbed out the window.

"Let's go fish in the creek," Wolfram said.

There was always good fishing where the creek emptied into the river.

Wolfram wore a combat pack and a canteen on his belt. We went to the

Stalingrad

garage and took our cane poles, which we had cut from a canebrake along the river, and walked up the newly paved road between the rows of dark ranch style houses.

The road ran along the top of the ridge and then ended. It was replaced by a dirt track that ran all the way to the creek. As the sun came up, we went down through the pines and into the oaks and hickories. Finally we stood on the banks of the creek where there were gums and poplars and cypresses. The creek was not out of its banks, but the brown water moved with a steady, powerful flow toward the river. It was a power we had learned to respect. Once, after the creek had flooded, we had found the complete skeleton of a dog hanging in a tree ten feet above the bank. The bones were clean and white, held together as if by some magic spell. I suppose that the tendons and ligaments had been the last to rot. The next day it was gone. I imagined those bonds all releasing at the same time and a rain of bones falling into the brown water. The creek had a name, but to us it was Dead Dog Creek.

We sat on a log and ate the apple pancakes Wolfram's mother had made. We drank two warm cokes. Then, after we applied war surplus mosquito repellent, we followed the trail along the creek toward the river. Later in Vietnam I would use repellent with the same sweet smell before I learned it was better to endure the mosquitoes than to advertise one's presence to the enemy.

The trail was easy to follow for the deer kept the vegetation beaten down. We usually said little to one another in the woods. We watched the ground for snakes; we looked for soft-shelled turtles. Once we caught a big one and my mother made turtle stew out of it. Soon we were close to the mouth of the river. So far it had been a good day. We had jumped a deer. We had seen two big cottonmouths slide off a log and into the creek.

"A canoe," Wolfram said.

The canoe floated in a big eddy a few yards out from the bank, its aluminum hull bright against the brown water. A little farther down the shady green tunnel made by the trees the river slid by the mouth of the creek in the sunshine. The river was moving fast, and its surface was littered with branches and trash.

"I wonder who it belongs to," Wolfram said.

"It belongs to us," I said.

I explained to Wolfram how we could paddle the canoe down the river and take it out where the railroad bridge crossed just below the water treatment plant. There we could drag the canoe up to the road. Colonel Varderman would help us take it home.

"I'll swim out to it," Wolfram said.

He took off his clothes. He was uncircumcised, the first person I had ever seen like that, like a Greek athlete on a vase. He swam out to the canoe. He put one hand on a gunwale and side stroked himself and the canoe to the bank.

There was nothing in the bottom of the canoe, not even a fishhook or a candy wrapper.

"No paddles," I said.

We scoured the banks of the creek and finally found a couple of pine boards, pieces of scrap left over from the building of all those houses, that could serve as paddles. We would have the current so all we really needed was something to steer the boat. Both of us had been in canoes before at Boy Scout camp.

We paddled the canoe out of the eddy and were caught up by the current, which bore us toward the river. The canoe felt light under me, responding instantly to every stroke of my makeshift paddle. We went out of the shady tunnel into the sunlight. I do not know how Wolfram felt, but I felt like a king. I imagined all the fishing trips we would go on in our canoe. In the summer we could float past the city and down to the Gulf of Mexico. We would camp on sandbars and cook catfish over driftwood fires.

As we entered the river, the current pushed on the canoe like a giant hand, and I felt the boat rolling over downstream. We both leaned upstream to correct this. Suddenly the river was in the boat. This was nothing like my experience in lakes. Sometimes at Boy Scout camp we would deliberately fill a canoe with water. The internal floatation tanks kept it from sinking. But we were no longer in the canoe. It was sideways in the current and moving rapidly downstream.

"Catch it!" I yelled.

Wolfram was closer to the canoe than I was. He swam toward it with strong strokes, but the distance between him and the boat rapidly widened. He still wore the combat pack. I shouted at him to slip out of it so he could swim faster, but he ignored me. The river made a curve, and the boat was swept into a stand of willows. I watched the boat shudder for a moment as it met the willows. Then one end rose and, accompanied by the sound of metal tearing, it folded in half just as easily as I might have closed my jackknife.

Both of us knew we did not want to be swept into those willows with the boat. We swam hard for the other side of the river, and our efforts just barely allowed us to clear the trees. Then we were past the ruined canoe. It seemed strange floating down the middle of the river on this beautiful morning. We were together now, borne on that brown flood through a corridor of green trees toward the Gulf of Mexico.

The river ran straight now. Ahead it disappeared out of sight around another bend. The water was up in the trees on both sides, and there seemed to be no good place to get off the river and avoid the fate of the canoe. Then I saw a break in the trees.

"A creek!" I said. "Swim to it!"

We swam as close to the trees as we dared. The current increased, and we shot along at a good speed. Then we were at the creek. We swam hard to escape the pull of the current and reached the safety of the slack water. I felt sand beneath my feet, the sandbar that was always at the mouths of those little creeks. We both stood up in water that came to our waists. The creek was a shady green tunnel. The river moved by in the sunlight.

"Look!" Wolfram said. "A hog!"

An enormous black and white hog floated past, riding high, like some sort of inflatable toy someone would use at Gulf Shores. It was on its back, its legs pointed stiffly in the air. It disappeared behind the screen of willows at the mouth of the creek.

"If we'd stayed in that canoe, we'd have been at the railroad bridge in half an hour," I said.

"I wouldn't want to get near that bridge in a canoe," Wolfram said.

He was right. I could see the canoe wrapped around a piling and maybe one or both of us entangled in the wreckage.

There was no trail along this creek. Our way was blocked by thickets of cane and briars. We cast about out into a stand of gums, keeping the morning sun at our back, because we wanted to walk west. We had not walked fifty yards before we ran into a dirt track. It ran south, parallel to the river. We walked for what seemed an hour. Neither one of us wore a watch. Then the track petered out. We sat on the ground and had a drink from Wolfram's canteen. We each ate another apple pancake. They had been wrapped tightly in foil and only a little water had reached them. I wondered if there was more food in the pack. Wolfram liked to produce food out of the pack during the course of our trips to the woods. He could never be persuaded to tell me beforehand what was in the pack.

"Matches?" I asked. I was thinking about what was going to happen if we had to spend the night in the woods.

"Wet," he said. "Finished."

"It doesn't matter," I said. "We'll be home in a few hours."

A woodpecker drummed against a tree. Then we heard its call as it flew off through the big timber.

"We'll have to go through the woods," I said.

"Yes, we can't be far from a road," he said.

I wondered what road he was talking about but said nothing. I supposed he was just wishing there was a road not far away. We walked off through the trees. Soon the land rose a little. We slowly picked our way through a tangle of blackberry bushes that were all in bloom and emerged on the shore of an oxbow lake. A head-high stand of bushes, which grew out into the water, kept us from actually reaching the lake. The bushes were covered with white blossoms. They formed a thick hedge all the way around the lake. Someone's red and white plastic fishing bobber floated in the dark, coffee-colored water. If we had been lucky, there would have been someone in a boat on the lake.

"There'll be a road out on the other side," I said.

Wolfram looked down at the bobber and nodded in agreement.

This oxbow lake was a large one. We were in the center of the bow on the outside edge. From where we standing I could not see either end of the lake.

"Which way?" I asked.

"South," Wolfram said.

He said it as if he were certain this was the right direction. There was too much brush along the edge of the lake to allow us to walk there, so we had to go back down through the blackberry bushes. The sun was directly overhead now. It was useless to try to steer by it. But all we had to do was follow the lake to keep from getting lost. Surely there was a road on the other side that would lead out of the river bottom.

But walking south alongside the lake proved to be a bad decision. After we had threaded our way through thickets of cane and briars, we found our way blocked by a cypress swamp. We stood on the edge of it looking at the stand of big cypresses rising out of the dark water.

"It probably goes all the way to the river," Wolfram said.

"You think so?" I said.

"All the way."

"I wouldn't be surprised if it did."

I tried to estimate exactly how long it would take us to walk around the swamp. And there might be impassable thickets along the river. I looked down the corridors of trees. I could see the other side of the swamp, and it seemed to me that the land rose there. It might be a ridge that would take us around the other side of the oxbow lake.

"Let's cross it," I said.

"Full of cottonmouths," Wolfram said.

"We wade around in those beaver ponds to fish. They're full of cottonmouths too."

"It might be deep."

"We can swim."

At the time there were no alligators. They had been hunted out. If a person went back there today, they would find a swamp like that full of gators.

Crossing the swamp proved to be easy. We only had to swim in a couple of places. We did not even see a snake. The land on the other side was higher but was covered with dense thickets of canes and briars. We decided to follow the slope of the land upwards. Wolfram took his hunting knife and made staves for us out of a couple of hickory saplings. We used these to beat a path through the briars. At least we were going in the right direction, directly into the mid-afternoon sun.

By the time we had made our way through those thickets it was late afternoon. We were walking through a stand of big pines. It was already growing dark beneath the trees.

"We'll hit a road soon," Wolfram said.

"Maybe," I said.

"There'll be a road."

"We may still be behind the lake. No way to get a bulldozer in here."

"I don't want to spend the night out here."

"Neither do I."

I was not afraid of spending the night in the woods, and I did not think Wolfram was either. We had camped by ourselves before. A neighbor had taken us coon hunting once, and we had spent the whole night roaming the woods, following the sound of the dogs. But our neighbor had known exactly where he was the whole time.

We were walking through a stand of oaks and hickories now. The land was lower. Then through the trees I saw a piece of the lake. We were still not completely around it. I thought how it would be if we walked down to the shore of the lake and there was a canoe or a johnboat. We could still be back home in time for supper.

"Let's walk to the lake," I said. "Maybe we'll find a boat."

"There's not going to be a boat," Wolfram said.

But the dream of the boat was in my head and I refused to be dissuaded. Wolfram went with me.

"We should go back to the pines," Wolfram said. "That's the highest place. There won't be so many mosquitoes."

"Come on," I said. "We have time to look."

Then ahead, in the gathering dusk, I saw the tree house. It was built of logs and was about fifteen or twenty feet off the ground. A ladder made from two by fours led up to it. We had come upon them before. They were built by deer hunters for use as shooting platforms. Deer seldom looked up. Once there had been panthers in the swamp that would lie in wait in trees, descending unexpectedly onto the backs of their prey. But the panthers had all been killed off long ago, and the deer were left with no ancestral memory of death dropping down from above.

"There'll be a road," Wolfram said.

"No, I think they came across the lake," I said.

We stood under the tree house. The ground was littered with cellophane wrappers and empty cans of beans and sausage. Brass rifle cartridges lay scattered about. Wolfram picked one up and blew across the end of it, making a whistling sound.

Then we walked down to the lake. My theory about the hunters coming by boat was correct. They had cut a path through the lakeside bushes. I imagined them doing it with a machete. Marks left by the grooved bottom of a johnboat were still visible in the earth. We could no longer see the other side of the lake, which had disappeared into the darkness. I imagined it was at least half a mile across, maybe more. A half moon began to rise above the trees, its light causing the perfectly smooth surface of the lake to look like polished metal.

"We can sleep in the tree house," I said.

We climbed up the ladder, reaching the platform through a hole cut in the floor. Someone had hauled an old rug up there. It smelled of mildew, but it was going to be better than sleeping on the bare logs. We sat there, looking out over the lake while mosquitoes buzzed about our ears. We put on more mosquito repellent.

Wolfram reached into the pack and pulled out a jar of herring. I had eaten that before and liked it.

"It'll make us thirsty," he said.

"I don't care," I said.

We fished the herring out of the jar with our fingers. Those herring had never tasted so good. Then the jar was empty. We licked our fingers clean. We drank the rest of the water from the canteen.

"What else have you got?" I asked.

Wolfram hesitated.

"Two more pancakes," he said. "We'll eat them in the morning."

We went to sleep. The first time I woke it was to the sound of dogs baying on the other side of the lake. The moon was down. Wolfram was sleeping soundly. I put more mosquito repellant on while I listened to the dogs. I did not imagine the dogs were on our scent. It was someone hunting possum or coon. But I expected by now Colonel Varderman and other men from the neighborhood were out searching for us.

I was thirsty from the herring. Wolfram had been right about that. But I decided I would wait until morning to share with Wolfram what little water was left in the canteen.

I slept again. The next time I woke Wolfram was gone. I heard the dogs off toward the river, their cries very faint. I longed for a drink of water. I imagined myself kneeling by the lake and scooping up water with my cupped palm. I raised my head and saw him standing beside the lake. He was wearing his combat pack. Wolfram was talking with a man, who was a head taller than him. There was no moon, so all I could see were their shapes silhouetted against the lighter darkness over the lake. They

Stalingrad

were speaking German. Wolfram and his mother sometimes spoke German to each other.

"Wolfram!" I called. "Wolfram!"

Wolfram turned towards me and raised his hand for me to be silent. For some reason I knew that I should obey. I was standing now. I could still hear their voices, now and then a German word emerging clearer than the others. I cannot remember any of the words.

I remember thinking that this man must be the owner of the dogs. Perhaps he was a former American soldier who had learned German during the occupation.

Then I watched Wolfram embrace the figure. And I knew that it was Albert, finally come back from the war. I wanted to shout with joy; I wanted to climb down the ladder and join them by the edge of the lake. I imagined the three of us dancing in a circle with linked arms, celebrating Albert's miraculous return. I would ask Albert how deep the snow had been in Siberia. I had seen snow only twice.

But for some reason I stayed there on the platform. And I thought of my own father lying dead in France beneath that green grass.

"Father!" I yelled, "Father!"

I woke flat on my back, looking up into the dark canopy of leaves. From deep in the woods came the baying of a single dog, a rich deep sound, not frantic but strong and steady. Then the baying of that dog was counter pointed by the voices of the rest of the pack, strung out behind the lead dog in that tangle of cane and briars.

The platform shook. For a moment I imagined Albert coming up the ladder. Wolfram's head came through the opening and then the rest of him. He sat down and took off his combat pack. I was completely awake now.

"What were you yelling?" Wolfram asked.

"Where have you been?" I asked.

"I saw a light on the other side of the lake. I yelled but no one answered. It's gone now."

I looked out across the lake. The darkness was pure and even. The sound of the baying was coming even closer now. Whatever the dogs were chasing was trapped between the river and the lake.

"What were you yelling?" Wolfram asked.

"I was dreaming," I said. "I don't know what it was. I was dreaming and then I woke up."

"Let's go to sleep."

"I'm thirsty."

He handed me the canteen. It was full.

"I filled it in the lake," he said.

I took a long drink. The water smelled faintly of fish or at least I thought it did. I felt something soft and fleshy slide down my throat. I hoped that it was a piece of duckweed and not a tadpole.

We lay down on carpet and went to sleep. The next time I opened my eyes it was morning. I raised my head and looked out over the lake. A pair of wood ducks were swimming along the shoreline. When I stood up the male, brilliant in his plumage, flushed first, followed by the female. Wolfram woke. He drank from the canteen and then handed it to me.

"Careful," he said. "Don't shake it."

He did not want me to disturb the sediment on the bottom.

We sat with our legs hanging off the edge of the platform and ate the two apple pancakes and drank the dark lake water.

I thought about telling Wolfram about my dream but decided not to. I wondered if he thought about his father often. His father was caught in some limbo in Wolfram's imagination, a dark figure against the white snow. For my father there was a white cross with a name on it and the company of his comrades. He lay in a place I could visit, but for Wolfram there was only the vast expanse of the Soviet Union, sealed from him forever by the Iron Curtain.

"I'm not walking through any more briars," Wolfram said. "Let's swim the lake."

It was a long way across the lake. In the light we could see that we were going to have to swim on a diagonal, perhaps three quarters of a mile, to reach the open space cut out of the lakeside bushes by the deer hunters to make a launching point for a johnboat. But we were both good swimmers. We had gotten off the river. I looked out across the lake, which lay smooth in the light from the rising sun.

"No more briars," I said.

We stood on the edge of the lake where the hunters had brought the johnboat in and out. It was where I had seen Wolfram and his father standing in my dream. I could not help looking for boot prints in the soft earth, but there were only the marks of our basketball shoes.

We took off our clothes. I put my socks and underwear and t-shirt inside my jeans. Then I pulled the belt of my jeans tight and tied the legs together, trapping air inside. We had learned to do this in Boy Scouts. I tied the laces of my shoes together and put them around my neck. I noticed that Wolfram was putting his clothes into the combat pack.

"You're going to swim all the way with that pack?" I asked.

He smiled.

"Sure," he said.

"If you have to drop it, you'll be walking home naked," I said.

"I won't drop it," he said.

I looked at him. In a few months we would both be tanned, but our skin was pale now. Our chests were smooth and hairless. Wolfram went into the water first, his body white against the dark water. I followed.

Wolfram did not have to drop his pack, but it turned out to be a long swim. Sometimes we stopped and rested by floating on our backs. Wolfram rested the pack on his stomach when we did that. The sky, which had been cloudless at dawn, was filling with white, puffy clouds. I thought now and then what would happen if one of us got a cramp. Those apple pancakes were rich, not an athlete's breakfast. Sometimes we swam side by side and sometimes Wolfram swam a little ahead of me, both of us using the breaststroke.

Then we were halfway. I wondered how deep the water was under us and how much closer to the shore we would have to swim before we could stand up.

"What's that?" Wolfram asked. "Is that a dog?"

I treaded water and looked at the gap in the bushes. A dog sat there on his haunches.

"Lost from the pack," I said.

The dog had seen or smelled us. Now it pranced about on the edge of the lake. We swam steadily. Long ago my jeans had become completely waterlogged. My shoes were heavy around my neck. I knew Wolfram's combat pack was even heavier. The dog began to bark.

It was not unusual for dogs to become separated from the pack during a hunt. If we were lucky we might run into the hunter out looking for it and get a ride home.

We made it to shore where we collapsed on the ground, both of us breathing hard. The coonhound leaped about around us and licked our faces. It had a collar with a brass plate riveted to it inscribed with a name and a telephone number. JOHNIE LEE HAUSER was the name on the plate. We put on our wet clothes and with the dog at our heels we walked away from the lake, following the set of tire tracks made when someone had driven a truck in to launch a johnboat. The tracks wound through the trees and soon hit a dirt road.

After an hour of walking we came out of the trees into someone's cornfield. On the other side of the field we saw a car go by on an asphalt road. Beyond the road a set of high-tension lines marched across the landscape. The cornfield would later become the site of a clay court tennis club where I would spend much of my time. We followed the track around the edge of the newly planted cornfield.

I felt good and I guessed Wolfram felt the same.

"Wait," Wolfram said.

He stopped and took off the combat pack. He unfastened the straps and reached inside and produced two apples.

Stalingrad

"You had these all the time?" I asked.

Wolfram laughed as if I had just said the strangest thing that he had ever heard.

"Sure," he said. "No apple trees in the Pearl River swamps."

The dog stuck his nose against the apple in my hand and whined.

"It's not the season for apples," I said.

That was a time when we ate things pretty much according to the seasons. You could not go to a grocery store and buy a watermelon in February.

"They came through the mail," he said. "In a box."

I thought of his mother's dream, of Albert with his sack of apples. Where had Albert gotten those apples in the middle of the winter?

"From Germany?" I asked.

"No, not from there," he said.

He took a big bite out of his apple. I bit into mine, the apple tasting sweet and firm. I thought of fall mornings and the scent of burning leaves. But there was something else too, a watery smell and maybe the scent of cypress needles. I thought of my father again. I would go to France. I would stand by his grave.

"Come on," Wolfram said. "Come on dog."

We all walked toward the asphalt road.

Land Clearing

Andrew Laird drove his truck along the highway and watched the fields of soybeans and cotton unroll on either side. It was a new truck, bought with cash from the profits of his land clearing business. ANDREW LAIRD LAND CLEARING was painted on both the driver's and passenger's doors. He passed a stand of pines, which stretched all the way to the Lynches River three miles away. *I'd like to clear all of South Carolina*, he thought. *So there wouldn't be a single tree. Just beans and cotton and corn.*

He passed a pasture enclosed with a white four-rail fence where there were horses and then cattle behind barbed wire. He passed a rectangular metal building where garbage trucks were parked. He turned off the highway and drove the quarter of a mile along the driveway to his father's house. Jack Laird lived alone. Andrew's mother had died the year before. The house was a brick ranch style. There were no trees along the drive and no trees around the house. His father hated trees.

One of his father's Jack Russell terriers ran out to greet him when he got out of the truck. He was wary of Claymore, because the dog had bitten him on the hand the week before. But this time Claymore was in a good mood. He ran up wagging his tail. Andrew petted him and Claymore licked his hand.

His father had been a demolition man during the Vietnam War, an expert in the use of plastic explosives and TNT, a magician, if a person chose to believe his stories, in the discovery and dismantling of booby

Land Clearing

traps. He always gave his dogs military names. His father had carried into battle the Luger his own father had taken off a German officer during World War II. "The last round for me," his father liked to say when he told war stories. Andrew had never been interested in his father's stories.

Jack Laird had liver cancer and was going to die soon. His big body was sprawled in a recliner in front of the TV. His nurses sat on the sofa. There were two because his father wanted them to be able to pick him up if he fell. He had a fear of lying there waiting for the ambulance while some puny woman struggled ineffectively with his bulk. One nurse was black and the other white. Andrew never bothered to learn the names of his father's nurses, because they were seldom around for long. His father was hard on nurses. He had fired one because she refused to wear a uniform. He wanted them dressed in white. "To prepare me for the angels," he liked to say.

They were all watching a movie on a big screen TV. Andrew looked out the picture window at his mother's rose garden. He watered the roses every time he came. If he had not they would have died early in the summer. Once a swimming pool had been there instead of roses. Andrew's older brother Billy had drowned in the pool behind the house when Andrew was six. He remembered his father filling the pool in with the bulldozer. He sat there on the machine with his mouth set in a hard straight line as if he were trying to will himself into metal, as if he wanted to become a permanent part of the machine. The air was filled with the stink of diesel fuel and freshly turned earth. His mother sat crying in the kitchen. His mother had planted the rose garden. It had taken truckloads of manure to make the fill dirt fertile.

His father paused the movie. A cavalry column was frozen in motion as the men rode across a desert landscape. A lightning bolt zigzagged down out of a dark cloud on the horizon.

"I got you a job," his father said.

"What kind of job?" Andrew asked.

The nurses got up and went out of the room. They all quickly learned that any business discussion between father and son was likely to be unpleasant.

Andrew had merged his unsuccessful land clearing business with his father's successful one when the old man got sick. His father was still running his garbage hauling company from his sickbed. Andrew hated the garbage business and hoped his father was not asking him to take it over.

"Clearing," his father said. "Two hundred acres."

"Where?" Andrew asked.

"Up on the Lynches River," he said. "Just outside of Bethune."

Andrew thought he knew the place.

"Billy Foley is fixing to expand?"

"That's right," his father said. "You're smarter than you look."

"I've been doing well. I've been making money."

"You ain't been doing shit. Making money off my leavings. That's all you've been doing."

Andrew looked at his father. His father's eyes were clear and bright. Andrew would have expected his eyes to be glazed and dull from all the morphine he was taking.

"Daddy—" Andrew began.

But he did not know exactly what it was that he wanted to say. His father had always viewed him as a competitor. When he had taken over the land clearing business, his father had acted as if he had stolen it. Andrew wanted to knock his father out of his chair and embrace him all at the same time. His father fixed his sharp gaze on him. It was how a circling hawk might look down on a rat moving through a field below.

"You clear that land," he said. "You do a good job. I want to see it."

Andrew pictured his father gazing with pride on the land. But he would never live to see it planted. Andrew doubted that he would last the summer.

His father pointed the remote at the TV. The column of cavalry sprang into motion. Thunder rumbled in the distance and lightning flashed.

"Stay and watch if you want," his father said.

Land Clearing

"No thanks," he said.

His father loved that particular movie. Andrew supposed he had seen the movie maybe ten or twelve times before he grew old enough to start school.

The old man's eyes were fixed on the screen. The nurses drifted back into the room and sat on the sofa. Andrew went out of the house, no longer thinking of his father but about the new project. He was five miles down the highway when he recalled that he had forgotten to water the roses.

They started working along the highway. First they cut a stand of pines and sold off the wood to the paper mill. Then, after they logged the valuable hardwoods, they began to clear the poplars and gums. They bulldozed the logs and stumps into huge piles and burned them. Andrew liked watching those fires burn at night.

On the day they started in on the trash trees, he noticed a green Land Rover stopped on the highway. A woman, (he thought it was a woman), watched them through binoculars. Now and then sun flashed off the lenses. Then he was sure it was a woman. From then on she was there at least once a day. The truck would stop on the highway and on sunny days the light would shine off her blonde hair. She would watch them for a few minutes and then drive off. One day, after he watched her truck disappear over a hill, he asked Carl and Bill, his dozer operators, if either of them knew who she was.

"Never seen that truck," Carl said.

"She's got money, driving that English truck," Bill said.

"Husband's money," Carl said.

Bill spat a stream of tobacoo juice onto the dry earth that had been ground to a fine powder by the heavy equipment.

"Or hers," Bill said. "Women these days are driving dozers. I've seen 'em."

Andrew decided that the next time he saw her truck he would drive out to the highway and find out who she was. She never returned. Andrew tried to put her out of his mind, but he found himself stopping work and looking toward the highway every time a vehicle that resembled her truck appeared. Once he was stopped by a highway patrolman on the interstate for speeding when he was trying to overtake what looked to him like a green Land Rover.

The work went smoothly. His father was no better and no worse. It seemed to Andrew that one day his father would vanish from his seat in the lounger and in full view of the nurses be bodily incorporated into one of the violent scenes that played constantly before his eyes on the television screen. His father would will himself out of life and into some sort of eternal digital existence.

It was not until they had reached the banks of the river that Andrew saw the woman again. She stood on the other side of the river where there was a bluff. Behind her the roof of a house rose through the trees. She waved at him. Then she yelled something, cupping her hands around her mouth. The dozer Bill was driving moved away. He could hear the songs of the birds again and then her voice.

"Trees, you—don't!" her voice came across the river. "You—"

He cupped his hand around one ear and then turned it toward her. He held out his hands, palms up. She disappeared. At the same time the dozer returned to work close to him, and even if she had had a bullhorn he would have been unable to hear her. Then he saw her, her blonde hair a bright spot against the tangle of cane, briars, and trees that covered the face of the bluff. He hoped she would be careful and not step on a snake. She disappeared again to emerge beside the river. It was low but not shallow enough to wade. There was an enormous blockage a few yards downstream, formed when a tornado had toppled a stand of big trees into the river. She crossed on that, picking her way among the tangle, surefooted, never making an awkward move.

He met her on the bank where they introduced themselves. Hannah Guiles was about his age, maybe a little older. Her eyes were blue. Her nose was sunburned and peeling.

"Couldn't you leave a few trees along the bank, as a screen?" she asked.

"Mr. Foley is expecting to grow cotton and beans right up to the edge," he said. "They don't grow in shade. But maybe I can cheat a little."

They stood there in the shade of a big poplar. The bulldozers had moved far away downstream.

"I never knew anyone had a house up on that bluff," he said.

"My husband discovered this place," she said.

"You bought it from John Self?"

"Yes."

"He didn't want to sell us the land but Walter was persistent. Walter died at Christmas."

"I'm sorry."

"It seems like a long time ago. Years ago. I wonder why I feel like that?"

He did not know what to say, so he said nothing. They stood together in the shade. Cicadas whined from the trees overhead. She looked back across the river toward the house. When she turned back to face him, she began to tell him about her husband, who taught languages at the state university. He had died on Christmas day of a heart attack in a Paris railroad station. Andrew tried to imagine both what such a railroad station was like and what dying there might be like. But the only images he could summon up were those from some of his father's favorite movies. Steam locomotives and German soldiers had not been present at her husband's death.

"I'm sorry," he said.

He felt uncomfortable saying it again but he felt that he must say something. It was as if he had been caught spying on her as she swam naked in the river. She stood and looked at him like she had just noticed that he was standing there.

"I don't know why I went on and on," she said.

"Sometimes you have to talk," he said. "Are you at the university too?"

She was. He imagined that all of her friends were professors. He had gone to Clemson where he had completed an engineering degree. He spoke no foreign languages.

She was a biologist. The red-cockaded woodpecker was her specialty.

"There's a few out on the refuge," he said.

On the wildlife refuge the federal government managed the long leaf pine forest to encourage the bird.

"Yes," she said.

"Lots of rattlers out on the refuge."

"I don't look for 'em."

He imagined her striding through the park-like forest wearing knee-high snake boots.

"Most of 'em down in the ti-ti," he said.

"That's right," she said. "I stay out of the brush."

They both paused for a moment and looked out over the wasteland where both dozers were at work pushing logs up into a huge pile. Puffs of black smoke spurted from a dozer's exhaust stack as a big log resisted its efforts.

"That blockage is causing the river to eat away at the foot of the bluff," she said. "In a few years it'll take part of my yard."

They both turned to look at the blockage. It was an unusually large one, the biggest he had ever seen.

"Dynamite it," he said.

"Yes, perhaps that's the only solution."

"You were watching us from the highway."

"I thought you were just logging the pines. I wanted to ask you to leave a few trees along the river."

"You never asked until today."

"I didn't think you'd pay any attention to me."

"Then we showed up right across the river from your house."

Land Clearing

"Yes, and I had to do something."

"I understand that."

"You know how to work with dynamite?"

"Yes."

"Could I hire you to do it?"

"No, but I'll do it. It'll make up for us taking the trees. I'll do it later today."

"I'll be home. You come by the house before you start."

He had used dynamite only a few times. He wondered if it would work well on the blockage. He would have to find a way to get it down under some of the big logs or it would be all smoke and noise and wasted effort.

She shook his hand. He watched her go back across the blockage up the trail to the top of the bluff. She stood in the spot where he had first seen her and waved to him. He waved back.

The dynamite was kept in the garbage truck shop. He was putting a box of it into the back of his truck when he saw his father's Cadillac pull into the yard. Every day his father had his nurses drive him over to the shop so he could take a look at how the trucks were being maintained. Andrew looked forward to selling the business when his father died. He did not want to spend the rest of his life overseeing the hauling of garbage.

His father got out of the front passenger's seat. He was not using his cane today, but he walked slowly. The nurses hovered a few steps behind him and then dropped back to just out of earshot when he reached the truck.

"You look good today," Andrew said.

"I feel good," he said.

He walked over to the truck bed and placed his hand on the case of dynamite.

"Run into a problem?" he asked.

"A blockage on the river," Andrew said.

"Why are you fooling with that?"

"For a friend."

He expected his father to stop asking questions at that point, but he was persistent. In a few minutes he had told him all about Hannah Guiles.

"Well, I hope you'll get something for all your trouble," the old man said.

His father began to cough, a long series of coughs that shook his body. Andrew reached over and patted him on the back. His father's body felt frail and insubstantial though the thin cotton shirt.

"Let's go see if somebody is bothering to change the oil in my trucks," his father said.

He reached out and took Andrew's arm. They walked together across the gravel and into the shop. The nurses trailed along behind them.

Andrew listened to his father talk with the shop manager. A worker had carelessly tightened the lug nuts on a tire with an impact wrench and had snapped a bolt. Now the truck was going to be down for half a day. The manager and his assistant were working on it.

"All that Smyra garbage sitting in the sun," his father said.

The manager assured him he had sent another crew to pick it up after they finished their route.

"Overtime," his father said.

They went back outside, his father still leaning on his arm. After he had helped him into the car and the nurse was preparing to drive off, his father rolled down the window.

"I'd like to see you clear that blockage," he said.

"Aren't you tired?" he asked.

"I thought you said I looked good."

"I did."

"Well, I ain't tired. What's the matter, you worried that I might get ahead of you with that woman?"

One of the nurses giggled. His father ignored her.

"You come on then," Andrew said. "Maybe I'll let you set the charges yourself."

When he drove up Hannah's driveway, he saw her sitting out on a deck built at the rear of the house. He supposed that from there she had a view of the river and the cleared land. Now a pall of smoke from the fires hung over it. The smell of burning wood was in the air.

Hannah came out into the yard and insisted on taking his father's arm. Together they helped him up the steps.

They all had drinks together. The nurses drank Cokes and complained, not seriously, that his father should not be drinking. His father kept looking at Hannah's breasts. She was not wearing a bra. He could clearly see her nipples through the thin cotton fabric of her blouse. The nurses knew he was looking and so did Hannah. Andrew realized that she had changed out of her jeans and t-shirt for him. He wished he had come alone.

His father asked to see the blockage. Andrew took one arm and Hannah the other, and they helped him walk across the deck. They all stood together at the railing and looked at the blockage, which they could make out through a screen of trees.

"I could do it," the old man said. "Half a case. One set of charges."

"Maybe," Andrew said.

"You'll have to get it down under that big log," his father said. "You don't do that and all you'll get for your trouble is a lot of noise and some dead cottonmouths."

"I'm using the whole case," Andrew said.

"You got enough wire to set it off from here?"

"No, I'm going to use a fuse and det cord."

"That'll be all right. Well, boy, get to it."

At the blockage Andrew found that there was space for him to crawl up under the big log. He divided the case into two parts. He wrapped each bundle of sticks with tape and connected the bundles with detonation cord. He set a blasting cap in each bundle. Then he took a stick and rattled it around in the crevice. He crawled under the log and wedged the charges between it and several smaller logs that lay across it. If all went as he planned, the blast should cut the blockage in half. The first high water would send the river through the new channel and sweep the remaining logs away.

As he lit the fuse and walked quickly away from the blockage and up the trail to the bluff, he hoped it would go as he had planned. His father would show him no mercy if it did not.

Although he was timing the fuse by his watch, it caught him by surprise just as he reached the top of the bluff. The roar filled his ears and he ducked behind a tree. He heard the debris raining into the trees below and then all was silent. A jay began to complain from the top of a pine. The acrid scent of the explosive filled the air.

He looked down through the trees and saw that the charges had done exactly as he had hoped. The huge tree was gone. One part of its trunk now stood straight up in the air. Splintered wood glistened in the sunlight. A passageway was cut deep into the blockage. He supposed that he might come out with a chainsaw and cut up some of the smaller logs to further clear the passage.

Now he no longer cared that his father had invited himself along.

He found Hannah and his father having another drink. The nurses were gone.

"They're watching TV," Hannah said. "They didn't even get to see the explosion. But we watched. It was magnificent."

"You could've planted the charges a little deeper," his father said.

"And I could've filled up a sack with cottonmouths while I was doing it," he said. "It wasn't much fun crawling up under that brush."

"I've kicked them damn snakes out of the way," the old man said.

"Well, you go on down there," he said. "There's probably more of 'em."

"If you don't do a job right, you just have to do it again."

Land Clearing

"First high water will clear it out."

"Maybe."

She stepped over and put her hand on Andrew's arm.

"Your father has been telling me about the garbage business," she said. "Come sit down with us. I'll fix you a drink."

"I'm giving up opium for martinis," his father said.

He looked at the old man. His face was flushed. Tomorrow he was going to have a bad day. Andrew knew that the nurses would blame it on him, and they would be right.

The nurses came out of the house. Their shift was almost over.

"Daddy, do you want to go home?" he asked.

"No, Hannah has invited us to dinner," he said.

The nurses left. They would meet the next shift. Andrew would drive his father home.

Hannah cooked steaks on a grill. His father did not eat with them. He had lain down on a chaise lounge next to the house and had gone immediately to sleep. He slept with his knees drawn up to his chest. He looked childlike, diminished.

The sun was low in the sky, and it was cooler on the deck. As they began to eat, a breeze came up from the river bringing with it the scent of burning wood and dynamite. It was still some time before dark.

"He taught my brother to swim when he was a baby," he said. "He taught me too. But Billy drowned."

He wondered why he was telling her this.

"I was an only child," she said.

Andrew recalled swimming in the pool with his father and Billy. It was an indistinct memory. His father was big. Billy had pushed Andrew's head under water. He had come up choking. His father and Billy had laughed. He searched for other pieces of that memory, but there were only those few images. Then suddenly he thought of the roses wilting in the heat. He would try to remember to water them when he took his father home.

"My father's wrong," he said. "The river will carry that blockage away at the first high water."

"I appreciate what you did," she said.

"We ruined your view. I know that don't make up for it."

"It's still a nice view."

"Yes, there's nothing prettier than a field of cotton or soybeans. And when he puts in corn it'll be almost like trees."

"I've got an apple pie. One I bought at the Piggly Wiggly."

"I've got nothing against grocery store pie."

She went into the house for the pie. He walked over and watched his father sleep. It was the deep sleep of a child, a child sleeping off a fever. He reached down and put his hand on his father's shoulder. His father stirred and mumbled something. She came out of the house with the pie.

They sat down and began to eat.

"I forgot to buy ice cream," she said. "I'll bet you like ice cream on your pie."

"No, this will be fine," he said. "We could make ice cream one day. There's one of those old churns in the garbage barn. One of the workers put it on the truck. Somebody had put it out on the curb. It was practically brand new. I wonder why he didn't take it home. I don't know. But it's there in the barn."

"We could get some peaches from Mr. Aiken," she said.

Mr. Aiken owned a big peach orchard. His children sold the peaches at a stand on the highway. He recalled that once his father had talked about going into peaches but had decided against it.

"No one ever had a bad crop of garbage," he liked to say.

"He grows some good ones," he said.

He imagined drinking martinis and turning the crank of the churn. He imagined lying in bed with this woman, her arms around him.

"Some more pie?" she asked.

"No thanks," he said.

Land Clearing

He wondered if he should ask her to go to a movie. They could drive to Columbia or Florence. He imagined himself watching a foreign movie with her, one with subtitles.

His father groaned and sat up. They both walked over to him.

"Daddy, are you hurting?" he asked.

His father nodded.

"I guess we better get you home," he said.

It was beginning to get dark. As he helped his father across the deck and down the stairs, he could see the fires burning on the land across the river. He supposed that after he was gone Hannah would sit on the deck and watch them burn.

They went across the dark lawn and helped his father get into the truck. He leaned his head back against the seat and immediately went to sleep. As he stood beside the driver's door, she thanked him again for the dynamite, and he thanked her for the dinner. Tomorrow he would drive over and invite her to a movie.

"Next time I'll remember the ice cream," she said.

"I'm serious about that churn," he said.

"Yes, that would be fun. You know, I stay up late. The Piggly Wiggly's open in Bishopville."

"After I take Daddy home I'll drive by."

"Can you eat another piece of pie?"

"I'll be hungry."

His father slept all the way home. At the house the nurses came out into the yard to help. By the time they got him into the house his father was wide awake. He did not seem to be suffering any ill effects from the gin.

"Sorry I got in your way," his father said.

"You didn't get in my way," he said.

"Sure I did. Right now you could be sitting in the dark with that pretty woman eating ice cream."

It was just like his father, pretending to sleep so he could eavesdrop.

"I'll see her again."

"Tonight?"

"Some time," he said.

His father settled into watching TV. Then he complained of pain and one of the nurses gave him an injection.

"I'm going," he said.

He put his hand on his father's shoulder. His father felt hot to his touch, as if he were running a fever. One of the nurses took his temperature but it was normal.

"You go on," his father said. "I'll be fine."

"Well, I'm going," he said.

"Go on, go on," he said. "The nurses can call you on your phone no matter where you are. Even if you're eating ice cream with that pretty woman. You keep that phone close."

"I always do."

"I know. I know."

Exasperated, he left his father sitting before the television.

He was going down the driveway when he realized he had forgotten to water the roses. He parked the truck and walked around to the back of the house. Someone had unhooked the hose, and he spent some time finding the end of it and attaching it to the spigot in the dark. He did not want to turn on the outside lights and have all of them come to the big picture window to see what he was doing.

As he was standing off to one side of the rose garden, waiting to see if he had set the sprinkler correctly, he saw his father walking slowly across the room. One of the nurses came up to take his arm, but he waved her away. Then he disappeared from view.

Andrew stood there in the dark, watching the water sweep over the roses. He would let it run all night. He had plenty of time to drive to Bishopville and reach the Piggly Wiggly before it closed. He thought of

Land Clearing 139

Hannah, and how his father would have liked to have her for himself. But even if his father had not been sick, he was not the sort of man Hannah would have been interested in. Then he wondered how he could be so certain about Hannah, a woman he barely knew.

He heard a shot. One of the nurses ran across the room. The other followed but stopped in the center of the window, frozen in place like a deer caught up in headlights. *So*, he thought, *this is his final gambit*. He would not be eating ice cream and apple pie this night with Hannah Giles. He stood there watching the sprinkler sweep back and forth. A mosquito buzzed in his ear. He ran through the events of the coming days in his mind: the arrival of his father's sisters from Arkansas, his father's funeral, the reading of the will. His father would be buried beside his mother in the church cemetery, on a sunny slope clear of the shade cast by the two big pecans.

"I don't want damn tree roots growing into me," he heard his father saying.

It was as if the voice was coming to him out of the night instead of from instead his head, this favorite saying of his father's.

He started to answer that voice, speaking the words into the night with no one to hear them but himself. But instead he suddenly realized how he could reply. He would make a large donation to the church in his father's name. When he asked the church board if he could plant a live oak beside his father's grave, they would surely give their assent. The oak would grow slowly, but it would put down deep roots. It might live a thousand years.

He laughed out loud at the idea, throwing his head back. Then he stood there motionless for a moment, listening to the sibilant sweep of the sprinkler. *It's not such a mean thing to do*, he told himself. *He'll lie in that cool shade.*

One of the nurses must have heard his laughter because when he walked toward the house she had pressed her face to the glass, her hands cupped around her head, and was peering out into the darkness.

The Child Soldier

Sam Knightly looked at the boy, who was hanging his head out of the window of the pickup. The wind whipped around the cab of the truck, bringing with it the scent of the poisons: insecticide and herbicide, recently laid on the cotton field they were passing. Dallas's hair was blond and long and very fine; and it looked to Sam as if the wind might blow it right off his head.

"Ooooo," Dallas called. "Ooooo."

Sam wondered if the boy was pretending he was a train or some sort of animal, a bird perhaps, possibly a peacock, that lived in the Elephant Mountains of Cambodia where Dallas had been born. Sam's son Peter and Martine, his French wife, both doctors, had been working in Cambodia. One day a group of Khmer Rouge soldiers had walked out of the jungle and handed over the boy to them. Peter and Martine had adopted him. When the French aid organization they worked for posted them to a new job, they came to spend a month in South Carolina. But Peter and Martine were dead, killed in an accident on the highway Sam was traveling.

The boy was curious and wanted to know the name of every tree and flower and bird. Sam named them when he could. He bought him field guides to birds, plants, and insects. Dallas carried them about in a backpack along with a notebook. In the notebook he listed the names of those he had learned and made drawings of them. The boy drew beautifully.

They passed the crossroads store on the Charleston highway Sam's

The Child Soldier

father had owned and that Sam had run for thirty years. There was a new gas company logo on it. The old pumps had been removed and replaced with new ones. Then they went through the curve where late one night, less than a month ago, Sam's son Peter had gone to sleep at the wheel, and the jeep had gone straight into a big pine. They were returning from a bird watching trip to the Ace Basin. Dallas had been asleep in the back seat and had emerged without a scratch. Martine was in the front seat with Peter. Air bags might have saved them, but the old Jeep Peter was driving had been built long before those were standard equipment.

Peter's death was the hardest thing that Sam had ever experienced, much harder than the death of his wife Esther ten years before. If Sam could have avoided driving down the highway he would, but that was impossible. The white blaze on the pine made by the impact of the Jeep was something that had haunted him. So he had come out early one morning with a chainsaw and cut down the pine, toppling it into Irwin Wallace's soybean field. He had offered to pay Irwin for any damage to his crop, but Irwin refused to take the money. Their deaths had triggered something in him besides grief. It was a sort of urgency. He felt uneasy. It made him think of the whine insects made in the fall just before the first frost.

"Ooooo," Dallas called again. "Ooooo."

"Dallas, is that a sound some animal makes?" Sam asked.

"Yes, Grandfather, a monkey," he said. "A monkey with white hands and no tail. Sometimes we ate them."

Peter had told him that the boy had been a soldier, that he had participated in many actions. And there had been the usual executions. But Peter also told him, and Martine agreed, that the boy seemed to be wholly unaffected by what he had experienced.

"The sweetest child," Martine said.

"He believes in ghosts," Peter said. "He says that Cambodia is full of the ghosts."

Sam had never been a soldier. One of his legs was shorter than the other, the result of an accident with a tractor when he was a boy. So he had remained at home when his friends were drafted during the Vietnam War. Most but not all of them came home again. He always felt he had missed out on something. He realized that Dallas was like his father. They knew things he did not know. "I loved those men," his father had once said of the men in his platoon. And Esther had pointed out to him more than once that he had never really loved her. He wondered if that was true. The boy was too young to know about love, but he knew everything about death.

Sam had temporary custody of the boy. He was taking Dallas to spend a week at his cabin on the edge of Marion Swamp, the place where Peter and Martine had planned to spend most of their leave. Sam's father had built it as a hunting cabin and had taken Sam there when he was a child. It was his favorite place in all of South Carolina. He and Dallas would fish and swim in the river together and get to know one another. He planned to gain permanent custody of the boy.

He turned the truck off the highway onto a gravel road. They went over a set of railroad tracks. Off in the distance, across a huge soybean field, was the stand of feathery-topped cypresses that marked the place where the river became Marion Swamp.

Dallas continued to make the sound imitating the monkey, the call rising over the hiss of the tires on the gravel. The gravel changed to dirt and they entered the woods. The bright sunlight was gone, and branches began to scrape the side of the truck. There was trash caught up in the trees from the last high water.

"Watch those branches," Sam said.

Dallas pulled his head back into the truck.

"Is it far?" Dallas asked.

"A couple of miles."

"Are there monkeys in these woods?"

"No."

"Cobras?"

"No, but plenty of rattlers and cottonmouths. You watch where you put your feet."

"Elephants?"

Then Dallas began to laugh and Sam knew that the boy had been teasing him.

The cabin was built on a bluff above the river. The bluff ran for several miles and there were other cabins. Sam could recall only one time when the water had come up into the cabin, which was built on pilings against floods. He had been about Dallas' age when he and his father had come out after the water went down and found a big catfish on the screened porch.

They unloaded the car and then went for a swim in the river. He showed Dallas how the rope swing worked. The boy was fearless. He climbed immediately to the topmost rung of the ladder they had made by nailing two-by-fours to a huge poplar and launched himself out over the river. Sam followed him.

"Good morning."

A woman was standing on the bank, dressed in cut-off jeans and a blue work shirt. She was blonde and as fair as Dallas. He guessed she was in her late forties or early fifties.

"I'm Meg Wentworth," she said. "I bought the Sutton place."

It was the next cabin downriver. He introduced himself and Dallas. Then he swam to the bank. They sat on a bench together and talked while Dallas played on the swing. Meg was from Charleston. She was a retired geologist who was still doing some consulting work in the southeast.

"I like swamps," she said.

"You came to the right place," he said.

Dallas launched himself off the swing, making the monkey call as he fell toward the water.

"I'd like one of those," she said.

"For your grandchildren?" he asked.

"No, I've never been married. It's for me."

Sam had thought that after Esther's death he would fall in love and marry again, but it never happened. Right now there was no one. The woman he had been seeing had moved to California. She wanted him to go with her, to get married. Now that he was retired there had been no reason really why he could not have gone. He tried to tell her he was not in love with her, but she had not understood.

"The Suttons have a swing," he said.

"Not anymore," she said. "Lightning hit that poplar. Split it right down the middle. But there's another one that'll work just fine."

"I'll help you put it up."

"When?"

"Anytime. Dallas and I are here for a month."

Then in response to her questions he explained about Dallas. He ended up telling her more than he thought he should. The soldiers had told Martine and Peter that the boy's mother was an American journalist. Ten years before she had come to write about the diehards who retreated back into the Elephant Mountains when the Vietnamese Army invaded Cambodia. But she had given up being a journalist. She stayed and fought with them. Her name was Rosa and she was from Texas. Rosa had died of malaria. And that was all they learned from the soldiers, who disappeared back into the jungle.

They tried to find some record of a journalist from Texas but were unsuccessful. She had not even been reported missing. The State Department knew nothing; the officials in Phnom Penh knew nothing.

Martine and Peter were concerned that Dallas refused to tell them any details about his life. The soldiers told them that the boy was a good fighter, fearless and dependable under fire. He was willing to talk about his mother's death, how the Khmer Rouge used the last of their medical supplies in an attempt to save her. That and the few things he revealed created the impression she had become a leader among them. Sam recalled that his father had said very little about his experiences as a Marine in the Pacific. He decided he would not press Dallas about his life with the Khmer Rouge.

"That poor little boy," she said.

They looked down at Dallas who was floating on his back, the current carrying him slowly down the river, his tanned body light against the coffee-colored water.

"But it hasn't affected him at all," he said. "I've never seen a happier child. Peter was never like that."

"I don't believe it," she said. "It makes it worse that he appears so happy. Just think how hard he has to work at that."

"I think you're wrong."

"I hope I am."

Dallas was now swimming back up to the pool beneath the rope swing. In him Sam saw himself as a boy. It was going to be good to watch Dallas do the same things he had done.

"You let me know when you've got a new cable," he said.

"I've got one," she said.

"Then we'll put it up today."

"I made a pot of gumbo. Come have lunch first."

He accepted. They all walked down the road to her cabin. They came upon a rat snake crossing the road. It was a big one, seven or eight feet long. Dallas asked him to name it and if it was dangerous. When the boy learned it was harmless, he chased it down and returned from a cane thicket with the snake wrapped around his arm.

"Are they good to eat?" he asked.

"I wouldn't," Sam said.

"We don't have to eat it," she said. "We've got gumbo. Let it go."

Dallas did as she asked. The snake crawled unhurriedly away into a gallberry thicket and disappeared.

He noticed the Sutton place needed some work. There were holes in the screen on the big porch, and the dock, where a red canoe was moored, was rotted out in places. After eating lunch on the porch, they began work on the swing. He nailed a series of short lengths of two-by-fours onto the tree to make a ladder that reached up to the big limb overhanging the water. He remembered when he had climbed up to replace the old rope swing at his cabin with a steel cable. He had been in his teens then. It was before the accident shortened his leg.

The limb was thirty feet above the water. He started out onto it with a rope tied around his waist he would use to pull the cable up. Then he realized this was going to be a difficult job for one person. He stopped and looked down at them.

"I'll come up," Dallas said.

"No, I'll be fine," he said.

But then the boy came up the ladder and out onto the limb to sit behind him.

"I want to help," the boy said.

They worked their way out on the limb. They had gone far enough now for it to begin to sway under their weight. But they were only a few feet away from the best spot to attach the cable. Sam decided to assemble the bolts that would hold the cable together and then work it out over the limb. They pulled the cable up. Dallas held the two pieces of cable while he tightened the bolts. Then he worked the loop into position and turned the bolts hard. He tossed the wrenches down to Meg.

"Let's jump," he said. "Hold your nose and your balls."

They both jumped off the limb at the same time. The dark water rushed up to meet him, and he hit the surface hard, the water tearing at his swimming trunks. His feet hit the sandy bottom. He pushed off and ascended a little behind Dallas.

After they attached the trapeze bar to the cable, Dallas tried it out. He swooped out in a high arc, higher than at Sam's cabin, and fell to the water. Sam took a swing on it and then Meg. Then they sat in the sun on a bench beside the pool while Dallas swam in the river.

"You come use it anytime you want," Meg said.

"You'll come to dinner tomorrow night?" he asked.

"I'd love to," she said. "I'll bring wine."

Then he and Dallas walked home. A bird called from the woods and Dallas asked him to name it, but Sam had no idea what kind it was. Dallas roamed ahead of him, darting in and out of the woods, until they were back at the cabin.

They played chess, a game Peter had taught Dallas, until the boy began to yawn. Then he went off to bed. Sam sat for some time on the screened porch and smoked a cigar. The night was filled with the trilling of tree frogs, which had climbed up on the screen. His screen needed repair too. He was going to have to replace a section where a storm had blown a limb through it. He decided he would cook venison for the dinner the next day. He went to the kitchen and took a roast out of the freezer. He put it in the sink and started to run water over it. Then he heard the sound of Dallas' voice from the bedroom.

It sounded to Sam like the boy was saying prayers. He wondered if they were Buddhist prayers. Peter had embraced that religion. Sam supposed he had no religion at all, although if someone asked he would have said he was Presbyterian. But then, as he walked carefully towards the boy's room, he realized it was names.

Dallas sat naked on the floor facing the window with his back to Sam. He was cross-legged, his hands folded together under his chin in the attitude of prayer.

"And Sakon and Chamroeun," Dallas was saying.

The boy turned his head. Sam wondered how Dallas knew he was there, for Sam was barefoot and the cypress floor had not creaked. The boy's face was serene. A frog trilled wildly from the screen.

"Are you praying?" Sam asked.

"No," Dallas said. "I'm remembering."

He stood up and turned to face Sam. He was uncircumcised, his body hairless.

"Remembering what?"

"People we killed."

"Why?"

"If I remember then it's like they're not dead."

"But they really are."

Sam wanted to reach out and touch the boy, but he knew his palms were damp. He did not want Dallas to know the effect his words were having.

"Yes, I know," Dallas said. "But they need to be remembered. I remember *all* of them."

"All?" Sam asked.

"Yes, and it's hard to do. There were so many."

"Did anyone know you felt that way?"

"No."

"Not even your mother?"

"No, she hated them. They all hated them. They thought they were nothing."

Sam had no idea what he should say.

"Are you all right?" Sam asked.

His words sounded hollow to him, inadequate.

"If you say their names they won't harm you," Dallas said. "I'm not afraid to sleep. Rosa was afraid."

"Your mother . . ." Sam began. But he did not know how to pose the question. He realized he was not exactly sure what he wanted to ask.

"Tell me about your mother."

"Rosa died of malaria," the boy said. "Rosa had bad dreams. I don't have bad dreams."

"Because you've said their names?" he asked.

"Yes. I've said their names. I can go to sleep now."

He got into the bed and curled up with his back to Sam.

"Sleep well, Grandfather," he said.

"You sleep well," Sam said.

He bent over the boy and kissed him on the cheek. When Sam stood up, Dallas' eyes were closed and he was breathing the slow, relaxed breaths of a sleeping child.

Sam went back out to the porch. He took up his cigar and poured himself a drink of whiskey. He wondered if naming the dead would be enough to achieve the serenity he saw on the boy's face. Or perhaps it was Buddhism. He recalled coming upon Peter meditating on the backyard deck early on the morning of the accident. Sam imagined meditating was sort of like prayer without words. Once Peter told him that he tried to think of nothing at all, a sort of even greyness. Sam could not understand how a person could think of nothing.

Before he went to bed Sam marinated the venison roast in juniper berries and milk. The evening of the next day Meg arrived with a bottle of wine and an apple pie. They ate dinner on the porch. While Sam and Meg were having coffee, Dallas went out on the river in the johnboat. Sam had showed him how to operate the trolling motor that afternoon and had cautioned him not to go into the swamp by himself without a compass. Dallas carried a backpack full of the field guides.

"He's really a normal child," Sam said.

As soon as the words were out of his mouth, he wondered why he had said them. It was as if he were trying to pretend that Dallas was his grandchild, that he had been born in the hospital in Charleston.

"Why do you want to think of him like that?" she asked.

He told her about Dallas' prayers.

"Maybe you should take him to see a therapist," she said.

"I will if he seems unhappy."

"But those prayers."

"My father never talked at all about the men he killed. Isn't this better?"

"I suppose."

"My father sure didn't try to remember those folks. At least I don't think he remembered on purpose. He hated them. They were yellow bastards. Japs."

"And the Japanese felt the same way."

"You know they did. You see, he's escaped that trap."

"I'm not so sure that he's escaped anything. He's just a child. But I don't suppose I really know anything about children."

Dallas brought the boat back to the dock and came up onto the porch.

"I saw a gator," he said.

"How big?" Sam asked.

"As long as the boat," Dallas said.

"Tall tales," Meg said. "He's become a southern boy already."

"I saw it," Dallas insisted.

"That's a pretty big gator for this river," Sam said. "Sometimes the water makes things look bigger than they are."

"I guess," Dallas said. "But it was big! Really big! I'm putting that gator in my book."

Dallas went to the hammock on one end of the porch and turned on the light over it. He opened his notebook and began to draw.

While Dallas drew and studied his field guides, Sam and Meg drank brandy and smoked cigars. Dallas fell asleep with an open field guide to birds lying across his chest. Sam turned off the light and walked Meg back to her cabin.

"It was a wonderful dinner," she said as they stood together at the door to her screened porch.

"I've got a freezer full of game," he said. "We can have dinners all summer."

"I'd like that."

He bent down and kissed her. She put her arms around him.

"You taste like cigars," she said.

"So do you," he said.

"I like the smell of cigars. I like the smell of the river."

He kissed her again. As he did he thought of waking up in her bed. It was what always appeared in his mind when he had kissed other women in cars, on boats, or like this standing on their doorsteps. He never thought of his own bed although they made love there too. But in the end he never was any closer to love than the first time he kissed them. He hoped it was going to be different with Meg.

"Let me cook for you and Dallas tomorrow night," she said.

"We're going fishing," he said. "We'll bring you some bass."

She kissed him again.

"You better get back," she said. "He might wake up. He could be frightened."

Sam did not think that a boy who had hunted other human beings in the Elephant Mountains would be frightened of waking up and discovering he was alone.

Then as if she could read his mind, she said, "He's just a child. Don't forget that."

"I won't," he said. "Good night."

"Good night, Sam. I can count on those bass?"

"Like the sun coming up in the morning."

He walked down the steps and across the yard and onto the road. Once outside the light from the cabin, he looked back. She was still standing on the porch. Then she turned and disappeared into the house. He felt elated. He jogged up the road, remembering how as a child he would run across the hard packed sand at the beach, in love with the speed of his body.

Back at the cabin he found Dallas was still asleep in the hammock. He decided to leave him there and went off to bed himself.

At daybreak Sam and Dallas used a seine in the shallow water over a sandbar to catch a bucket full of minnows. Then they took the boat out of the river and into the swamp. It was one of those perfect days, the sky blue and without a cloud. It was shady in the swamp. The dark water was covered with patches of bright green duckweed. It was difficult to move through the swamp because of the fallen trees left when a hurricane came through a few years before. Sam had used a chain saw to cut a path to his favorite place to fish and had sunk Christmas trees there to provide cover for the bass.

Sam heard a woodpecker drumming on a cypress. Then the bird flew and gave its cry. They both watched it go off through the cypresses with its jerky style of flight. He knew it was a pileated woodpecker and named it for the boy. Dallas looked it up in his bird book. He began making a sketch of the bird in flight in his notebook.

When they reached Sam's favorite place to fish, they quickly caught a limit apiece of bass using cane poles and minnows. Sam sculled the boat into the shade of a cypress. He got himself a beer out of the ice chest and a Coke for the boy.

"Where does this swamp go?" Dallas asked.

"It's really the river," Sam said. "It spreads out here and then about ten or twelve miles to the south it becomes the river again."

"It's full of ghosts."

Sam took a drink of his beer and regarded the boy who sat in the bow facing him. Dallas did not seem to be upset.

"How do you know that?" Sam asked.

"I can feel them," Dallas said.

"Who are they?"

"People who cut the trees, soldiers, slaves."

"Why are they here?"

"I don't know."

"If I were a ghost, I'd pick another place to haunt."

The boy did not smile in response to his remark. Sam wondered if Dallas was teasing him again.

"Are you afraid of them?" Sam asked.

"No, but I wish I knew their names," he said.

This was a reaction to the horrors of the boy's life in Cambodia, Sam told himself. His father sometimes had nightmares. Sam would wake to his shouts in the night and then hear his mother's calm voice trying to soothe him.

The Child Soldier

"Draw me a picture of a ghost," Sam said.

And as soon as he had said it he was sorry for his words. He was no therapist. He was a business major in college who had ended up running a crossroads store for most of his life.

Dallas opened his notebook and began to draw. In a few minutes he had produced a rough sketch. He handed the notebook to Sam.

The boy had drawn a naked black man poling a pirogue through the swamp. Sam felt as if he had stepped into a pool of quicksand. He was unsure what he should say. The boy might have read about escaped slaves or had been told stories by Peter.

"You *saw* this man?" Sam asked.

"No, but he's here," Dallas said.

Sam looked around him. The sun was well up now. A flight of cattle egrets, the sunlight shining off their white feathers, flew over.

Sam realized this was not haunted house ghosts, but something darker, something serious.

"Are you sure you're not afraid of them?" Sam asked.

"They can be scary if they're restless," the boy said.

"Restless?"

"They haven't had a funeral. Cambodia's full of them."

"And why do you say their names?"

"It's like prayers for them. Like that priest prayed for Peter and Martine."

"And this man?"

"I can sort of see him. He's all covered with mud. He's scared."

Sam decided that Dallas did not *see* anything. It was with his imagination that he saw. What he recalled were those people he and his mother and the Khmer Rouge had killed. He could probably *see* them anytime he wished.

Then Dallas looked up at another flight of egrets and said, "I won't forget them."

Sam wondered if the boy was referring to the dead in Cambodia or those whose spirits he imagined still lingered in the swamp. He decided not to ask.

It was already hot, even in the shade. Sam wished he could slip over the side and lie like a turtle in the cool mud at the bottom of the lake.

"You don't need to be worrying about dead folks," Sam said.

"Someone's got to worry about them," Dallas said.

Sam hoped the boy would never mention his views about the dead to some social worker. They were going to have to do an interview with one when they returned from the cabin.

"It's not your job," Sam said.

He was wondering exactly how he should coach Dallas for his interview. It might be worse to say something to him about the dead. It might be better not to call attention to that.

"I don't think I should stop," Dallas said.

"Why?" he asked.

"I don't know why."

Talking with Dallas was not exactly like talking with a child and not like having a conversation with an adult either. He decided he would ask Meg if she felt the same. And some time this month Dallas might talk to Meg about the dead. He was going to have to prepare her.

"You know, the way to catch big bass is to come out here at night," he said. "Once I caught a nine-pound bass right here."

"With minnows?" Dallas asked.

"No, with a jig with a pork rind skirt on it. You use a real short line and a stout cane pole. You splash that jig around in the cover. I don't know if they hit it because they're hungry or if it just makes 'em mad."

All the way back they discussed tactics for fishing for large bass at night.

After they cleaned the fish, he sent Dallas with the three largest ones to Meg. When Dallas returned, he showed him how to rig a jig with a pork rind skirt and promised him that one night soon they would go after some big bass. After they had some lunch, they both went to sleep, Sam in the

The Child Soldier

hammock and Dallas on the couch in the living room.

Sam dreamed of standing on the dock and watching Peter swimming in the river. The sun was directly overhead, and the light glittered off the surface of the river. Then suddenly something pulled him under. There was no splash, no disturbance. He just vanished. The river flowed on, its surface smooth and glass-like. Sam dived into the river, but instead of swimming to rescue Peter, he felt himself sinking straight to the bottom. He heard Peter screaming.

"Grandfather?" a voice said. "Grandfather?"

He looked up. Dallas standing over him.

"Dallas?" he said.

"Were you dreaming, Grandfather?" Dallas asked.

"Yes, I was."

"A bad dream."

"Yes."

"You were calling Peter's name."

"I was dreaming about him when he was a boy. It's nothing. Just a dream."

"You're ok?"

"I'm fine."

Sam got up and busied himself with replacing the section of torn screen. While he worked, Dallas, wearing a Walkman, lay in the hammock and read a book about whales. He was playing a compact disc of whale songs, one Martine had bought him. As Sam worked he dropped nails and cut a piece of wood to the wrong measurement. He felt like he was still partly in the dream, sinking to the bottom of the river while Peter's cries were all about him, like love songs of whales.

They had dinner on Meg's porch. After Dallas finished dessert, he asked if he could take the boat out on the river until dark.

"Does an animal that sings live in the river?" he asked.

"Gators grunt in this river," Sam said. "Nothing makes noises like whales."

Dallas went back down the road to their cabin. He and Meg had coffee together on the porch. He wondered if he should tell her about their talk in the swamp as he listened to her explain her plans for a new dock.

"Anything you build here is likely to get washed away," he said.

He wanted to love this woman. He wanted it to be something permanent.

"I know that," she said. "I don't mind."

He told her about the conversation he had had with Dallas in the swamp.

"That poor little boy," she said.

"He's a boy but he's also not a boy," he said. "He helped kill people."

"You think that makes him a man?"

"No, but it makes him different."

"He needs someone to love him."

"I'm going to raise him and love him if the state of South Carolina lets me."

"They've got to."

She reached out and took his hand. They sat talking about his plans for Dallas and drinking coffee until it grew dark.

When after an hour Dallas did not return, they both walked to the cabin. He expected to find the boy in the hammock listening to whale songs and drawing. But the cabin was dark. There was a piece of paper on the door. It looked like a large white moth had come to rest on the screen.

He turned on the light and they read it together.

GONE TO CATCH A BIG BASS

He explained about night fishing.

"He's going to get lost," he said.

"Could he find his way back by the lights of the cabin?" she asked.

"Maybe."

She walked through the cabin and turned on every light.

"I think I should go look for him," he said.

She wanted to go with him. They would use her canoe.

She sat in the bow with a big flashlight while he paddled the canoe. A gator grunted from somewhere deep in the swamp. A startled pair of wood ducks took flight as she played the beam of the flashlight over them. Soon they were close to the place where they had been fishing, an open space in the swamp surrounded by tall cypresses that had escaped the loggers.

"There he is!" she cried.

He followed the light and saw the johnboat. Dallas was sitting motionless in the stern with his head bowed. He seemed to be in the same attitude as when Sam had watched him saying the names of the dead.

"Dallas," Sam called.

"Come here," the boy said.

Sam paddled them across the open space.

"It's so big," the boy said.

They were beside the johnboat now. He brought the canoe up parallel with it. Meg was next to Dallas. Sam looked down and saw that the boy had landed an enormous bass. It was more than nine pounds.

"That's got to be the biggest bass to ever come out of this swamp," Sam said.

"It'll just fit on a platter I've got," Meg said.

Sam began to realize that both he and Meg were more excited than the boy. Dallas should be beside himself with joy. Instead he remained in the attitude of meditation.

"I went fishing with Rosa once," the boy said. "We threw frags into a pool. Then we waded around and picked them up. We were hungry. Rosa had bad dreams."

Sam felt that the boy was starting to slip away to some place where he would be terrified and alone.

"It's a great fish," Sam said.

He reached down and touched it. The half moon was rising over the trees and light fell on the silver scales.

"Rosa had bad dreams," the boy said. "Rosa had bad dreams."

Then he continued to say it over and over as if it were a sort of mantra.

Meg leaned over and put her arms around him. Her movement caused the canoe to rock. Sam took hold of the johnboat's gunwale with both hands to steady the canoe.

"It's ok," she said. "It's going to be ok."

Sam could think of nothing to say. Dallas was sobbing. Something called from deep in the swamp. He was not sure whether it was animal or bird.

"Do you hear that, Dallas?" Sam asked.

Dallas stopped crying.

"What is it?" Dallas asked.

"I don't know," Sam said.

"It was a gator," said Meg.

"Maybe," Sam said. "We're going home now, Dallas. You and I'll run the boat. Meg can follow in the canoe. We're going home."

He slipped out of the canoe and into the johnboat. Then he steadied the canoe while Meg took the center seat.

Dallas moved to the bow.

"Are you going to have bad dreams?" he asked.

"Not often," Sam said.

Sam walked across the boat, running his hands along the gunwales for balance and keeping his body low. He put his arms around the boy.

"And maybe you will too," Sam said. "But not often."

"You promise."

"I promise."

Then with Dallas in the bow with the big flashlight and Meg trailing a little behind them in the canoe, they started out of the swamp. The animal called again. They all turned their heads to the sound, but no one said a word.

Sam and Meg sat on the porch and smoked cigars. Tree frogs trilled from the screen. Dallas lay in the hammock wearing his Walkman. His eyes were closed. Sam supposed he was listening to whale songs again.

"We'll fix your screen tomorrow," Sam said. "I've got enough wire left over."

"We'll have Dallas' big bass for dinner," she said.

"With corn on the cob?"

"Yes, and a salad with those Florida tomatoes I bought."

Dallas took off the headphones and picked up his notebook. He began to recite the names: "kingfisher, rat snake, red-tailed hawk . . ."

Sam took Meg's hand and throwing his head back watched the fan spin the bluish cigar smoke about the porch while the frogs trilled and the boy chanted the world.

Queen of the Night
(inspired by the photographs of Cy DeCrosse)

Richard Carter woke from a dream of Mexico. The sound of guitars was still in his ears, but the strongest remembrance was the sweet scent of a flower, overpowering his senses and making him feel as if he had injected an opiate into his veins. He lay in bed, looking up at the ceiling fan turning slowly above him and hoped he could slip back into the dream. He had smelled the flower only once, seventy years ago. He was ten, traveling with his parents. His father was a Texas oilman, rich and busted a dozen times, before he died poor of a heart attack in a rented room in Galveston. Richard was in high school then, living with his mother in Atlanta.

He closed his eyes and drifted close to sleep again. Then he found the smell, strong, as if the flower were blooming on the balcony outside his bedroom window. The name came to him. Queen of the night. Someone's garden. That was where it had been. His mother's voice was telling him that the flower bloomed only once every seven years. The people held a fiesta to celebrate, musicians roaming the streets, people dancing.

Richard made his living as a photographer. He had tried fashion photography, but he always felt uncomfortable working with models. For the past forty years, he had specialized in cars for magazine layouts. He was in demand. He lived alone. His fourth wife had left him a year ago. All his marriages had been childless. He supposed that by now he had learned enough not to attempt marriage again.

Queen of the Night

It was April and very pleasant. He had breakfast on the balcony of his Bay Street house and watched the ships in Charleston Harbor. And suddenly in this city, old for America, he felt the weight of his years. As long as he stayed healthy he could take photographs of cars. But after that? He had plenty of money. He would not die poor like his father. He had made sure that would not happen to him. If he got sick he would hire someone to look after him. He would die in this house. By the sea.

He cleared away the breakfast dishes and cleaned the kitchen. Then he went to his computer and looked up the flower on the web. *S. grandiflorus*, the night-blooming cereus. And it struck him suddenly, as he looked at the picture of the flower, its huge white petals filling the screen, that he would take no more photographs of cars. He would photograph night-blooming plants. He would make platinum prints, expensive and difficult, but certain to retain the image forever. Like gold, incorruptible, lying at the bottom of the sea.

He would begin with the queen of the night. He spent two days on the computer searching for someone who had a cereus under cultivation due to bloom sometime soon. Finally he discovered one at The University of Arkansas. The botanist in charge of the flower was Mary Lee Hull. He wrote her an e-mail. She replied.

>Richard,
>
>Sure you can come up here and photograph my queen. She's due about the first week in August. She's photosensitive so you'll have to use a strobe or she'll close right up. Where can I find your work?
>
>Mary Lee

He wrote back and told her that he took photographs of cars.

At the end of July, Mary Lee sent him an e-mail informing him a bud was developing on the plant. They were watching it closely. He packed his equipment and drove to Arkansas.

He checked into a hotel in the little Ozark town and called Mary Lee.

She told him the bud would probably open in the next few days. She invited him to dinner.

Her house was on a ridge with a view of the university below it, the huge bowl of the football stadium dominating the landscape. He was met at the door by a woman in her fifties.

"Mary Lee?" he asked.

For some reason he had expected her to be much younger.

"No, I'm her daughter Sarah," the woman said. "You've never met my mother?"

"Only on e-mail," he said.

Sarah took him through the house, which as he expected was filled with plants, and into the kitchen where her mother and two sisters were at work. Sarah introduced him to her sisters Amy and Han.

Amy looked much like Sarah, tall and thin with blonde hair. Han was Oriental, much younger than her two sisters. Mary Lee did not look that much older than her Occidental daughters. She had her white hair pulled back. Her eyes were bright blue. He thought that she moved like a dancer. His second wife had been a dancer.

"My daughters have come home for the queen," Mary Lee said.

While her daughters finished work on the meal Mary Lee took him into the living room. There they talked about how he planned to shoot the flower. He would use a soft strobe to illuminate the plant and would shoot it against a painted background he had already prepared. He wanted to create the effect of the flower blooming high in the crown of a rain forest tree with the light of the full moon upon it.

She told him about her daughters. Sarah taught high school science in a nearby town. Amy was a biologist for the forest service. Han was Vietnamese. She was in her senior year at the University. Mary Lee had adopted her after her parents, who worked at a chicken plant in a nearby town, were killed in a car crash. Mary Lee's first husband, a pilot, died in the Pacific during World War II. Her second husband, the architect who built the house, died of a brain tumor when the girls were young.

As they ate dinner, he described his dream of Mexico.

"I wish we could grow them in our garden," Mary Lee said.

"Can you remember the name of the town?" Amy asked.

"No, all I remember is the smell of the flower," he said. "And the sound of music."

"I've been at two bloomings," Sarah said. "Amy has been at three."

"This will be my first," Han said.

After dinner the daughters did the dishes while he and Mary Lee sat on the sofa in the dining room and drank whiskey.

"Have you ever been in a canoe?" Mary Lee asked.

"A few times," he said.

"I'll like to show you a river tomorrow."

"The flower?"

"Nothing will happen until right after sunset. One of my graduate students has got the watch until it blooms. Kristina will call me. It happens synchronistically with sunset. It won't be tomorrow night. Maybe in three or four days. Saturday is what I'd guess."

"Is the river far?"

"Not far. Don't worry, we'll be back in plenty of time. It's a beautiful place. Bluffs and limestone cliffs. I'll bring a waterproof bag for your cameras if you'd like. And dress for swimming. Those deep pools are wonderful places to swim this time of year. So cool on a hot day."

He agreed to meet her at the hotel early in the morning. He drove back to the hotel and went to sleep, hoping as he had every night since the first time that he would dream again of the flower. So far he had not.

In the morning, after a dreamless night, he met her in the lobby of the hotel before sunrise. Her truck, with a red canoe up on it, was parked at the curb. The sleepy young desk clerk waved to her. He wondered if the woman had been one of her students or a friend of Han.

They went through a drive-through at a fast food restaurant for breakfast. Then, while they ate a sausage and biscuits and drank coffee, she drove them over winding mountain roads. They descended from a high ridge down a gravel road to the river, which swung in a smooth curve along the base of a series of limestone bluffs. There was a concrete launch ramp for canoes. This section of the river was managed by the federal government. They planned to float down to a bridge where there was a store. They would hire someone to drive them back to her truck.

They took the canoe off the truck together and carried it to the water.

"Russell, my second husband, loved to kayak," she said. "He was the one who showed me this river. I used to be able to portage this boat by myself. Now I can't."

She directed him to take the bow.

"It's an easy river," she said. "The only problem we'll have is finding enough water to float this boat."

They went down the river, the boat caught up in the gentle current. He began to take pictures of the bluffs. She pointed out a scissor-tailed flycatcher perched on a dead cottonwood. He watched a fish dart away in the clear, greenish-colored water to seek shelter in the darkness of a deep hole.

"Catfish?" he asked.

"No, small mouth," she said.

He thought of the flower, waiting for the darkness so it could spread its petals and release its perfume into the night. He hoped she was right about calculating the opening.

By lunchtime they had both gone over the side many times to cool off. She had taken off her shorts and T-shirt and wore only a Speedo. He wore a pair of running shorts. He welcomed the places where they had to walk the boat down through a shoals. He had stopped taking pictures and had returned his cameras to the waterproof bag.

She turned the canoe into a gravel bar at the base of a limestone bluff. They sat on a blanket in the shade of a stand of willows and ate the sandwiches she had packed and drank cold beer from the cooler. She told him the bridge was a short paddle away.

"So you've devoted your life to the study of night-blooming flowers," he said.

"No, I wrote my dissertation on prairie grasses," she said. "Right after Russell died I got interested in those flowers. Do you want to go swimming? This is a good place. There's a hole out in the middle of the river that must be twenty feet deep. It's spring fed. The water's so cold it'll made your head hurt."

He already marveled at her energy. The sun seemed to have no effect on her at all. His knee was bothering him. He had slipped on a rock when they were walking the boat down a set of shoals. He had injured it playing basketball, in the days before arthroscopic surgery.

"I want to close my eyes for a little while," he said.

"You rest," she said. "I'll go for a swim."

He lay back on the blanket and closed his eyes. He heard the sound of the gravel beneath her bare feet as she walked toward the river. He listened to the rush of the river and the songs of the birds as he drifted off to sleep. He hoped he would dream.

When he woke her face was in his field of vision. She was smiling, her blue eyes bright against her tanned face. Her wet hair was plastered tightly against her skull. He thought she was beautiful.

"Did you dream of the flower again?" she asked.

"No, I don't think I dreamed at all," he said.

He sat up on the blanket. She knelt beside him.

"Could I take some pictures of you?" he asked.

"I look awful," she said.

But he persuaded her and shot up the rest of his film. He did not feel awkward working with her. He could tell that the camera liked her face. He believed he was going to be pleased with the results.

Then they packed up their gear and made the short paddle to the bridge.

On the way back to town he asked her if he could see the plant so he would be able to plan the way he wanted to shoot it. She drove to the arboretum.

The plant was a vine that grew in a tangled mass in a corner of the building. The bud was completely developed but still tightly closed. He quickly saw where the best place would be to place the backdrop. He would hang the strobe from a beam to simulate moonlight.

"It doesn't look like much," he said.

He tried again to remember what the flower in Mexico had looked like, but still he could recall nothing but the smell and the sound of the music.

"Just wait until you watch it open," she said.

When she dropped him off at the hotel, he asked her to dinner that night and she accepted. He went up to his room and iced his knee. Then he showered and took a nap. Again he did not dream.

The knee felt better when he woke. He went out to find a place to develop the color film. The black and white film he would develop himself when he went back to Charleston. Then he returned to the hotel.

He met her for dinner at a restaurant on the square just as the sun was starting to drop behind a line of hills. She wore a black dress and a single strand of pearls. Now his knee was bothering him. He planned to ice it again before he went to sleep. After they were seated, she put a phone on the table.

"So Kristina can call," she said. "I knew you'd worry."

They had a leisurely dinner. Then they lingered over brandy and coffee. They were the last customers out of the restaurant, the busboys already beginning to mop the floor. She walked with him to his hotel where she had parked her truck.

"I usually run every morning," she said. "Come run with me."

He explained to her about his knee.

"You could ride a bike," she said. "We have plenty of those at home."

He agreed to meet her at her house at seven. Afterwards they would have breakfast.

"I hope you dream of Mexico tonight," she said.

He wanted to ask her up to his room, but was afraid it was too soon. He wanted to kiss her. Instead they shook hands. He watched her drive off in her truck through the deserted streets.

In the morning his knee felt better, but he decided not to risk running on it. So he rode the bicycle. She ran with a smooth stride up and down the hills around the University. It looked to him like she could run forever.

After she cooled down they went to a café, which had once been a gas station. They sat at an outdoor table under a green awning.

"Did you dream of the flower?" she asked.

"No, of basketball," he said. "I dreamed all night long of basketball. I was shooting a jump shot. I never missed. You know, I never had a jump shot."

"What are you going to do today?"

"Pick up color film I shot of you. Read."

"Could I go with you for those pictures?"

"I'd like that."

They sat and drank coffee until lunchtime. They saw Han on the square with a boy. She waved at them but did not cross over to their table.

"He's a sweet boy," she said. "I've forgotten his name. Han would be angry with me."

"Why did you adopt her?" he asked.

"Her father worked for me at the arboretum for a time. He was good with plants. I don't know why he thought he'd have a better future with chickens."

"So you knew her."

"Yes, she'd come to work with him sometimes. I'd take her out for ice cream."

"Let's go pick up my film."

They drove to the drugstore in a nearby shopping center. Then at her suggestion they left the packet unopened and went through a drive-through that specialized in barbecue, which they took to the town park.

They sat at a picnic table not far from a set of deserted tennis courts. There was a swimming pool at one end of the park. Music and the shouts of children drifted over to them. They looked at the prints.

"Look at my hair," she said.

But he was pleased.

"No, these are not bad," he said. "Not bad at all. The best I've ever done with a model. I'll work on them when I get home. I'll send you something really fine. And a print of the flower, of course."

Then they ate the barbecue sandwiches and the greasy onion rings.

"I'll have to run an extra five miles tomorrow," she said.

And then out of nowhere a memory appeared, no clue as to what had been the trigger. He recalled living in New Orleans when he was in his twenties. He lived with a girl in an apartment in the French Quarter. He could not remember the name of the street. There were jalousies over the windows, closed against the direct sunlight. It was dark but hot in the room in those days before air conditioning. Dust motes drifted about in shafts of sunlight. They had made love without regard for the heat, their bodies slick with sweat. He could not recall the girl's name.

"Are you thinking of the queen?" she asked.

"I'm sorry," he said. "No, I was thinking about the time I lived in New Orleans. When I was a young man."

"You rode streetcars."

"Yes."

He wondered if she had somehow guessed at the nature of his reverie. That was how he wished he could spend the afternoon with her. She was exactly the right sort of woman to make love to behind jalousies. Now they called it having sex. He did not want to have sex with her. He wanted it to be more than that.

"Richard, neither of us has time for long romances," she said. She put her hand on his arm. "Let's go to the hotel. I've got a house full of children."

"I'd like to take you to New Orleans some time," he said. "I know a hotel in the French Quarter."

"That's still there?"

"Maybe."

They lay together on the bed. Lovemaking was not that different from when he had been twenty expect for the absence of desperation he had felt to embrace as many women as possible. Now that had been replaced with something else. He was comfortable with women in a way he had not been when he was young. He liked their company, whether having drinks at a café or in bed.

She had put a plastic bag full of ice on his knee.

"You should get that knee fixed," she said.

"It doesn't usually give me any trouble," he said.

He wondered what she expected now and at the same time he wondered what he expected. He thought of the girl he had lain with behind the jalousies so long ago. And he tried to remember exactly what he had felt for her. At the time he had thought it was love. And then he had learned to recognize the difference between love and desire. Or thought he had learned. There had been his four wives. Perhaps he still did not know how to tell and might never know.

"You'll go back to Charleston to make the prints?" she asked.

"Yes," he said.

"I want to see where you live. By the sea?"

"The harbor."

"After you make the prints you call me. I'll fly down."

He imagined her running through the streets of Charleston early in the morning and he riding beside her on a bicycle. No hills for her to climb there. She would run along the Battery and then up Bay Street past his house. She would talk to him as she ran, her shoes making little splats on the asphalt. The wind off the harbor would rattle the palm fronds and toss her fine white hair.

The bag of ice slipped off his knee. She picked it up and held it in place.

"Could the queen grow in Charleston?" he asked.

"The winters are too cold," she said.

He imagined moving south down the Florida coast, far enough south so tropical plants could flourish. They would have a garden. They would watch the big white flower slowly open in the moonlight.

"Damn, but that's cold," he said.

"It needs to be cold," she said.

He ran his hand from her neck down the length of her body, stopping at her calf where he felt the smooth bulge of her runner's muscles. His body was not in that sort of shape and was not likely to be ever again, no matter how many miles he rode a bicycle.

"Let's stay right here," he said. "Until it's time for dinner."

"I have to go home and change," she said.

She lay her head on his chest.

"I believe you'll run again," she said.

"Maybe in Charleston, where it's flat," he said.

"You don't like our hills?"

"Not even on a bicycle."

He wondered what his heart sounded like to her. He supposed she had some kind of runner's heart, large and strong, pumping oxygen-rich blood throughout her body. It was as if his body was an ancient tool he had borrowed from a museum, still serviceable but irreplaceable and prone to breakage.

"Go to sleep," she said. "Go to sleep and dream of Mexico."

He closed his eyes and slept but did not dream.

They went to dinner that night. The next day they had breakfast together and then she went off to the arboretum. He sat in the café on the square and read articles she had written on the queen of the night. They spent the afternoon in his room. And over the next three days they went out to eat together and made love. The bud was not opening as fast as she had predicted. She told him she believed the blossoming would be delayed at least one and maybe two days.

On the night it had originally been scheduled to bloom they had dinner together. As the sun began to set, she put her phone on the table. Before they had dessert and coffee she gave Kristina a call just to make sure. But the bud still showed no signs of opening. Then they had their dessert and coffee and again were the last people out of the restaurant.

They walked together across the deserted square.

"Amy is leaving in the morning," she said. "They're releasing some mountain lions in the national forest and she has to be there. It's her project. She's been on the phone ten times a day about those lions. Just like us and that plant. So I need to get home early. I don't see as much of her as I'd like to."

"Too bad the queen didn't cooperate," he said.

"I'd say sunset of the day after tomorrow. I may get fooled again but that's what I think."

They reached her truck. He kissed her and watched her drive off.

That night he dreamed of the plant, the same dream he had had in Charleston. When he awoke, the rich smell of the blossom seemed to be hanging in the room. Just then the phone rang. It was Mary Lee. He half expected her to tell him that Kristina had gone to sleep and had awakened to discover the plant had opened. But it was not that at all. A friend of Mary Lee's, who lived in the town, had died during the night.

It was not unexpected. Her friend had been sick for months. But Mary Lee seemed to be shaken by her death.

"Dora and I started the first grade together," Mary Lee said.

The funeral was not going to be for a few days. One of Dora's cousins was coming from New York.

"I'll watch the plant bloom and then bury Dora," she said.

Then he told her about his dream.

"So you're certain it hasn't bloomed?" he asked.

"No, I talked with Kristina not ten minutes ago," she said. "She agrees with me. It's going to be tomorrow. I'll call you. The girls are helping me make some food to carry over to Dora's sister."

He lay back down on the bed, intending to close his eyes for only a few minutes. When he awoke it was noon.

After he had lunch, he spent the early afternoon taking pictures of the university, whose architecture was a mélange of styles. The afternoon was oppressively hot, and he walked from patch of shade to patch of shade on the tree-lined campus as he took pictures. He liked the stone buildings that had been built in the late nineteenth century with their cupolas and turrets. After he had shot up all his film he walked down the hill to the town and returned to the hotel. He had a message to call Mary Lee.

She told him they were going to meet at the arboretum at five. She would drive by and then he could follow her in his car. He gathered up his equipment. He had brought several large-format cameras. When he reached the arboretum, he would decide which one to use.

Then he went to the café on the square and had a glass of iced tea. The afternoon seemed to him to have become even hotter, not quite as hot as a summer afternoon in Charleston when no breeze was coming off the harbor, but quite uncomfortable. He sat in the shade of the awning and read a book until just before five. He walked back to the hotel where he found Mary Lee waiting in the lobby.

He followed her out to the arboretum. When they arrived the parking lot was filled with cars.

"My friends," she said. "They've come to see the queen and *you*."

In the lobby a table had been set up with wine and food. She introduced him to her friends, mostly middle-aged people from the university. Han and the boy were there. Mary Lee remembered the boy's name, which was Roger. Then Richard went to set up his equipment.

A young woman sat in a folding chair beside the plant. She held a glass of champagne in her hand. Mary Lee introduced him to Kristina.

"See, she's right on the edge of opening," Mary Lee said.

The bud had become larger than the first day he had seen it. It was swollen and looked ready to open at any moment. He positioned the backdrop and set up the camera and the strobe. Then they left Kristina to watch the plant and returned to the lobby where even more people had arrived. He switched to bottled water, intending to stay sharp for the task ahead of him.

The sun had just dropped behind a line of hills and he was engaged in conversation with a one of Mark Lee's colleagues when Kristina came up and tapped him on the shoulder.

"It's starting," she said. "I saw her move."

They all went back into the arboretum. He checked the focus on his camera again and tested the strobe. For the next two hours they all stood about in the darkness of the artificial jungle, a little starlight coming into the room through the glass ceiling, and waited for the queen to open. A fleshy tearing sound began to come from her, like an orange being slowly pulled apart by a fastidious eater. Various sweet scents filled the room as the bud slowly unfurled. Then the one overpowering scent from his dream. He closed his eyes and tried to imagine the garden in Mexico but could not.

"Seducing us with sweetness and beauty," Mary Lee said.

Finally, after two hours, the enormous flower was fully open, its white petals surrounded by spokes of gold. A sigh came from the crowd. Mary Lee put her arm around him and kissed him on the cheek. Then she stepped back as he began to shoot exposure after exposure of the flower. The strobe popped on and off, its soft light illuminating the blossom.

Gradually the people left. Richard and Mary Lee and Kristina sat in the darkness filled with the perfume from the flower. The flower itself was a soft white splotch. The strobe went off with its unceasing regularity. He got up and turned it off. The moon was rising over the hills. They could all see it through the panes.

Mary Lee opened another bottle of champagne, the cork flying off to land with a rustle in a stand of plants. She filled their glasses.

"To the queen," she said.

They all drank. By the time half the bottle was gone Kristina announced that she was going home. She left them sitting together in the darkness.

"I want to see *this* plant bloom again," she said.

"I know," he said.

"Now you'll go to Charleston and make prints."

"Yes. All my equipment's there. You'll drive down with me?"

"Yes. After we bury Dora."

He imagined them driving through the Arkansas delta, huge fields of cotton, soybeans, and rice on either side of the highway, and then crossing the river at Greenville.

"We'll wake up every morning and look out at the sea," she said.

And he wondered if it were going to be as easy as that. She might remain to live with him in the house on Bay Street or after a few weeks she might go back to Arkansas.

He imagined himself making the prints. A tedious, careful process was required to produce the images that appeared to be lit from within by their own soft light. His negatives had to be perfect, his printing technique had to be perfect, and if not then the shoot of the flower was all wasted. He would have to search for another plant about to bloom.

Then it struck him that he might be able to locate the town in Mexico. They could drive down along the Pacific coast and until he saw something that triggered a memory: a hill, a town church, a clump of trees. And he might dream again of the town, providing other clues. They might drive into it on the evening a flower was blooming, finding their way to the garden by following the sound of guitars.

"You're thinking of the flower?" she said. "Your prints?"

"Yes," he said. "I'm thinking of the flower in my dream, the one in Mexico. We could drive down. Look for the town. We could get lucky. A flower might be ready to bloom."

"I'd like that," she said. She walked over and sniffed at the flower. "The petals are so soft."

"It's perfect," he said.

"But not tomorrow."

"No, not tomorrow."

He wished he could explain to her how the prints of the flower were going to look. And how the prints he planned to make of her were going to look. Those pictures he shot at the river. But he knew that he could never explain how her image would emerge from the final acid bath, how she would be wrapped in light.

"What if we don't get to see her bloom again?" she asked.

"It doesn't matter," he said. "It won't matter at all."

Pinecones

The death of Dean Henderson's father, who lived in South Carolina and who Dean had not seen in five years, coincided with Dean's losing his job as a route salesman for a wholesale grocery company. Dean had been caught fishing in a pond behind a crossroads store in Georgia when he was supposed to be working his way back towards the company headquarters in Charlotte. The store owner was one of Dean's best customers. Dean had watched in disbelief as Mr. Foster, the owner of the grocery company, stepped out of his white Cadillac and stood on the gravel lot dressed the way he always dressed in the summer, in a white suit and a blue tie. He stood there looking out over the pond, shading his eyes from the sun with one hand. Dean sculled the johnboat into the bank, where he was met by his employer.

"Catching any?" Mr. Foster asked.

Dean for a moment had thought that everything was going to be all right. In June he had been salesman of the month.

"No, sir," Dean said.

"Well, from now on you'll have plenty of time to fish," Mr. Foster said. "Don't come back to the office."

Mr. Foster never offered any explanation as to what he was doing in rural Georgia. Dean imagined he was there visiting a sick relative or attending a funeral.

Three months later Dean still had not found a job. He was being hounded by bill collectors. He had been evicted from his apartment. What little money he had he used to keep his car, a new Lincoln Continental, from being repossessed. Then his father died.

He planned on spending several weeks in the Carolina sandhills after the funeral. The sandhills were the bed of an ancient sea. The soil was not good for farming, but it was good for growing longleaf pines. A big tract of it was taken up by a national wildlife refuge and a state forest. He would do some deer hunting; he would clean out his father's trailer. Then he would give up on Charlotte and go to Atlanta to look for a job.

His father had been much older than his mother, who had died when Dean was a boy. Dean's earliest remembrances of his father were of an old man, a person older than some of the grandfathers of his friends. Now the old man was dead at ninety-three. The man who'd come to read the electrical meter him found him lying on the couch, an opened but untouched bottle of beer on the table.

Dean spent the night before the funeral in the trailer, which still smelled of his father, a mixture of sweat, tobacco, and whiskey. No one came to the funeral, for the old man had outlived his friends. Some cousins in Arkansas were the only relatives Dean knew about, but he had no idea where in Arkansas they were living. Years ago they had left Pine Bluff to live somewhere in the Ozarks.

So it was just Dean and a preacher, whose church the old man never attended. It was one of those perfect October afternoons, the sky without a cloud, the kind the old man disliked. He liked days with a little rain so that a man could walk quiet in the woods. Dean buried his father in the churchyard beside his young wife.

Several years before he had made it clear to Dean that he no longer wanted him to come down to hunt deer, that he wanted no company at all. Dean's father made his living mostly through illegal activities. That was what he and Dean had fallen out over. His father was growing marijuana on the refuge. Dean had refused to help.

He called his father from time to time, but the conversations were usually brief and left Dean feeling sorry that he had called at all. "Selling godamned groceries," the old man had said once. Dean had not responded but wondered what his father had against groceries.

There was a house on his father's land, but it had long ago been abandoned. The house, which belonged to his mother, had taken a direct hit from a live oak during a hurricane. His father had planned to repair it and had gone so far as to remove the oak. The limbs and sections of the trunk were still stacked at one side of the house. The blue tarp he had nailed over the hole in the roof was in tatters. Now squirrels lived in the kitchen cabinets and hornets had built a nest on the dining room chandelier. One day someone would set the house afire just for the thrill of watching it burn.

When Dean drove up to the trailer, set in the shade of a big live oak, Rachel Habersham's truck was parked beside it. She was the daughter of the superintendent of the wildlife refuge whose boundary was a quarter of a mile away from the trailer, the entire side of his father's one hundred acres of land flush up to it. Here the refuge was a tupelo gum and cypress swamp. Her father had retired and Rachel had been appointed to his position. Dean and Rachel had gone to school together.

She was dressed in her uniform, her dark hair pulled back in a ponytail.

"How many bushels of pine cones do you reckon your daddy has got in the barn?" she asked.

"How many do you think came from the refuge?" he asked.

"Plenty," she said. "Why don't we take a look?"

In the three months before Christmas there was a hot market for longleaf pine cones, which were used to make decorations. Signs appeared on the windows of crossroad stores advertising wholesale prices for new-crop long leaf cones. The cones were huge, and it was easy to pick up a bushel. The best hunting was on the refuge where harvesting of the cones was forbidden. Many people also made their living off collecting pine straw, which was sold for mulch. For both of these crops the refuge had been his father's favorite territory. He did it at night. Despite the efforts of Rachel's father and then Rachel the old man had never been caught.

The barn door was secured with a chain and padlock. Dean had not bothered to search for the key yet.

"What exactly does a refuge cone look like?" he asked.

"Same as any other," she said. "I just want to see those pine cones. It doesn't seem possible that a man in his nineties could fill that barn. I sure tried hard to catch him. I've got the mosquito bites to prove it."

"I don't have the key."

"How'd he do it?"

"I don't know. What does it matter now? You can't put a dead man in jail."

"I just want to know."

Dean pictured his father moving through the woods at night carrying trash bags full of pinecones. He then poled the pirogue through the swamp and deposited the bags on an island. He had hewed the pirogue out of a cypress log with an adz, refusing to use a single modern tool. The bags remained hidden in a stand of gallberry, an evergreen that grew so thick a pack of dogs chasing a coon would have had difficulty moving through it. On rainy nights he transferred the bags to the barn.

"There's a pair of bolt cutters in the trailer," he said.

"You don't mind?" she asked.

"Why should I?"

"Let's get those cutters."

They walked across the grass to the barn. They had dated in high school. The old man had not liked that.

"You don't know what you might say to that girl," he had said.

The old man was not the reason they had stopped dating. She had fallen in love with another boy whose father owned the water heater plant just outside of the small town. She had married Jack McGill and then divorced him.

"You ever see Jack?" he asked.

"No," she said.

"What's he doing?"

"Running his daddy's plant."

They reached the barn. On one side his father had nailed the skulls and antlers of the deer he had killed. He killed mostly for meat, with no regard for state game laws. But he also liked to hunt big bucks and many of the racks were fine ones.

He handed her the cutters.

"You do it," he said.

She cut the chain. He swung the door open. They stepped into the semi darkness of the barn.

"Looks like he was fixing to sell some pines cones," she said.

Two cotton wagons were half full of cones, and the livestock stalls his father had converted to wire bins were full.

"Waiting for the price to get right," he said.

"Once my daddy thought about putting some kind of chemical on our cones," she said. "The kind they put on money to catch bank robbers. Fluoresces under ultraviolet light. He put it on a few but your daddy never poached those cones. I wonder how he knew."

"He was smarter than a trapwise fox," he said. "He just knew."

"What you gonna to do with these?"

"Sell 'em."

"You should destroy 'em."

"No, I believe he picked up every one of these on private land." He took a cone out of one of the bins and ran his hand over it, a perfect new-crop cone. "Had permission too."

"Where's the pine straw?"

"Up in the loft. But it looks like he wasn't paying mind to anything but pine cones."

"I'm sorry he's dead."

"You'll get to stay out of the woods at night."

"There a plenty of others who *try* to do it."

Pinecones 181

They left the barn. He thought that he should look hard for the key or buy another lock. The pinecones were too valuable to leave in an unlocked barn. The next time he went past Mr. Black's store he would stop in and see what he was paying for a bushel of new-crop cones.

The day he discovered a rub on a sapling, made by a big buck, he found where his father had hidden the pirogue on the edge of the swamp. A wheelbarrow, the type with double pneumatic tires favored by suburban gardeners, was hidden under the camouflage netting. He supposed this was how his father had taken the pirogue from the barn to the edge of the swamp. He was much too old to carry it by himself any longer. He brought the cones out along a deer trail that ended behind the barn. Someone else might have been tempted to cut a path down to the swamp for a pickup. But Dean supposed that was one of the reasons why his father had never been caught. He was very careful.

He took the pirogue out into the swamp to look at the island. He poled the boat through the shallow water, cutting a path through patches of green duckweed as he weaved his way through the maze of cypress knees. It was as hot as a day in August. He was thankful for the shade of the cypresses.

The island was not much larger than the barn. He made his way through the tangle of gallberry and vines, following what looked like a game trail, but he knew his father had made it. He came into an open spot, no bigger than the kitchen in the trailer. His father had made it by training the branches of the gallberry over the open space, so that if someone flew over the island in a helicopter they would see nothing but a uniform stand of the evergreen. The gallberry cave was empty.

He sat there for a time in that cool dark place, a few mosquitoes buzzing about his ears, and thought of how difficult it must have been for the old man to move that many pine cones out of the refuge, store them on the island, and then on a suitable night transport them to the barn.

Dean had been living at the trailer for two weeks. It seemed to him that he had never traveled about from small store to small store selling ice cream, canned tuna, and cow feed. As far as he knew no woman had ever set foot in the trailer. He wondered how his father had lived like that for so many years.

He planned to stay until he shot the buck. The tracks he had found were those of a big deer. When the season opened in two weeks he would rattle him up, using the ancient set of antlers he had seen used for the first time by his father. Then he would go to Atlanta. The money from the sale of the pines cones in the barn would get him started. Sometime in the middle of November he expected the price to hit its peak. He still had one credit card whose account had not been frozen. He would use that to buy groceries.

It was the day before Halloween and in two days he planned to hunt the buck. He was cooking breakfast when he saw Rachel's truck pull into the yard. He met her at the door.

"How about some biscuits and Daddy's bacon for breakfast?" he said.

"Biscuits and bacon would be good."

She drank coffee while he pulled the biscuits from the oven.

"Dean, will you take me to the Halloween party over at Matthew Johnson's?" she asked.

"Think I might be out collecting pine cones on Halloween?" he said.

"Taking pinecones from the refuge is a federal crime. I see you've locked up the barn again. I sure hope you haven't been filling up those cotton wagons with refuge cones."

"You'll have to be nicer than that if you want me to take you to that party."

"Mr. Black was up a nickel last time I was at the store. You'll get yourself a nice price." She looked around the trailer like she did not think much of it. "Dean, I thought I was in love with Jack but I was mistaken. He was in love with water heaters. But I wasn't in love with you either. I don't think I've ever really been in love."

Instead of answering her, he brought the skillet to the table.

"Let's eat," he said.

They both concentrated on their food. He thought of the night she had told him that she was going to marry Jack after graduation. He had wanted to cry but had not. She had. When he told his father about what had happened the old man had laughed at him.

"Sonny, that's why women ain't allowed in this trailer," he said.

"You know, my father died alone right over there on that sofa," he said. "He didn't even get to start drinking one last beer."

"Is that what you're planning on doing, drinking that last beer? Will that satisfy you?"

"No, I wasn't saying that."

"You sure didn't seem to care one way or the other when I told you I was marrying Jack."

"I cared. And I'll take you to that party. Where're you living?"

"With Daddy."

"Same place?"

"Yes."

Then they drank coffee and talked about his chances of killing the big buck until she said she had duties to attend to on the refuge.

The party was like a high school reunion. Their class had had their tenth reunion earlier in the year but he had not attended. They both drank too much. She spent the night in the trailer with him. He enjoyed the feel of her tanned, athlete's body. She had gone to the state university on a basketball scholarship. He told himself that it was nothing permanent. In a few months he would be living in Atlanta.

He rose before light and went out of the trailer with his father's rifle. She had not awakened. The alarm would wake her later. Today she was supervising the burning of a tract of pines. The undergrowth, mostly scrub oak, was kept burned to produce a park-like forest favored by the red-cockaded woodpecker, an endangered bird the refuge was interested in seeing do well. The longleaf pines, because of their thick bark, were immune to the fire that killed the oaks.

He took up a stand in a gallberry thicket where he had a view of the rubbed sapling. Then he began to work the antlers, trying to convince the buck there was a rival in the area. But the buck never appeared. Once the sun was well up over the pines, he slung the rifle and walked back to the trailer.

She was gone but had left a note.

Dean,

We'll be burning up near Laurel Creek Church. Come out and you can have half of my lunch. Hope you got your buck.

Love,

Rachel

As he was eating breakfast a car drove up into the yard. He met the man on the porch. He was middle-aged and wore a cheap suit. Dean wondered what had reduced him to this sort of job. Usually collections in the field were a younger man's game.

"I guess you've come about the car," Dean said.

"That's right," the man said. "You're three months behind."

Dean invited him into the trailer and sat down at the kitchen table and wrote him a check off his credit card account.

"Mr. Henderson, you need to get yourself a job or a cheaper car," the man said. "Does that truck run?"

His father's pickup was parked next to the barn.

"No," Dean said.

"Then get it running," the man said. "Do that or find a job. I'd do both if I were you."

"I will," Dean said.

"Which one?"

"I haven't made up my mind."

"I'd make it up if I were you. I'd settle on something. Somebody like

Pinecones

me'll find you no matter where you go."

"I'll be right here."

"Good, that's good. This is beautiful country down here. No work but beautiful country. Everyone's working in Charlotte. Finding a job is easy."

"Just like you."

"I've done a lot of things in my life. Least I'm working. I wouldn't mind sitting down here at deer camp but I need to work. I've got obligations."

My father, lived out his life right here in this trailer, he thought.

"Get yourself a job, son," the man said. "You want to keep driving that big car then you get yourself a job."

"I appreciate you coming all the way done here to give me this good advice," Dean said.

The man sighed.

"Well, you keep up those payments. Then I won't have to come back."

The man left. Dean decided that he would take Rachel up on her offer of lunch.

Rachel was easy to find. All he had to do was follow the smoke. They ate across the sand road from where they were making the burn. The breeze kept shifting and blowing the smoke over them. They ate country ham and biscuits from Mr. Black's store.

"Mr. Black says the price won't hold for long," she said.

"I ain't in a hurry," he said. "It might go a little higher."

"I wish there was something on the refuge for you. I've already got a crew of burners hired for the season."

"Maybe I could go to work making water heaters."

"You working for Jack. That would be something."

"I'll have to go to Atlanta and find a job in sales. That's my talent."

"After you sell those pine cones."

"Yes, after that."

It appeared to him that she wanted to say something but she was silent.

"Amy Black makes good biscuits," she said. "Makes'em from scratch every morning."

"Let's go to Leesville tonight," he said. "See a movie."

"Yes, let's do that."

The smoke swirled about them and they closed their eyes against it.

"I wish you'd stay a while," she said.

"I wish I could," he said. "Too bad I can't go to work for Jack."

They sat on the thick carpet of pine needles and talked about possibilities for him in the region until it was time for her to go back to her crew. He kept thinking of the feel of her body against his. He wanted her there every night.

Rachel came to the trailer every day as soon as she got off work. She usually did not spend the night, because she did not want to have to explain her actions to her father. Now they had spoken of love. He was considering commuting to Charlotte sixty miles away. But first he had to find a job.

Then just after she left the solution came to him. He would continue with his father's life. Pines cones and pine straw. And he might find a job of some sort in Leesville. He would start collecting cones this very night. He knew exactly where Rachel would be, home with her father. She would not be likely to go out again.

He took some trash bags from his father's supply and walked down through the pines to the swamp. It was a cool night. When he reached the swamp, a half moon was rising above the cypresses. He had not taken any light with him. He could recall all the times his father had said: "You take a damn light into the woods and they're gonna catch you for sure." He reached the swamp and took the cover off the pirogue. Then he poled it through the swamp and past the island to the refuge.

When he was a boy his father had taken him with him a few times, but mostly the old man liked to go alone. He believed that taking another person doubled his chances of being caught. Dean remembered walking out of the same gums up into the pines. He walked a mile before he started to gather pinecones. Then he quickly filled four trash bags. That was another of his father's maxims. Never fill more than four bags. Two bags could be tied together and a pair slung over each shoulder. A fifth made walking too hard.

He returned to the pirogue and deposited the bags on the island. Then he poled the pirogue to its hiding place and walked up through the pines to the trailer. He drank a beer and went to bed. He would have liked to watch TV but his father never allowed a set in the trailer. He had sold the set and the satellite dish Dean had given him one Christmas as a peace offering. As Dean drifted off to sleep, he thought with satisfaction of the bags lying hidden on the island. He tried to imagine how many bags he would have to carry to fill the cotton wagons, how many trips across the swamp it would take. He would go out every night after Rachel left. This, he imagined, was how his father must have often gone to sleep, dreaming of pinecones filling the wagons.

Toward the end of November there were plenty of rainy nights. He used them to move the pinecones from the island into the barn. Even though the price fell off by three cents he kept on collecting. He was determined to fill the wagons.

He and Rachel had started talking about marriage. She thought the house could be repaired. He had replaced the tattered tarp with a new one. And on a morning when there was a heavy frost, he had removed the hornet's nest from the chandelier.

He had driven to Charlotte a few times to interview for jobs but no one had made him an offer. He told people he had been selling groceries in California. He even made up the name of a company he worked for and a description of his territory. Once or twice he even considered telling the truth but stopped himself just in time. He had no idea what was wrong. It was as if he were sending out some sort of signal all his potential employers recognized but of which he was unaware. He made sure that whenever it was possible that they got a look at the big car, the emblem he thought would demonstrate to all that he could sell.

"We can put a new roof on the house with the pine cone money," he said. "I can do the work."

They were watching the evening news on TV. Rachel had brought an old set from her house. He had put up an antenna. The reception from Charlotte was surprisingly good. The trailer no longer smelled of his father, the stink of his tobacco replaced by the scent of her perfume. He had thrown out the old mattress in the bedroom and washed all the linens and towels. He had scrubbed the walls and floor.

"Don't talk to me about that pine cone money," she said. "We'll save up for that roof."

The night before he had brought the last bags up to the barn in a cold drizzle. The cotton wagons were full.

"No need for those cones to go to waste," he said.

"Burn them," she said.

"I can't."

"Why?"

"They're a part of my father."

"Who didn't want to see you for years. Why was that?"

He thought of the day he told the old man that he would have nothing to do with marijuana farming. What his father had needed him for was to carry water up from a creek for the plants. Some people hauled in gasoline-powered pumps to do the job. They were the ones who got caught and ended up in prison in Columbia.

"He wanted all those big bucks for himself," he said.

"That sounds like him," she said. "So you'll burn them?"

"I can't."

"It's not that much money. Maybe two or three thousand dollars. That won't look like much when you get a job."

"A dollar looks like a lot right now."

She got off the sofa. She was crying but refused to acknowledge it, the

Pinecones

tears running untouched down her cheeks. She picked up her purse and wrapped the strap around her hand as if she were preparing to fight her way through a crowd of thieves.

"Those cones *are* your daddy," she said. "And he's laughing at you right now. You have to decide."

Then she walked out of the trailer without waiting for his reply. He did not try to stop her.

The next day was cold with a high blue sky. After breakfast he unlocked the barn. Then he began to pile the cones in an open space between the barn and the pines. When he finished around lunch time, he guessed there were close to eight hundred bushels of cones. He called Rachel.

It was dark when Rachel drove up to the trailer. She walked in with a bottle of whiskey in her hand.

"Daddy would've approved of that," he said.

"I suppose," she said.

After they had a couple of drinks, they turned the lights of the Lincoln on the cones. They sat on the hood and had a third drink.

"I was going to use the money to keep them from repossessing this car," he said.

"Get a job," she said.

They finished their drinks. He sprinkled kerosene over the cones. He touched a match to each pile and they caught fire quickly. They burned with a quick, intense heat, filling the air with the pine-scented smoke. The heat was at first pleasant but then it became too hot, forcing them to retreat a few yards. For a moment he was concerned about the car, but then the fire faded and the red-hot piles collapsed upon themselves, sending sparks swirling up into the darkness. They stood there sipping the good whiskey until the fires burned themselves out.

"You're free of him," she said.

She kissed him, her mouth smelling of whiskey and her lips warm against his.

"Maybe I am," he said.

He found a job in Leesville working in the produce section of a grocery store. Somehow he just could not convince anyone to hire him as a salesman. He sold the Lincoln and paid off most of the note. Then he got his father's pickup running. All it needed was a new battery. The engine was in perfect condition.

They spent their weekends working on the house. Their plan was to get married as soon as it was livable again. He tore off the cedar shakes and decked the roof with plywood. Then he put on asphalt shingles.

He never told her about how his father and later he had removed the pinecones from the refuge. The pirogue and the wheelbarrow were still hidden beneath the camouflage netting.

They worked hard on the house. They planned to be married in June. In May, when he was installing doors on a closet one Sunday afternoon while Rachel was in Washington, DC on refuge business, he found a canning jar full of marijuana seeds on the top shelf. His father had been too cautious to keep it in the trailer or the barn. The hornet's nest in the dining room was certain to keep people out of the house during warm weather.

He ate dinner that night with the jar on the table before him. He considered how one good crop of marijuana would pay for the bathroom Rachel wished they could afford. He could say that he had gotten a raise or that he had worked overtime.

The idea that had seemed so good that evening seemed even better in the morning. It was safe to go on the refuge in daylight because Rachel was not due to return until the next day. He called in sick and took the can and a spade down to the pirogue. He poled the boat across the swamp. It was a hot day. It seemed as if summer had already arrived. The trees were in full leaf; the birds were singing. He watched an alligator swim off and disappear behind a cypress. Once he was on the refuge land he began to plant the seeds in stands of the gallberry. He had learned this from his father who never planted his crop in patches, just a few plants here and there. They would be invisible from the air. No one would care to walk those gallberry thickets in the summer, alive with cottonmouths and rattlers.

He went to sleep that night tired from the planting but happy. He imagined tending his crop while Rachel slept in the house. He would carry milk jugs of water up from the creek, one for each plant. A pinhole in the bottom of each jug allowed the water to soak slowly into the earth. The well-watered plants would grow tall and lush in the summer heat. On a few nights in August, he would harvest the bud-laden heads slowly and carefully and hang them on racks hidden in the gallberry to dry. He and Rachel would be married and living in his mother's house by then. And he would go on with his secret life, his father's blood showing him the way through the dark woods.

Nicolae and the Devil

A friend in Paris, who had met Nicolae only once and knew him solely by reputation, always spoke of the sculptor with admiration. "He lifts blocks of marble!" our friend said. He was awed by Nicolae's success with women, who invariably fell in love with him but never he with them. Nicolae seemed to regard their presence as the natural order of things, no more surprised by their affections than by his ability to work marble. Our friend was unaware that the secret of Nicolae's success was not his strength but his indifference.

We arrived in the summer at our house in the foothills of the Pyrenees, eager for a break from teaching, to discover from our neighbors that Nicolae had made a large sculpture of a devil. We drove over to Nicolae's atelier to see it the next morning.

Nicolae and the other Romanians had had a party at his atelier the night before to celebrate the completion of the devil. Wine bottles lay scattered about around a heap of ashes, the soft dust imprinted with the marks of bare feet where they had danced about the fire. A boom box sat on the plush red seat of an elaborately carved chair. Someone had left a cowboy hat with a raven's feather stuck in its band on top of a stack of bricks.

We were sorry we had missed the party. We'd have eaten eggplant and sausages and drunk the heavy red wine of the region. At dawn we'd all have gone swimming in a nearby lake, the usual ending for Romanian

Nicolae and the Devil

parties. Last year Meg and I stood naked in waist-deep water and watched the sun come up over the mountains, while the Romanians played rugby on the beach. I remember how her breasts had been gilded by the rising sun. I have never loved her so much as at that moment.

We stood before the devil, twelve feet high and made of granite and black marble. It was half male and half female, one hip curving out in feminine softness, the other lean and hard, while a stone cock hung from one side of its groin and pudenda sprouted from the other. The head was marble, the open mouth full of pointed teeth. The eyeless and noseless face was a smooth expanse of polished marble. There were the usual cloven hooves, horns, and pointed ears. It had a long plumed tail that Nicolae had managed to make look light and feathery. But everything else about it was heavy. That was its chief quality. The massive devil towered above us.

"Quetzalcoatl," I said. "The feathered serpent."

Meg repeated this in French to Nicolae, a short, powerfully built man with a thick black beard and dark eyes, the sort of man who caused so much difficulty for the Roman legions. He laughed and nodded his head in agreement.

The teeth had appeared in Nicolae's sculpture after the death of Gwyn, an American artist who worked in sculpture in the manner of Bosch. Just before they were to be married, she had gone to the hospital in Toulouse for a fertility test. The test had elevated her blood pressure, and her heart, which had a defect no one knew about, was unable to stand the strain. Nicolae was devastated. We saw him the next day, and I have never seen a man in so much pain.

After that the toothed heads began to appear. They were brutal but beautiful things.

"A wonderful devil," I said.

"A handsome devil," Meg said.

Nicolae walked up from his atelier to join us.

"What better person than me to make a devil," he said. "I am from Translyvania."

He explained how he had made the devil for a satanic cult.

"They are Americans," he said.

The Americans had a house in a little village above Limoux, he told us.

"What are they doing here?" I asked.

Nicolae shrugged his shoulders and puffed on his pipe.

"They want it for their garden," Nicolae said. "They have a big house, almost a chateau."

"Have you seen them?" Meg asked.

"No," Nicolae replied. "They remain in the house. They have a gardener. He gives me instructions. Tomorrow I will install it."

"May we go along?" Meg asked.

"Of course," Nicolae said. "I have hired a truck. Be here at six o'clock. Bata and I want to do the work before it gets hot."

Bata was one of several Romanian artists who worked at The Forge, a group of houses and old buildings the French government had sold to the Romanians at cheap rates. Bata was in the process of converting one of the buildings into a house and atelier. Nicolae had been helping him. He was generous toward the refugees. Only a few were good artists, but Nicolae gave them places to live and money and kept them afloat. After a few years most drifted away to settle elsewhere in France, made uncomfortable in the end by Nicolae's success.

When we left, Nicolae was standing before the sculpture. He relit his pipe and blew a puff of smoke toward the devil.

"What do you think," Meg asked.

We were driving up the side of a mountain on a twisting road. Genets, brilliant yellow flowers on long reed-like stems, were still in bloom. They grew in masses on the slopes. Already it was too hot for them at lower elevations. Soon these too would be gone.

"I think it's wonderful," I said.

"No, I don't mean just that."

"What do you mean?"

"The change. It's playful. That tail."

"Those teeth didn't look playful."

"Oh, I think he's changed. He's gotten over Gwyn."

"Maybe."

We reached the crest. Off to the west was Spain, the snow newly melted off the highest peaks. Below were the red tile roofs of a village. Our village was on the other side of the narrow valley at the foot of a range of mountains that rose to form a plateau.

"You'll see that I'm right."

The tail was playful. I conceded that.

We went home and I spent the afternoon painting the shutters. Meg went off to look for the wood man who kept our *cave* stocked with firewood. He had no telephone so one had to go up to his house in person. A friend in the village had told her that he was getting ready to raise his price for a cord of wood.

I was up on the ladder painting the last of the bedroom window shutters when Meg and Madame Jordy came around the side of the house.

"I was right," Meg said.

"About the wood?" I asked.

"No, about Nicolae," she said. "He's closed the museum."

By that she meant that he had removed Gwyn's statues and paintings and drawings from his house. After her death he had filled the house with them, covered the walls. A strange composite bird-man had resided in the kitchen. I could remember the cats playing with the feathers on his arms and Nicolae picking a white cat up and tossing it out the kitchen door while the grey one ran for cover.

Madame Jordy had been the messenger of this news. Our neighbor praised my work on the shutters. Then the women disappeared around the side of the building, probably going to sit in Madame's garden, of which she was especially proud.

That night we sat on the balcony with a bottle of wine and a couple of cans of anchovies and a loaf of bread. We were too tired to cook. Off on the hill above the village we could see the outline of the Cathar chateau in the moonlight. The Cathars were a people who believed that the visible world was the creation of the devil. Sometimes I wondered what they saw when they looked at the fir-covered mountains or at a hillside carpeted with genets.

"No more teeth," Meg said. "The devil is the last of it."

"I hope so," I said. "It's time for him to change."

And I thought that even if he quit making those fanged figures, the fangs would not go away. They would be someplace else, even sharper in his imagination than in marble.

When we arrived at The Forge, a flatbed truck and crane were already there. Two men, dressed in blue overalls, sat together in the cab of the crane. Nicolae and Bata stood beside the devil drinking coffee.

Nicolae spoke to the men in the truck. One got out and attached the cable from the crane to a hook Nicolae had set in the back of the devil's neck. The crane operator took up the slack on the cable. We all stepped back.

The devil rose from the ground. Then the crane pivoted, swinging it toward the flatbed truck. With a pop the hook broke and the sculpture fell to the ground, making a heavy sound in the soft dust. It lay on its back, its eyeless face turned toward the sun. For a moment everyone stood in stunned silence. Then, realizing that the devil was unharmed, Nicolae and Bata began to laugh. The crane operator had gotten out of his cab and was standing on the truck bed looking at the other man, who was examining the broken hook.

"This devil doesn't want to go to Limoux," Meg said.

"Nicolae should have known that hook wouldn't hold," I said. "That monster must weigh a couple of tons."

"Hindsight," she said.

After some consultation the men wrapped nylon-covered steel cables

Nicolae and the Devil

around the hips and trunk of the devil. They were good at it. When the crane again lifted the devil off the ground, it balanced. The crane operator smoothly swung the devil up and over the truckbed, then lowered it to rest there. The truck, stabilized by hydraulic supports, creaked as the devil's weight came down on it.

"We're in business," I said.

But the men were unable to retract the hydraulic supports. They examined gauges in the cab; they traced the hydraulic lines, looking for leaks. They shook their heads.

"He's not going to Limoux today," Meg said.

And I agreed with her. It was spooky. The sun was well up now; it was beginning to get hot. The light was brilliant off the devil's face.

One man crawled under the truck to inspect the hydraulic lines, a wrench in his hand. He worked at something and then yelled at the other to try the mechanism again. This time the stabilizers retracted smoothly.

We followed the truck around the outskirts of Limoux and then turned to go back up into the hills to the village. This was unfamiliar country to us.

The road gained elevation. Soon Limoux was far below us. Then we reached the village. The narrow winding streets were barely wide enough for the passage of the trucks.

We went up a hill to the highest point in the village. There on the ridgetop, overlooking the vineyard-covered valley below, was the house. It was long and narrow, surrounded by a high stone wall with bits of broken bottles set into the top. One section had no bottles. Instead razor wire gleamed in the sunlight. We were seeing the house from the rear.

"They must have magnificent views," Meg said.

At the gate Nicolae spoke into the intercom. The gate swung open. Then the driver carefully drove the flatbed truck into the yard. We had parked our car outside the walled yard beside Nicolae's van. We watched the crane operator drive inside, the boom tearing a limb off a pine tree and bringing down a shower of cones. The sharp scent of pine sap filled the air.

Nicolae had prepared a pedestal for the devil in the garden. Or what was going to be a garden. Evidence of construction was everywhere: piles of stone, plastic irrigation pipe, plants with their roots wrapped in burlap.

As the crane operator prepared to lift the devil again, we investigated the house. In an open window we saw the back of a computer. But all the other shutters were closed. By a pine tree there were two dog houses and empty water and food bowls. By the size of the chains it looked as if the dogs were big or enormously strong.

"Rottweilers?" Meg asked.

"Maybe, or pit bulls," I said.

We had hoped for worshippers in hooded robes who would gather around the sculpture and sing chants.

"At least someone could come out and say the Lord's Prayer backwards," I said.

"They may wait until it's installed," she said. "They'll do it at midnight."

Now the devil was dangling in the air from the crane. Nicolae and Bata guided the steel rods set in the base of the sculpture into the holes prepared for them in the concrete pedestal. Everything went smoothly. Soon the devil stood gazing toward the house.

Nicolae mounted a ladder with an electric cutter in his hand. He cut off the broken hook and began to grind down the jagged edges. Sparks flew everywhere. He never wore goggles or a mask when he used electric tools on marble. He would end up covered from head to foot with the fine white dust. He had had problems with his lungs, but he still refused to wear a mask.

"I've got to pee," Meg said.

"Go knock on the door," I said.

"I'm not going in that house. Those bushes over there will do fine."

She went off into the tall bushes which grew at the windowless end of the house.

Nicolae and the Devil

Bata mixed mortar. He handed up a plastic bucket of it to Nicolae along with a piece of stone to cover the place where the hook had been set. Nicolae tapped the stone into place with the handle of the trowel.

Meg returned.

"They have the most marvelous garden," she said.

At that moment a young woman came out of the house. Her head was shaved and she wore a white cotton dress that left her arms bare. Her skin was milky white. When she drew closer, we saw that she had a devil's head tattooed on one arm. It was a conventional devil done in blue and red and black ink. She walked straight past us without even acknowledging our existence and went up to Nicolae.

"She's beautiful," Meg said. "She could be a model."

We tried to eavesdrop on their conversation, but they were not speaking French.

"She's Romanian," Meg said. "I wonder if he knew that she was here."

Bata joined us.

"Who would have thought there would be a Romanian girl in this place," he said.

The woman, whose name was Anna, invited us into the garden. It was filled with flowers, mostly roses. The sweet scent from them was everywhere. We sat under an awning and looked off into the valley below. Far to the west we could see the big mountains rising up in row after row into Spain. Anna brought us bottles of the local sparkling wine, Blanquette de Limoux. We ate sausages and bread and drank the cold wine.

Nicolae spent all his time talking with Anna. We talked with Bata. Anna returned to the house for more blanquette.

"Tomorrow she will come to my atelier," Nicolae said.

That was all he would tell us. He laughed at our questions about her.

Anna visited Nicolae's atelier. We speculated about whether she would fall in love with him.

"I wonder if the cult allows its members to fall in love?" I said.

We were having dinner on our balcony. It was a hot night. Moths the size of hummingbirds circled the candleflames.

"She's going to fall in love with him," Meg said. "Whether they allow it or not."

We had heard conflicting rumors about the cult. Some said they were altruistic, devoting themselves to the care of dying AIDS patients. Others took a darker view. There was talk of animals being sacrificed and of orgies at the house. Supposedly the cult was under investigation by the French police. Nicolae would tell us nothing.

"Anna is my friend," he said. "She does not wish me to talk about the cult."

Then Nicolae's work underwent a change. He began making sculptures of Anna in the classical mode. They were technically perfect, but that was all they were, perfect. No one's imagination had played on the material. The figures might as well have been stamped out with a machine.

"He's fallen in love with her," Meg said.

"Infatuated perhaps," I said. "But not in love."

"Are you blind?"

"A few statues doesn't mean anything."

"Love is what they mean. And she's destroying his work."

"Do you think she means to destroy it? Do you think she knows what she's doing? How bad they are?"

"Oh, she knows. She knows."

"Now you're just like the people who believe they have orgies up there."

"I wouldn't be worried if it were orgies. Or a few dead chickens."

"What can we do?"

"Nothing."

"Just watch."

"Yes, watch."

So we watched. Anna spent more and more time at Nicolae's atelier.

She had begun to grow her hair. It came out red. At the end of the summer we saw them in Carcassonne. They were walking down the street with their arms entwined about each other.

"She's in love too," Meg said.

"Then why would she destroy his work?" I asked. "On orders from the cult?"

"Oh, she's not doing that. I never meant it was that. She knows but she can't help herself. She's like Narcissus. How could she not resist letting him make her image, over and over?"

Meg watched them until they disappeared around a corner.

"I imagine that he knows now," she said. "That he's in love."

"And that she's destroying his work?"

"Maybe even that. And he doesn't care."

"I wonder if she still lives with the cult?"

"Bata says she does. I don't think she'll be there much longer."

Then we learned that Anna was in the hospital in Carcassonne. She had slit her wrists. At Nicolae's atelier. When Nicolae discovered her, she was smearing her own blood over one of the statues he had made of her. She was going to be all right, Bata said. This very day Nicolae was bringing her to stay at his house until she recovered.

We left to return to America soon after that. At Christmas we received a card from Nicolae. It had a picture of one of the Anna sculptures on it. He wrote that she was well.

"I wonder if he will marry her?" Meg said.

"It won't be in a church," I said. "Not with that tattoo. Everyone in the region knows about her. But they could go to Paris. They could go anywhere they want."

In May we returned to France for another summer. Nicolae invited us to dinner. Anna's hair had grown into a shining red mane. She was just as beautiful as the first time we had seen her but in a different way. She and

Nicolae seemed to be very much in love.

From Bata, who was also a guest, we learned that she now lived in Nicolae's house. Bata did not think she had gone back to the house above Limoux after her suicide attempt.

"She is bad for his art," he said. "Nothing but Annas everywhere. All in the style of the Renaissance. A waste of a great talent."

The next day, when at Nicolae's invitation we visited his atelier, we were shocked even though we had been prepared by Bata. The atelier was filled with Annas. They spilled out into the yard. A circle of them, speckled with bird droppings, stood where the devil had fallen from the crane. It looked as if he had been working day and night on them since we left.

And Anna moved among them with her shining hair. I thought that for her it must be like she was walking in a hall of mirrors. Her skin was as white as the marble, the only defects the tattoo of the devil on her left arm and the scars from her suicide attempt. She did not try to conceal either of them.

"It's grotesque," Meg said.

We were driving back to our house.

"They're not selling," I said. "Bata says that since the devil he's sold almost nothing. He won't even show the old pieces."

"He's got to get clear of her."

"He can't."

"Yes, he's in love."

Bata told us that he had persuaded Nicolae to hold a local exhibition of his old work. A gallery owner in Toulouse had come up with the idea of having the exhibition at one of the Cathar chateaux.

"Perypetuse," Bata said. "They will have to take the pieces up by helicopter. No one with heart trouble will be able to come. It is crazy. Everything he has done since he met that girl has been crazy."

Perypetuse was a Cathar chateau off the road to Perpignan. It was built atop a mountain at such a height and in a position so strong, the

Nicolae and the Devil

approaches so precipitous, that no one had ever mounted an attack on it. Even the climb from the parking lot to the chateau was formidable. It was not a place to go for anyone frightened of heights.

We planned to go the second day. We were sitting on the balcony after dinner, drinking the last of a bottle of wine. Meg had just struck a match to light the candles when we heard Bata call up to us.

"Come to report on the sales," I said.

She looked over the edge of the balcony.

"I don't think so," she said. "Something's wrong."

We heard Bata coming up the three flights of stairs at a run. He burst onto the balcony.

"She killed him!" Bata announced.

Then he began to cry. We put the wine away and got out a bottle of whiskey. We all had a drink and sat there huddled in the darkness waiting for Bata to tell us what happened.

Finally he began. The exhibition had gone well. The work on the Annas had created a sort of thirst for the old pieces. But that was all we got out of him. Bata was unable even to start the real story. He sat in silence and drank. We sat in the darkness and waited. I think we both knew he was so fragile that if we pushed him we might hear nothing at all.

When I filled his empty glass, he started to talk.

"I knew something was wrong," Bata said. "She walked up and down among his pieces, those beautiful things. I could tell she wanted the room filled with herself as he had filled his atelier."

I could imagine her walking amid those pieces with her white skin and that shining hair. Nicolae would be dressed in black boots, black pants, a wide belt and a sheepskin coat and hat. It was his Romanian peasant's outfit. He wore some version of it to all of his exhibitions.

"She picked up one of the pieces, that head I liked so well, and smashed it against the wall," Bata said.

Then he paused. We could not see his face as he talked. He had pushed his chair back into a dark corner.

"Bata?" Meg said.

"Do you have ice for this whiskey?" Bata asked. "Americans always have ice."

"No," I said.

"Warm whiskey on such a hot night," he said.

"Please tell us," Meg said.

She had taken my hand in hers and was squeezing it hard.

"She ran out of the room and onto the battlements," Bata said.

Then he told us how they all followed and found her standing on the wall with a drop of a thousand feet beneath her feet.

"She jumped," Bata said. "It was as if she intended to fly. I would not have been surprised if instead of falling she had swooped over our heads. Flew like a falcon. She kept her arms spread all the way to the bottom. But she never flew. Then Nicolae went over the side after her. He did not try to fly. He knew better. He knew exactly what he was after."

"Why?" I asked.

"He was teaching her to carve marble," Bata said. "They made many of the Annas together. I think that in the end she made them better than Nicolae. She had a talent for such things."

"He was in love with her," Meg mused.

"Love," Bata said. He stood up and spat over the balcony. "What he had, what she had, was not love. It was something else. If that is love then there is no love. Only everyone caught within themselves. Tomorrow I will go to his atelier and smash those Annas."

Bata never smashed the Annas. They are stored in one of the rooms at The Forge. The other artists use them when they are in need of a piece of white marble, transmuting them into other things, usually of poor quality. Bata left and went to live elsewhere. From time to time we would see a notice of one of his exhibitions, but then over the years we lost track of him.

Every summer we return to our house. We both like the idea of growing old together, of loving each other long and completely. As long as we can climb the stairs we will return.

    Sometimes, as we sit together on our balcony on one of those soft summer nights, we find ourselves silent. Often we are both thinking of Nicolae and Anna. We have talked of them over the years, how our love is different. How lucky we are that it is different. But at those times, those dark nights on the balcony after the candles have almost burned out and we are sitting there, sometimes holding hands and sometimes not, I think we both feel that some huge moth has blundered into the light and has brushed our faces with its powdered wings before disappearing into the darkness.

Fishing on Sunday

When I was a boy, I lived with my mother in a trailer on the banks of the Black Warrior River. My father was dead, killed one night when, drunk, he drove his truck into an eighteen-wheeler out on the Birmingham highway. My mother cut up chickens for a living, standing before a never-ending stream of carcasses moving toward her on an overhead belt. She was constantly having trouble with infections from the minor cuts that resulted from her work. One of my clearest memories of that time is of her standing at the kitchen sink and looking at her hands and crying. She never complained about the work, but she was vain about her hands.

At the beginning of my freshman year in high school, Raymond Smart came to live with us. My mother had had men friends before. Some came to pick her up at the trailer, but more often she met them in Birmingham to go dancing at one of the clubs there. Sometimes she stayed over on Saturday night, leaving me with one of my cousins, but she always came home on Sunday morning to take me to church.

I can recall the day when I realized those men were her lovers, that she had spent the night in some man's arms. I don't think I was jealous or even shocked, just curious as I watched her dress before going off to meet one of them, making herself pretty in front of her bedroom mirror. At the time I had begun to try to imagine, as I lay in my bed and held myself in my hand, what it would be like to make love to a girl.

Raymond moved in, maybe a year after I began to think seriously

Fishing on Sunday

about girls. He worked at the trailer plant. From him I learned that the workers called the trailers they made "coaches." They liked to pretend they were making those silver Airstream trailers, real trailers that you could pull behind a car and drive right out of Alabama to a place like Montana. Sometimes he talked about buying one and driving up to Canada, maybe even Alaska, to fish. That was his dream. He'd sit in front of the TV and watch those fishing shows with the same enthusiasm that my crippled grandmother watched television evangelists. He had a bass boat he was making payments on. He liked to fish at night, and he did that three or four nights a week, coming home at daybreak to eat breakfast with my mother. He said he was after a million dollar bass, a world record that would bring the fisherman who caught it endorsements from tackle manufacturers. I don't know if that was true, but Raymond believed it.

I think Raymond wanted to marry my mother, but she wasn't interested in marrying again. I can imagine him pressing her on the subject in that insistent quiet way of his. I never heard him raise his voice to her, and he certainly never did to me. He was a gentle man, who often massaged my mother's feet after she came home from her work. She'd sigh in a way that at the time embarrassed me. He suited me because I was quiet like him.

Raymond often would look at me and say things like, "Still waters run deep." I can picture him saying that, sitting on the couch massaging my mother's feet, himself barefoot and shirtless, because of the summer heat, his lean but muscular chest, like the chest of a fighter, just as smooth and hairless as mine. He claimed his Cherokee blood was the reason. And maybe he was telling the truth, because his face did have an Indian look to it.

Then Raymond got fired from the trailer plant. He said it was because of a faulty alternator in his truck which made him late for work. He was unable to find another job. The boat dealer repossessed the bass boat. Raymond was friendly with the man who came to get it. They stood around and smoked cigarettes and drank a beer together. Then Raymond helped him put the boat on the hitch. I watched them from my bedroom window.

I was lying on my bed reading *The Red Badge of Courage* for my English class.

Raymond watched them drive off with the boat. Then, walking with his head down, he came back to the trailer. I heard him fooling around in the living room for a time. Finally he wandered back to my bedroom. He usually was careful not to disturb me when I was doing my schoolwork. He stuck his head around the corner of the doorway.

"You reading?" he asked.

"That's right," I said.

He came into the room and stood by my bed.

"You could read that to me but that'd take a long time. I ain't got that much time. You're a smart one all right. Still waters run deep."

My teachers thought I was smart, sure to be class valedictorian, and that would win me a scholarship to the University at Tuscaloosa. Raymond was excited about that because he was a devoted football fan. I might be a source for fifty-yard line tickets.

I did wonder about his complaining that he had no time to read. To me it appeared that he had nothing but time. He'd lie around the trailer all day smoking the cigarettes my mother had bought him and watching television. There was not even any work to do in the garden. It was early September and only a few tomato vines were left. Raymond and I had not been good about working it. A nice stand of Johnson grass had sprung up where the squash was supposed to be. It appeared to me that he had given up looking for a job, although just before the evening meal, which my mother cooked after she came home from work, he'd make a great show of going through the classified ads in the Birmingham paper. Then he might complain about the fact that the steel industry was mostly gone from Birmingham, that once a man could make good wages there.

One Friday night, just after Raymond had said the blessing over the pork chops, he started in on those vanished steel mill jobs. I could tell it was something my mother did not want to hear, and I tried to catch Raymond's eye, but it was too late. He was caught up in his lament over

Fishing on Sunday

those cold furnaces, enamored with the sound of his own voice. He was not looking at either one of us as he finished his speech, delivering the last words in the direction of the screen door, through which we could see the empty space where the bass boat had once been parked.

He looked up to my mother for sympathy like he always did, but instead was met with the sight of her holding out her hands toward him. It had not been a good day for her. There were bandages on three of the fingers of her left hand.

"My hands are ruined," she said.

"Why they ain't," he said. "The hands of a nymph is what they are."

He smiled at her, pleased with himself. We'd been studying Greek mythology in school and Raymond had got stuck on those nymphs. I think he imagined them as table dancers in a Birmingham bar. She did hesitate for a moment, temporarily rendered speechless, hearing that word come out of his mouth. But it was too late for sweet talk.

"I'm ruining my hands so you can sit here and watch TV and smoke cigarettes," she said.

"I've been looking," he said.

"Ha, you haven't half tried."

"It's tight in the trailer business."

"Do something else. Work at McDonald's."

"Nobody knows coaches like I do."

"What are you saying? That you've got a skill?"

"Nobody ever complained about my work."

"You never made coaches. You made trailers. Just like this one. That start to fall apart soon as folks move in."

She looked up at where the ceiling sagged.

"I wonder how many studs somebody like you left out of this one. The first time a tornado comes by here it'll fall right down."

Raymond had told us how they often cheated on the construction and slipped inferior work past the inspectors.

"Building trailers is no different from cutting up chickens," she said.

"It don't take a college degree to do it."

Now my mother had begun to cry. Raymond got up and tried to comfort her, but she pushed him away. She retreated to the bedroom. We sat at the table and tried to eat, but neither one of us had an appetite. We cleared the table and washed the dishes. Then we watched TV until it cooled off enough to sleep. When I went to bed, Raymond had all the lights turned off. Bathed in the bluish glow from the screen, he was watching a fishing show.

I woke early and found Raymond asleep on the couch. My mother's car was gone. She had left a note on the refrigerator. She had gone with her sister to a flea market at the town of Warrior.

I spent the morning reading while Raymond watched TV. When it got too hot to stay inside, we both went out and sat in a couple of easy chairs under a big sweet gum. Raymond had bought the chairs at a yard sale along with a plastic tarp, which he threw over them when it rained. But the chairs had been left uncovered a few times during storms and now always smelled musty.

"Nothing like a sweet gum for shade," Raymond said.

"Yes," I said, "nothing like it."

Raymond always said that about the tree. He was a man who reduced all of life to a few favorite phrases.

"Your mama is a good woman," he said.

"Yes, she is," I said.

I took up my book and began to read. I hoped he would not start in on "still waters run deep," but he was silent, reflective in a way that I had seldom seen him. He looked up into the thick, green canopy of star-shaped leaves as if he was waiting for some sort of mystery to be revealed to him. Then the phone rang.

Raymond got up, moving faster than I was used to seeing him move, and ran for the trailer. I guessed it was my mother. I imagined him standing in the kitchen, which by this time of day was like one of those steel plant furnaces, and saying sweet things to her. He was inside so long that

Fishing on Sunday

I had returned to my book. Suddenly he was there standing over me.

"We'll be fixing our own supper," he said.

We made hamburgers out on the grill and ate them under the sweet gum. Raymond drank a few beers. He offered me one, and I accepted. It wasn't my first. I thought I would miss my mother not being there but I didn't. I liked being alone with Raymond, who was treating me like a man. We sat under the tree where it was already dark, although in the open you could still read a newspaper, and drank the last of the beer. It had taken me a long time to finish just one, but Raymond had gone through a six pack. He didn't appear drunk.

"She's not coming back tonight," Raymond said.

"We'll see her in church tomorrow," I said.

"We ain't going to church."

"Mr. Wade is getting baptized. Don't you want to see that?"

Marion Wade had spent his youth making money in the strip mining business. He drank and chased women and treated his childless wife badly. People liked to say that strip mining was the right business for him, that he was digging his way right down to Hell and that one day the Devil would rise up out of the bottom of one of those coal pits and snatch him away. Now he was saved and as was the custom at our church he was going to be baptized in the river right after the morning service.

Raymond explained that we would fish the section of the river above the low-water bridge where baptisms were held. We could watch the ceremony from a platform built high in the branches of a big poplar, which grew on the banks of the river just above the bridge. The platform was used as a launching pad for a tree swing. Someone had fastened a cable high in the branches of the tree. You could swing out over the pool and then drop into the water. I had spent many summer afternoons there. No one would be using the swing, because if you tried that now, you'd be likely to hit a rock and break both your legs. The water was that low.

"We don't have a boat," I said. "And if we did the river's too low to float one."

"Billy Clay said I could borrow his canoe," Raymond said. "We'll walk it down the shoals, ride it in the deep places."

"It'll be too hot to fish. They'll be lying down at the bottom of the pools. Maybe we could do it at night. That's when they're feeding."

I knew that the fish would be easy to find. They'd be hemmed up in a few of the big pools.

"I got a way to get'em," he said.

Sometimes people used seines. Hand generators were common. People who used them said they were placing a long distance call to the fish, which stunned by the charge flopped about on the surface. And occasionally some total outlaws used malathion or whatever poison was handy.

"We're gonna gig'em," he said.

What Raymond had in mind was a five-tined frog gig attached to a basswood pole. We spent the rest of the evening making the gigs. We cut long inch-wide strips of rubber from an old inner tube and attached them to the butt of the poles. At the ends of the strips we tied loops, which went over our wrists. We practiced on a cardboard box and the system worked beautifully. The rubber cushioned the shock against our wrists when the gig reached the end of its tether. And you could quickly retrieve it and make another throw.

I went to sleep dreaming of spearing fish in the river. I don't think Raymond slept at all. I woke up a couple of times during the night and heard the sound of the TV. When he woke me it was still dark. I could smell the breakfast he had made. We ate quickly and then drove the truck to Billy Clay's barn where the canoe was stored. It was an aluminum canoe made to look like an Indian birchbark, the kind I sometimes saw on TV in old movies. The ends were raised, and there was the silhouette of an Indian chief in a war bonnet painted on the bow. We put it in the bed of the truck and headed for the river.

We crossed the bridge just as the sun was coming up. The water, covered with patches of mist, was low. All the rocks at the shoals were exposed, piles of open mussel shells, their white insides brilliant in the sunlight, scattered here and there. The mussels had been fished out of the shallows by raccoons.

We drove down a rutted dirt track to the river and unloaded the canoe. We had brought two ice chests, one for the fish and one for beer and soft drinks. With me at the stern and Raymond at the bow we walked the canoe out into the river. The rocks were slippery. We both stumbled as we wrestled with the heavy canoe, the metal grating against the rocks. It was slow going, but we finally reached the first pool. That's what the river was, a series of deep pools separated by shoals. It probably dropped four or five feet a mile between where we were and the low water bridge.

"Just big fish, boy," Raymond said. "Nothing but bass and catfish. Others'll be too small or full of bones."

Bass, gar, bream, carp, and catfish all lived in the river.

The pool was perfectly clear. We were wearing pairs of Raymond's polarized fishing glasses, which allowed us to see right through the glare of the sun off the water. The moment I put my foot into the pool, the water warm as a bath, I saw a fish dart away. Raymond told me to spread out.

"We'll hem'em up at the foot of the pool," he said.

Fifty yards away there was, I knew, a three-foot drop. But no water was flowing over it now. Raymond had tied the painter around his waist and pulled the canoe along after him. We moved slowly, our spears held high, watching the water like a couple of wading birds.

I speared the first fish, a bass of three pounds. The vibration from the fish's struggles shot right up the spear shaft and into my hands, its weight bending the shaft as I lifted it out of the water. It quivered on the tines in a way that let me see into the heart of it. It was different from catching one with a pole.

Raymond whooped.

"That's it, boy!" he shouted.

Then he speared one, and I speared another. It was easy. The water was clear as out of the tap at the trailer and shallow. There was no place for the fish to hide. And they had been made sluggish by a combination of the heat and the lack of oxygen in the water. We put our catches in the big ice chest, where they flopped around and banged against the sides for a while.

"We're gonna have us a big fish fry," Raymond said.

We fished out the pool. Raymond drank a beer to celebrate, and I drank a Coke. Then we slid the canoe down over the rocks to the next pool.

"Ain't this a beautiful river," Raymond said.

I agreed that it was and looked forward to hearing that from him the rest of the morning, which is exactly what happened.

The fishing was even better in the second pool. Raymond speared a bass of at least seven pounds, a very large fish for the small river. I speared a big catfish, which finned me badly in the left hand when I tried to take it off the gig. I bathed the wound in a patch of swift water in the shoal below the pool and my hand felt better. Raymond drank another beer while I did it.

"I reckon your mama is getting ready for church about now," he said.

"And Mr. Wade is getting ready to be baptized," I said.

I didn't want to talk about my mother. I hadn't thought of her a single time since I started fishing. I wondered if Raymond had had her on his mind the whole time.

The next shoal was at least a mile long. We followed the main course of the water through it, trying to float the canoe whenever possible. The sun was well above the trees now, and it was hot. A breeze brought us the stench of somebody's hog lot. Today they'd be hosing down those hogs to keep them from dying of heat and walking chickens in the chicken houses to keep the same thing from happening to them. Raymond liked to tell the story of a bird dog he once had that got into a chicken house and killed every chicken in it. From then on the dog was interested only in chickens, no good at all for quail.

In the next pool the fish were concentrated in an area of cool water, a place where a deep spring bubbled up out of the limestone. When I walked into it, the water waist deep, the change in temperature came as a pleasant shock. I speared a bass almost as big as Raymond's seven pounder. We hung on the edges of the pool and waited for a fish to swim by. It was easy. After we'd filled the ice chest to the top with fish, Raymond took the beer and Cokes out of the second ice chest.

We returned to the pool. It seemed as if there was a supply of fish in it that would never be depleted. We whooped in delight as we speared them and taunted each other when one of us made a bad throw. I was wild with joy. I wanted that feeling of a fish quivering on the tines to go on forever. Finally, just as we filled the second chest, only a few small bass and catfish swam in range of our spears.

We pulled the canoe over into a patch of shade. Raymond drank his last beer, and I drank another Coke.

"They're probably starting for the river," Raymond said.

I looked downriver. There was a half mile of shoals and then the big pool and tree swing. When I turned back to Raymond, I saw that he was crying. I looked away, knowing he'd be ashamed if I saw him. I'd been taught not to cry, and I knew he'd learned the same thing. So I looked back down river, that long avenue of shoals, which was rocks, clumps of river grass, and bright spots of water between green walls of trees.

"I reckon I'll be living someplace else right soon," Raymond said.

I turned back to look at him. He was adjusting the loop of the rubber strip around his wrist. The rubber had put a black mark around his wrist and rubbed the skin raw just as it had mine.

"She won't stay mad for long," I said.

She'd gotten angry at him before over his staying out fishing for bass all night long.

"It's not a matter of her being mad," he said. "Women ain't like men."

He waded out into the pool. He stood motionless, like some great extinct wading bird. His arm moved forward and the spear darted into the water. He pulled in a gar, one of those long thin fish with a mouth full of needle-like teeth. He walked to the bank and put his foot on it and pulled out the gig, leaving the gar to flop about on the hot rocks. He took up a position in the pool again, this time spearing a carp, which he shook off the gig and left floating belly up in the pool.

"Come out here, boy," he said

I took up my spear. There was nothing in the world for me but those fish, especially the gar, which looked liked they'd swum right out of some dinosaur-filled swamp. I didn't feel the heat or worry about how that rubber strap was taking the rest of the skin off my wrist. I was just as excited as before, but my excitement was of a different kind. When I had one of those big gars on the tines it was like I had crawled along a narrow passage into the heart of a pyramid and had opened some pharaoh's sealed tomb, standing astonished at the glitter of all that gold. For I don't know how long we speared those trash fish, eaten only by the desperately poor.

We did not stop until we had speared all the fish in the pool. For a time we stood there silently, both of us looking down into that perfectly clear water in which nothing moved except schools of minnows and a few bream too small to be worth spearing. I felt both elated and frightened, still so excited that the spear shook in my hand.

"We got every damn one of them," Raymond said.

He said it without heat, coldly, with an absolutely flat and inflectionless voice.

I looked across the pool. Now I felt sad. I wished I had not speared a single fish I did not intend to eat or watch somebody else eat.

We left the pool and sat sweating in the shade. We shared the last can of warm Coke, which tasted and smelled of fish. The surface of the pool was littered with dead fish, which soon would swell and rot in the heat. I looked up, expecting to see vultures circling, but the sky was perfectly clear, not a single cloud or vapor trail to mar that expanse of blue.

"Let's go see Marion Wade get himself baptized," Raymond said. He paused and looked out over the pool. "This sure is a beautiful river."

I gazed out over the pool and tried to think of something to say, but I could think of nothing. The pool was perfectly calm, shining in the sun like a polished piece of metal.

"Yeah, this sure is a beautiful river," Raymond said again.

He looked at me, as if he were expecting me to agree.

"We better hurry up or we're gonna miss the baptism," I said.

We walked the canoe down through that long shoal and arrived at the tree swing pool. From time to time Raymond had checked on the fish. Some ice was left, but not much, and he was worried about them going bad. He kept talking about the big fish fry he was going to have, how my mother would make hushpuppies and cole slaw and we'd invite all our kin.

We beached the canoe in the shade and climbed the ladder to the platform. No one was at the low water bridge yet, which we had a good view of through a screen of branches. Then we heard the sound of tires on the gravel.

"It's them," Raymond said. "I wonder if Marion'll change his mind."

"Would he do that?" I asked.

"You can never tell about Marion," Raymond said.

I thought about Marion being cleansed of his sins in the same river where we'd fished. It wasn't just that we had broken the law. It wasn't that at all. And nobody would care if we killed every carp and gar in the river. It was something else, but I couldn't put a name on it.

"What happened back there?" I asked.

"Where?" he asked.

"At the pool. Where we speared all those fish."

"We killed some fish. That's all."

I could tell that he didn't know, that it was something he didn't understand. And I didn't expect him to understand, but it seemed to me that I should be able to. I could also see that not understanding didn't bother him. He could kill every fish in that pool every day of his life.

"Look at'em," he said.

I peered through the screen of branches and saw Marion Wade dressed in a white robe being led by the preacher and the deacons down to the water. A big crowd was watching, brought out by the conversion of such a great sinner. I saw my mother, wearing a blue dress, standing on the low-water bridge.

"I wonder if that old bastard has got cancer," Raymond said. "I wonder if he knows he's going to die soon. Hedging his bets."

We watched the baptism. It seemed to me that the preacher held Marion Wade under an extra long time, as if he wasn't sure that the baptism would take unless he did it that way. Marion Wade came up sputtering and gasping for air. Everyone hugged each other and the crowd began to sing a hymn, the sound drifting up through the trees to us. The sound of the singing made me feel good.

In the end the baptizing turned out to be a waste of time, because Marion went right back to drinking and seeing those women in Birmingham. Just before Christmas one of his women shot him and then set his Cadillac on fire with him in it to cover up the crime.

Then the singing stopped. We watched them climb out of the river.

"Boy, you go run down through the woods," Raymond said. "Get your mama to wait for us. We can't afford to take the time to walk back to the truck. These fish'll spoil in this heat. I'll bring the canoe down when they all clear out."

I went off to do as he asked. I slipped out of the bushes, where I had been hiding so the preacher and deacons wouldn't see me and learn I had been fishing on Sunday, just as my mother was getting into her car with her sister. She didn't get mad. Later I knew that was because she'd already made up her mind about Raymond. She made a fuss over the cut on my hand, and I tried to pretend that it didn't hurt at all although it did. It ending up getting badly infected. I still bear the scar.

We hung around and waited for Raymond to show up with the canoe. As soon as the last car left he appeared, paddling the boat up that long pool from the tree swing.

"We got every damn fish in this river!" he shouted.

My mother and her sister laughed, and I did too. I'd never seen Raymond so excited.

Raymond did throw a big fish fry. But he never did get a job, and one day I came home to find him gone and my mother crying. He'd gone to Louisiana to work in the offshore oil fields.

I ended up graduating second in my class, beaten out by a girl from Warrior. So I got a job in the trailer plant. I could save enough money there in a year to allow me to start college.

The men at the plant often spoke of Raymond. His ability to find clever ways of fooling the inspectors had made him famous. It was said that in a week Raymond could leave enough two by fours out of a series of trailers to frame a new one.

My mother never spoke of him. She had begun to study for the GED exam. There was a course she took at night at the community college. On those nights when she wasn't in class and on weekends both of us spent our time reading. She was good at math problems but not so good at reading and I helped her as much as I could. I didn't think that she had much chance of passing on the first try. She talked about finding a better job in Birmingham after she got her degree, how her hands would heal and they'd be beautiful again.

One April night, the day after she had finally passed the GED on the third try, we were celebrating by eating steaks. We sat out under the sweet gum tree.

"I suppose that Raymond has moved on from Louisiana," she said.

That was the first time she had mentioned his name since he left. It had been more than a year. There was no new man in her life as far as I knew. I was dating Tanya Littlejohn, who was a year behind me in school. She was eager to get married after graduation. I was not so sure. I was not so sure about anything. If I married her then I would have to work at the trailer plant for at least another year before I went to the university.

"I reckon he has," I said. "But he might stay a long time. The fishing's good off those rigs."

"I'm fixing to get me that telephone operator job," she said.

She was going to Birmingham to apply for the job, had been talking about it for weeks.

My mother looked at her hands.

"Raymond was always good to me about my hands," she said. "He said they didn't bother him at all."

I thought of plunging my gig into one of those long silvery gar and then feeling the weight of it on the shaft. I remembered Raymond laughing.

My mother threw her head back and looked up at the sweet gum.

"Raymond always said this tree makes the best shade," she said.

As she continued to talk about Raymond, I realized he had meant much more to her than I had imagined. I hoped she would get that telephone operator job, that she would meet some man in Birmingham who would treat her well.

I considered how difficult the next few months were going to be for me. I thought I was in love with Tanya. She was pressing me to stay at the plant and attend the community college. She said that going down to the university would make her nervous. If I stayed in the hills, I could see us living in a doublewide. Our children would be baptized in the river. I wished I knew exactly what I should do.

My mother had stopped talking about Raymond, but I couldn't stop thinking about him way down in Louisiana out on one of those drilling platforms. Sometimes I considered going down there and getting a job myself, maybe on the same rig with him. There I would make much more than working at the trailer plant. After six months or a year, I could come back and marry Tanya Littlejohn. We could go to the university, escape from life in the hills. No child of ours would ever be baptized in that deep, still pool above the low water bridge.

I wondered if Raymond would be glad to see me. Life there was easy to picture in my mind. We would fish off that platform, for fish liked to school around the steel legs. No trash fish this time. Eating fish. Dolphins. We would catch one rainbow colored dolphin after another, the fish irides-

Fishing on Sunday

cent, shimmering in the light. We would pull them in until our arms were tired.

But I never went to Louisiana. Instead I got a job in the trailer plant and worked there for a year, but I did not marry Tanya Littlejohn. There was this basketball player she had been serious about once. One day in July, just before I was getting ready to leave for the university, she told me she was going to marry him. I was relieved but did not tell her so. I think she knew it anyway. We shook hands.

Things at the university went well for me. My second year I got a scholarship so there was no need to return home to work in the trailer plant in the summers. I never heard anything from anyone about Raymond. My mother never spoke of him, and I never asked. Then in the fall of my senior year I saw him at a football game during halftime.

He looked just the same as he came up the steps. I wondered how he had managed to get a seat that close to the field. A woman was on his arm and they were laughing at something Raymond had just said. I got out of my seat and went up to him. He seemed glad to see me and introduced me to the woman, who spoke with a Mississippi accent.

"You come down for the game?" he asked.

"I go to school here now," I said. "How was Louisiana?"

"I never made it there," he said. "Would've been good fishing off them platforms. I work for a company that digs tunnels."

He went on to explain about it, how his job was to help with the shoring up. How they were based in Birmingham but traveled all over the southeast. I tried to imagine that, Raymond down in some tunnel with a light on his hard hat, wrestling with a piece of timber. I supposed that might be a dangerous line of work, but I did not ask him if it was.

"You're putting'em in instead of taking'em out," I said.

He laughed.

"Well, I was thrifty with them studs," he said.

The band was marching off and the team was coming back on the field and the woman tugged at his arm. He had found himself a real Alabama fan.

"You tell your mother I'm fine," he said.

"I will," I said, knowing I was not going to mention our meeting at all.

"I should've gone to Louisiana," he said. "Fished off them platforms."

"You'll get there," I said.

He rested his hand on my shoulder for a moment, smiled, and then was gone. I watched them until they took their seats and merged with the crowd. How he had gotten fifty yard line seats I'll never know.

I sat down and thought about that day on the river, the feel of a quivering fish on my spear. I got all tight inside as I considered the rest of it: my mother, Tanya Littlejohn, the trailer plant. Then I realized the crowd was on its feet, everyone cheering. I stood up with them and yelled too, joining Raymond, the Mississippi woman, the whole stadium, my body loose and easy, the whole of my life spread out before me like an endless open plain.

Walking to Carcassonne

Richard Purvis was walking over the Pyrenees from Spain just as his father had more than fifty years before as a young lieutenant in the company of a band of Spanish guerrillas. He supposed his father had traveled mostly at night. He and the *guerrileros Espanols* joined forces with the French maquis to mount an operation against the Germans. It was June. German troops could not be sent to Normandy if they were being pressed in southwest France.

It was cold in the mountains. He had put on a sweater under his parka as he stood on the highway and watched the little train of the Pyrenees, *le petit train jaune,* cross the road on the narrow gauge tracks and then go clattering away along the mountainside whose immensity quickly turned it into a toy train.

A few days later he walked past a lake, the source of the river beside which his father had died. His father had been leading the rearguard of the band that had ambushed a German convoy. As his band was taking captured war materiel to their base in a nearby town, they had been ambushed themselves. But because of his father, who had held the road against the Germans with two other men, the maquis had escaped.

He ate his lunch of bread and cheese beside the river, here only a tiny rivulet, scarcely big enough for trout. Treeless pasture stretched away in all directions; cowbells clanked in the distance. Off across the high valley was a ski hotel built at the base of a network of runs cut across the face of the mountain.

Richard the Lion Hearted.

He had discovered that dedication in a Conrad novel a cousin had given his father on his birthday. It was a sentiment that seemed to him to have come straight out of Walter Scott. The same sort of thinking had caused his great-grandfather, a cavalry commander, whose photograph was on the wall of his uncle's house in Savannah, to initiate charges by speaking in a firm, clear voice to his men: "The gentlemen of the Effington Light horse will turn the corner."

So for Richard that was the mystery, what he could not understand, how anyone could be so free with his life. Nothing his father had done beside the river that day had any effect on the outcome of the war. Yet he and the two other men had held up the Germans, knowing that they would most likely die as a result. Richard had avoided service in Vietnam because he was the sole surviving son of a veteran killed in action. His cousins had all gone and two of them had been killed.

Richard had written to the office of tourism in a village close to where the action occurred and had received an account of it from a schoolteacher. The French had put up a marker commemorating the action. His mother, now dead, had kept a framed photograph of it in her bedroom. She had not remarried. There was no grave. The Germans had thrown the bodies into the river. Richard was to meet with the schoolteacher when he arrived. The teacher had written that he would be able to produce an eyewitness to the action.

Today for the first time his body felt really good under the weight of the pack. He had lost weight. He was becoming lean and hard. He lay on his back and watched a hawk turning in slow circles overhead. The hawk gave a shrill cry as its shadow passed over him and then disappeared behind a ridge.

He considered how he had failed at a series of businesses, including, in the end, his family's hardware store, which a cousin had taken over and saved from bankruptcy. There were the three failed marriages, the third gone with the store. Now he had made this trip on a small inheritance from one of his uncles. He had come to Spain to investigate importing cheap shotguns, a scheme that had the potential to make him a rich man. But instead of flying into Madrid where the company that manufactured the guns had its headquarters, he had flown into Barcelona. He had told himself that he should wait, not go to Madrid until he felt more optimism for the new venture. That was what he had always done after one of his businesses had failed, wait patiently until some new idea filled him with enthusiasm. But the failure of the hardware store had been different. There was something about it that laid a heavy hand on his desire to succeed.

He lay there a long time, watching a line of clouds form over the mountains to the east and waiting for the hawk to return, but it never did.

Over the next few days, he followed the river down out of the high mountains. Power plants had been built along its course, the water falling through giant tubes that came down the mountainsides from the high lakes. Fishermen were in the river after trout.

Then he walked down into a gorge where the river ran beside the highway. Now the fir trees were gone and the mountainsides had a dry Mediterranean look, covered with scrub oaks, pines, and aromatic shrubs. The hum of cicadas was in the air. This was the road his father had defended against the Germans. He looked at the map and estimated he was only thirty or forty kilometers away from that spot. And beyond that the river came out of the mountains and into the wide valley that held the ancient walled city of Carcassonne. After viewing the city he would take a train to Madrid and then fly home to Savannah. That night he went to sleep in a campground beside the river listening to French and Spanish voices and what he thought might be German.

His father had listened to those voices and had known what they were saying. That was one reason he had been sent to France. He had been at the state university when the war started, a French major, intending to go off to graduate school. He had hiked in the Pyrenees as a student.

At noon Richard walked into the schoolteacher's little village, which boasted of thermal baths, a brand new casino out on the road to Carcassonne, and a Roman church. He went to a café and ordered a beer, then called the schoolteacher, who gave him directions to a restaurant beside the river.

He walked past the Roman church and through an iron gate to the grounds of the combination restaurant and spa. He found Jean Camon, a young man in his twenties, seated at a green metal table under the shade of a huge tree. Richard had long ceased to wonder if his father had walked past a certain tree or had looked at a certain vista, but for some reason the thought of his father sitting at the green table under the tree appealed to him. The place looked old enough.

"I was wondering if my father ate here," Richard said.

"No, this place housed German officers," Jean said. "They loved the waters."

"Just like the Romans."

Jean laughed.

"Yes, they were famous for their love of baths."

"And the Germans?"

"They destroyed the Romans and would have destroyed us. What do you think you are going to find out there on the route to Carcassonne?"

"I don't know."

Jean looked a little younger than Richard's children from his first marriage.

Jean then explained that his grandfather fought at Dien Bien Phu. On Bastille Day he stood on the square of Jean's village wearing his medals. Jean wondered if his father would have returned to Vietnam if his grandfather had died there.

"I suppose the jungle has taken it back," Richard said.

"Yes, growing fast in a few months," Jean said.

A swan with five cygnets in her train walked past them across the grass and disappeared behind a boxwood hedge.

"He might not have wanted to go back there," Richard said. "He might not have needed to."

"And you have this need?" Jean asked.

"I walked over the Pyrenees."

"We will have lunch. Then I will take you to the place where your father was so brave."

"The eyewitness?"

"The old man lives in this village. He will be waiting for us. He would be here but his wife is sick. Her sister will care for her while we are gone."

"Something serious?"

"Yes, something that bathing forever in these waters cannot cure."

They had lunch. Fish soup, *confit de canard*, and *crème de Catalan*. They drank a bottle of the local heavy red wine. After they had coffee and Jean rolled himself a cigarette, Richard told this stranger about his three wives and the hardware store and his hopes to start an import business.

Then they were both silent. Jean was rolling another cigarette. Somewhere in the town an old man, probably one of the maquis, was waiting for someone to come care for his wife so he could explain to the American lieutenant's son exactly what happened one day beside the river. He felt annoyed with Jean. What did this boy know about anything? Just things he had learned out of books in school.

Jean looked at his watch.

"Let me smoke this one," he said. "Then it will be time to go to the old man's house."

They sat, not talking, while Jean finished the cigarette. Richard listened to the rush of the river that ran out of sight behind a stone wall and the hum of the cicadas. He paid the bill, despite Jean's protests. They walked along a stone walkway toward the iron gate.

"The old man is German," Jean said.

"What?" Richard said.

He was not sure that he had heard correctly.

"Yes, a German," Jean said. "He was a part of that action on the road.

He was in love with a French girl from this village. After the war he came back for her. The old man has a bad hip. How do you say? Ah, yes. Hip replacement."

"He came back for love?"

"Yes, love. We will go in my car to his house."

Richard did not think that he had ever really loved any of his wives, certainly not the way the German boy must have loved the French girl, abandoning his country for her.

The old man, dressed in the blue pants of a French workman, a sport coat, and heavy brogues, was standing at the door of his house. He was toothless and short with a mane of white hair. His eyes were blue. He carried a small canvas sack by a strap slung over his shoulder.

After introductions the old man got into the back seat and Jean drove them through the town and across a bridge over the river. Jean and the old man were engaged in conversation.

"We are talking about his wife," Jean said. "He thinks that she will die soon."

Jean turned the car onto the highway, which followed the river on their right. A set of train tracks ran on the other side of the river. Beyond the tracks the brush-covered mountainside rose almost straight up, and on the other side of the road there was an identical mountainside. He caught glimpses of white water now and then through the trees. The cicadas were loud in the brush; a dry, dusty scent mixed with the smell of the aromatic shrubs.

They crossed a bridge over the river and went under a railroad bridge. Then they drove past the stone foundations of what must have been the old railroad bridge. The old man turned in his seat and spoke to him, smiling as he did, his tongue protruding from his mouth as he formed the words without the help of teeth.

"He says your father's band blew up the bridge," Jean said.

The road twisted through the mountains, following the course of the river. Then Jean pulled the car off on the side of the road next to the river.

"The monument is around the bend," Jean said.

They all got out of the car. On the other side of the road was a sheer rock cliff where the roadway had been blasted out of the rock. Marks were on the rock where holes had been drilled for the charges. There was no room to walk beside the cliff. Cars and trucks flashed past, appearing suddenly around either curve of the road. The silence following their passing was filled with the ferocious, insistent hum of the cicadas and the rush of the river, unseen behind a screen of shrubs.

"We must go slowly because of the old man's hip," Jean said. "Pay attention to the cars."

A low stone wall was built a few inches from the road on the riverside. For a time they were able to walk on the gravel between it and the road, but then the path disappeared as the road came right up to the pavement.

Jean helped the old man up onto the top of the wall. With Jean in the lead and the old man between them, they walked along it. As they came in view of the curve, Richard saw that there was a sort of alcove in the cliff on the other side of the road. An iron fence was built across the opening and inside on a stretch of raked gravel a slab of pink marble was set in the ground. A bright bouquet of flowers filled a vase attached to the slab. Except for the flowers, the scene was identical to that photograph he had known from boyhood.

"We must help this old man," Jean said.

They each took one of his arms and listened for the traffic. Car after car passed. A motorcycle came roaring down the road, taking the curve between two cars going in opposite directions. Then there was a lull, the only sounds the river and the cicadas.

"*Vite!*" Jean said. "Quick!"

They walked quickly across the highway, the old man between them, their hands on his arms. Then they stood at the iron fence, safely behind a series of concrete posts set into the ground as a barrier against the traffic. The sunlight was hitting the marble at such an angle that the reflection made it impossible for him to read the writing. Next to the cliff a seep came out of the mountainside and formed a tiny pool. The vegetation around it was luxuriant.

Jean produced a key and unlocked the iron gate. They all walked onto the gravel and stood before the monument. Richard read his father's name, 1st Lt. Richard Purvis, cut into the marble. There was a French name and a Spanish name beneath it. No one spoke for a few moments as they all looked at the names.

Then the old man began to speak, pointing down the highway in the direction of Carcassonne toward where the road curved out of sight. He spoke for some time until Jean held up his hand.

Jean explained how the old man's platoon ambushed his father's band three kilometers from the marker. But it was an imperfect ambush because the man who was assigned to hit the lead truck with a *panzerfaust*, an anti-tank rocket, missed, and although there were losses, his father's band was able to disengage and carry off a good part of the war materiel.

His father took up a position at the marker, a Thompson machine gun in his hands. Two other men covered the approach from the river where there was a thick tangle of vegetation and many rocks. It was easy for two men to do that in a narrow place if they had courage.

The mountain kept the Germans from flanking them on one side and the river made it difficult to do it on the other. Even if they crossed the river and gained the railroad tracks there was no field of fire from there onto the maquis position. And the bridge was out so they could not cross behind them. There was no approach to the village from that side so it was impossible to gain possession of the highway bridge.

Then the old man pointed across the river toward the mountain and began to talk again. Richard looked at the shrub-covered mountainside and wondered what the old man was talking about. He was excited, moving his arms and hands about as he spoke.

Jean explained how the old man's sergeant sent him across the river to climb the mountainside until he had a clear field of fire on the maquis

Walking to Carcassonne

position. He was the best shot in his platoon, and killing the American who was covering the road with the machine gun would be easy.

The old man was silent. He stood there looking up at the mountainside. Then he looked directly at Richard, his blue eyes lively, his tongue working to form the words.

"He says that those three devoted themselves to acts of foolish bravery that day," Jean said.

Richard considered his father's predicament. He was a young man and those others most likely young men too, their whole lives before them, who knew they were probably going to die in order for a few other men to escape with those trucks loaded with war materiel. Better to drive the trucks into the river and then scatter into the high mountains where the Germans would never find them.

The old man was talking again, pointing up at the mountainside across the river, talking slowly and seriously.

Richard learned from Jean that the river was high and the old man almost drowned crossing it, in the process losing his rifle. But he still had a pistol and he decided to climb to where he could see the man with the machine gun clearly and shoot up all his ammunition at a range of what he guessed would be a least three-hundred meters.

The old man paused and took a book out of the canvas sack. As he leafed through it, Richard saw that most of it was filled with handwriting. Here and there were drawings of soldiers. He stopped at a drawing of a beautiful girl who sat on a rock beside a river.

"*Ma femme,*" he said.

"It is his wife," Jean said.

The old man continued to leaf through the pages, passing by photographs and documents he had pasted into the book. Then he turned a page and there was a drawing of a soldier wearing a beret crouched behind a rock, a Thompson machine gun in his hands.

The old man began to talk again, jabbing his finger at the picture as he spoke.

"He says that he fired his pistol at your father," Jean said. "He fired until he had no more ammunition. Then he watched the action through, how do you say?"

Jean formed his fingers in circles and placed them over his eyes.

"Binoculars?"

"Yes."

The old man pointed again at the picture of Richard's father. The old man started to talk again and pointed toward the thick wall of shrubs on the other side of the road.

Jean explained how the old man's sergeant sent men against the maquis by the river and killed them both. Richard's father held the road still but the men coming up from the river were approaching his flank. He knew his friends were dead because they had stopped firing. He would have known that because they were armed with Russian rifles. The sound was easy to distinguish.

Richard walked to the edge of the road and put his hand on the piece of the cliff behind which his father crouched. Jean continued to translate.

His father had good discipline with the machine gun. He made his ammunition last as he retreated back along the road. The old man thought he was intending to take a position at the foundations of the destroyed railroad bridge. That was when one of the men came up onto the road from the river and killed him.

The old man took up the book again and turned through the pages until he reached a drawing of Richard's father lying face down on the road, one hand still on the Thompson. He continued to turn the pages and revealed a drawing of a stretch of rapids with a group of soldiers standing with their rifles slung and looking out over the water. To Richard it did not seem quite real and he turned about and looked at the rock wall and the road, those places that had held the presence of his father. Then the old man spoke briefly and put his hand on Richard's shoulder.

Jean told him how the sergeant ordered the bodies thrown into the river. He was not a cruel man, but he had lost three of his brothers on the

Russian front. That old man regretted that Richard's father's body was lost, that he only had the monument.

"Ask him if he would have acted as my father did?" Richard asked.

Jean spoke to the old man who thought for a moment and then grinned and spoke.

"He says that your father was young and he was young," Jean said. "He says that all young soldiers are filled with foolish bravery."

Richard walked over to the monument, the gravel crunching under his boots. He stood before it and listened to the hum of the cicadas and the drip of the seep.

Foolish bravery, he thought.

The old man and Jean walked up to stand beside him. The old man spoke again.

Jean explained that for the old man it was a strange action because he had been an observer, instead of a participant. That had not happened to him many times. He watched men die on both sides. He watched them throw the bodies into the river. It gave him a strange feeling. The old man thought that was what it was like to be God or a general.

"Ask him how he did it," Richard said.

"He will only tell you that it was foolish bravery," Jean said. "What is it that you wish to know?"

"How my father stood right here when he knew he was going to die. I couldn't have done that."

"I do not know. You know the old man's answer."

The old man spoke again and Jean translated.

He told Richard that the old man had said that if he had not lost his rifle he would have easily killed Richard's father. Then they would have overtaken the trucks carrying the war materiel.

They all went across the road again, Jean and Richard on either side of the old man, and walked along the top of the stone wall and then beside it to the car. Jean drove them back to town. No one spoke until Jean stopped the car in front of the old man's house. Richard felt the old man's hand on his shoulder and then the old man was speaking.

"He wants to give you his drawing of your father," Jean said. "The one that shows him fighting from the rock."

"No," Richard said.

"Yes," the old man said.

"You will have to take it," Jean said.

Richard liked the idea of seeing the drawing just once, only for a few seconds. He had done nothing to deserve to possess it.

"Tell him I can't take it," Richard said.

Jean spoke to the old man.

"Yes," the old man said. "Yes."

"If you do not take it you will offend him," Jean said.

"Tell him thank you," Richard said.

Jean spoke to the old man, who reached out and put his hand lightly on Richard's shoulder again.

Richard turned and looked at the old man, who was sitting with the journal open on his lap. He held a pocket knife in his hand. Carefully he cut the page out of the journal, the knife making a rasping sound as it cut through the heavy paper. Then he handed the sheet to Richard, who sat for a moment with it in his hand, looking at his father crouched by the rock, the Thompson on his shoulder.

Jean and the old man got out of the car. Richard got out. He shook hands with the old man and thanked him through Jean for the drawing. Then the old man smiled at them and disappeared into his house.

As Jean drove Richard to the campground, he explained he was leaving that afternoon for a weekend backpacking trip in the Pyrenees. He dropped Richard off at the campground next to the river.

"He has never talked to me about that action," Jean said. "I think it was disturbing to him."

Richard did not know what to say in reply so he said nothing. He thanked Jean for his help and watched him drive off.

He stood there with the page in his hand and wondered how often the old man was accustomed to take out his journal and leaf through it. He wondered what the old man thought as he remembered the past, a person more comfortable as a participant than as a spectator of war.

That night he slept well beside the river, drifting off to sleep to the sound of the water rushing over the rocks. And he knew that Jean was sleeping somewhere in the high mountains and that the old man was asleep in his house with his dying wife.

In the morning he loaded his backpack and walked into the village and had breakfast in a café. He considered taking the train from the village to Carcassonne and then on to Madrid. But the thought of beginning the negotiations with the gun manufacturer did not excite him.

Out on the highway it was already hot as he walked along beside the river. The cicadas were wild in the shrubs. He passed the monument to his father and the other fighters, but he did not cross the road to it. He walked on around the bend into new country, territory that on that day so long ago had been filled with German soldiers. His body felt good, the weight of the pack resting easy on his hips and shoulders. He tried to put everything but the physical act of walking out of his mind.

After a few kilometers the road straightened and the river widened. Now as far as he could see plane trees lined the road, and he walked out of the blinding sunlight into that cool corridor. The river was marked by a line of trees, and there were fields of sunflowers, some taller than a man, on either side of the road. He passed a sign to Carcassonne. The image of the walled city, its turrets and towers rising out of that yellow and brown and green landscape, filled his mind. But beneath that pleasant vision was still the mystery of his father and himself, something that could not be explained by the drawing he had buried deep in his pack.

Foolish bravery, he thought. *Foolish bravery.*

With these words in his head he walked along the shady corridor, now feeling the weight of the pack for the first time, knowing that the walk was going to be much harder when he emerged from the green tunnel and into the sunlight. But right now the weight was not so bad and he gave himself up to the act of walking, just as he imagined his father had so many times as he climbed to a place of refuge in the high mountains.

Then he realized how unpleasant it was going to be to get on the train to Madrid. He could go to other places. Paris. Rome. He had enough money to live comfortably in either one of those places for several months. But he knew he would go to Madrid. It would be hot there; he would have to wear a suit. He could see nothing to his life but an endless string of such ventures, all of them ultimately failures.

The pack was beginning to feel not only heavy but uncomfortable. It pulled on his lower back. He stepped off the road and dropped the pack and began to rearrange the contents. When he was satisfied, he sat down beside it and took a drink of water.

In Madrid he would negotiate hard so there would be money left over for a prostitute. Not a simple girl but someone who spoke good English, a girl he could take out to the best restaurant in the city. After sex they would sit on the balcony of his hotel, for he would take a room with a balcony, and look out on the lights of the city. Then he would explain to her how he was going to put those Spanish shotguns in every discount store in the United States. And she would believe him. She would believe every word.

Scott Ely was born in Atlanta, GA, and he moved to Jackson, MS when he was eight. He served in Vietnam (somewhere in the highlands near Pleiku). He graduated with an MFA from the University of Arkansas, Fayetteville. He teaches fiction writing at Winthrop University in South Carolina. His previous book publications include STARLIGHT (Weidenfeld & Nicolson); PITBULL (Weidenfeld & Nicolson, Penguin); OVERGROWN WITH LOVE (University of Arkansas Press); THE ANGEL OF THE GARDEN (University of Missouri Press). His work has been translated in Italy, Germany, Israel, Poland, and Japan. There were also UK editions of the novels published.

Previous (and forthcoming) Magazine Publications:

Playboy, Southern Review Baton Rouge, LA; Antioch Review; Gettysburg Review; New Letters; Shenandoah; Five Points; 21st A Journal of Contemporary Photography.